Wilt on High

Tom Sharpe was born in 1928 and educated at Lancing College and at Pembroke College, Cambridge. He did his National Service in the Marines before going to South Africa in 1951, where he did social work for the Non-European Affairs Department before teaching in Natal. He had a photographic studio in Pietermaritzburg from 1957 until 1961, when he was deported. From 1963 to 1972 he was a lecturer in History at the Cambridge College of Arts and Technology. He is married and lives in Dorset.

Also by Tom Sharpe
in Pan Books

Tom Sharpe

Wilt on High

Pan Books
in association with
Secker and Warburg

First published in Great Britain 1984 by Martin Secker and Warburg Ltd
This edition published 1985 by Pan Books Ltd,
Cavaye Place, London SW10 9PG
in association with Martin Secker and Warburg Ltd
9 8 7 6 5 4 3 2
© Tom Sharpe 1984
ISBN 0 330 28765 6
Photoset by Parker Typesetting Service, Leicester
Printed in England by Cox & Wyman Ltd, Reading

Chapter one

'Days of wine and roses,' said Wilt to himself. It was an inconsequential remark but sitting on the Finance and General Purposes Committee at the Tech needed some relief and for the fifth year running Dr Mayfield had risen to his feet and announced, 'We must put the Fenland College of Arts and Technology on the map.'

'I should have thought it was there already,' said Dr Board, resorting as usual to the literal to preserve his sanity. 'In fact to the best of my knowledge it's been there since 1895 when—'

'You know perfectly well what I mean,' interrupted Dr Mayfield. 'The fact of the matter is that the College has reached the point of no return.'

'From what?' asked Dr Board.

Dr Mayfield turned to the Principal. 'The point I am trying to make—' he began, but Dr Board hadn't finished. 'Is apparently that we are either an aircraft halfway to its destination or a cartographical feature. Or possibly both.'

The Principal sighed and thought about early retirement. 'Dr Board,' he said, 'we are here to discuss ways and means of maintaining our present course structure and staffing levels in the face of the Local Education Authority and Central Government pressure to reduce the College to an adjunct of the Department of Unemployment.'

Dr Board raised an eyebrow. 'Really? I thought we were here to teach. Of course, I may be mistaken but when I first entered the profession, that's what I was led to believe. Now I learn that we're here to maintain course structures, whatever they may be, and staffing levels. In plain English, jobs for the boys.'

'And girls,' said the Head of Catering, who hadn't been listening too carefully. Dr Board eyed her critically.

'And doubtless one or two creatures of indeterminate gender,' he murmured. 'Now, if Dr Mayfield—'

'Is allowed to continue,' interrupted the Principal, 'we may arrive at a decision by lunchtime.'

Dr Mayfield continued. Wilt stared out of the window at the new Electronics Building and wondered for the umpteenth time what it was about committees that turned educated and relatively intelligent men and women, all of them graduates of universities, into bitter and boring and argumentative people whose sole purpose seemed to be to hear themselves speak and prove everyone else wrong. And committees had come to dominate the Tech. In the old days, he had been able to come to work and spend his mornings and afternoons trying to teach or at least to awaken some intellectual curiosity in classes of Turners and Fitters or even Plasterers and Printers, and if they hadn't learnt much from him, he had been able to go home in the evening with the knowledge that he had gained something from them.

Now everything was different. Even his title, Head of Liberal Studies, had been changed to that of Communication Skills and Expressive Attainment, and he spent his time on committees or drawing up memoranda and so-called consultative documents or reading similarly meaningless documents from other departments. It was the same throughout the Tech. The Head of Building, whose literacy had always been in some doubt, had been forced to justify classes in Bricklaying and Plastering in a 45-page discussion paper on 'Modular Construction and Internal Surface Application', a work of such monumental boredom and bad grammar, that Dr Board had suggested forwarding it to the RIBA with the recommendation that he be given a Fellowship in Architectural Semanticism – or alternatively Cementicism. There had been a similar row over the monograph submitted by the Head of Catering on 'Dietetic Advances In Multi-Phased Institutional Provisioning', to which Dr Mayfield had taken exception on the grounds that the emphasis on faggots and Queen's Pudding might lead to a misunderstanding in certain quarters. Dr Cox, Head of Science, had demanded to know what a Multi-Phased

Institution was, and what the hell was wrong with faggots, he'd been brought up on them. Dr Mayfield had explained he was referring to gays and the Head of Catering had confused the issue still further by denying she was a feminist. Wilt had sat through the controversy in silent wondering, as he did now, at the curious modern assumption that you could alter acts by using words in a different way. A cook was a cook no matter that you call him a Culinary Scientist. And calling a gasfitter a Gaseous and Liquefaction Engineer didn't alter the fact that he had taken a course in Gasfitting.

He was just considering how long it would be before they called him an Educational Scientist or even a Mental Processing Officer, when he was drawn from this reverie by a question of 'contact hours'.

'If I could have a breakdown of departmental timetabling on a real-time contact hour basis,' said Dr Mayfield, 'we could computerize those areas of overlap which under present circumstances render our staffing levels unviable on a cost-effective analysis.'

There was a silence while the Heads of Departments tried to figure this out. Dr Board snorted and the Principal rose to the bait. 'Well, Board?' he asked.

'Not particularly,' said the Head of Modern Languages, 'but thank you for enquiring all the same.'

'You know very well what Dr Mayfield wants.'

'Only on the basis of past experience and linguistic guesswork,' said Dr Board. 'What puzzles me in the present instance is his use of the phrase "real-time contact hours". Now according to my vocabulary . . .'

'Dr Board,' said the Principal, wishing to God he could sack the man, 'what we want to know is quite simply the number of contact hours the members of your department do per week.'

Dr Board made a show of consulting a small notebook. 'None,' he said finally.

'None?'

'That's what I said.'

'Are you trying to say your staff do no teaching at all? That's a downright lie. If it isn't . . .'

'I didn't say anything about teaching and no one asked me to. Dr Mayfield quite specifically asked for "real-time"—'

'I don't give a damn about real-time. He means actual.'

'So do I,' said Dr Board, 'and if any of my lecturers have been touching their students even for a minute, let alone an hour, I'd—'

'Board,' snarled the Principal, 'you're trying my patience too far. Answer the question.'

'I have. Contact means touching, and a contact hour must therefore mean a touching hour. Nothing more and nothing less. Consult any dictionary you choose, and you'll find it derives directly from the Latin, *contactus*. The infinitive is *contigere* and the past participle *contactum*, and whichever way you look at it, it still means touch. It cannot mean to teach.'

'Dear God,' said the Principal, through clenched teeth, but Dr Board hadn't finished.

'Now I don't know what Dr Mayfield encourages in Sociology and for all I know he may go in for touch teaching, or, what I believe is called in the vernacular "group groping", but in my department . . .'

'Shut up,' shouted the Principal, now well beyond the end of his tether. 'You will all submit in writing the number of teaching hours, the actual teaching hours, each member of your department does . . .'

As the meeting broke up, Dr Board walked down the corridor with Wilt. 'It's not often one can strike a blow for linguistic accuracy,' he said, 'but at least I've thrown a spanner in Mayfield's clockwork mind. The man's mad.'

It was a theme Wilt took up with Peter Braintree in the public bar of The Pig In A Poke half an hour later.

'The whole system is loony,' he said over a second pint, 'Mayfield's given up empire-building with degree courses and he's on a cost-effectiveness kick now.'

'Don't tell me,' said Braintree. 'We've already lost half

our textbook allocation this year, and Foster and Carston have been bullied into early retirement. At this rate I'll end up teaching *King Lear* to a class of sixty with eight copies of the play to go round.'

'At least you're teaching something. You want to try Expressive Attainment with Motor Mechanics Three. Expressive Attainment! The sods know all there is to be known about cars in the first place, and I haven't a clue what Expressive Attainment means. Talk about wasting the taxpayers' money. And anyway, I spend more of my time on committees than I do supposedly teaching. That's what galls me.'

'How's Eva?' asked Braintree, recognizing Wilt's mood and trying to change the subject.

'*Plus ça change, plus c'est la même chose.* Mind you, that's not entirely true. At least she's off Suffrage for Little Children and Votes at Eleven Plus. After those two blokes from PIE came round soliciting and went away with thick ears.'

'Pie?'

'Paedophile Information Exchange. Used to be called child molesters. These two sods made the mistake of trying to get Eva's support for lowering the age of consent to four. I could have told them four was an unlucky number round our way, considering what the quads get up to. By the time Eva had finished with them, they must have thought 45 Oakhurst Avenue was part of some bloody zoo, and they'd broached the topic with a tigress in cub.'

'Serve the swine right.'

'Didn't serve Mr Birkenshaw right though. Samantha promptly organized the other three into CAR, otherwise known as Children Against Rape, and set up a target in the garden. Luckily the neighbours put their communal feet down before one of the little boys in the street got himself castrated. The quads were just warming up with penknives. Well, actually, they were Sabatier knives from the kitchen, and they'd got quite good with them. Emmeline could hit the damned thing's scrotum at eighteen feet, and Penelope punctured it at ten.'

'It?' said Braintree faintly.

'Mind you, it was a bit oversize. They made it out of an old football bladder and two tennis balls. But it was the penis that got the neighbours up in arms. And Mr Birkenshaw. I didn't know he had a foreskin like that. Come to think of it, I doubt if anyone else in the street did either. Not until Emmeline wrote his name on the damned French letter and fixed wrapping paper from the Christmas cake round the end and the wind carried it ten gardens at peak viewing time on Saturday afternoon. It ended up hanging from the cherry tree in Mrs Lorrimer's on the corner. That way you could see BIRKENSHAW down all four streets quite clearly.'

'Good Lord,' said Braintree. 'What on earth did Mr Birkenshaw have to say about it?'

'Not much yet,' said Wilt, 'he's still in shock. Spent most of Saturday night at the cop shop trying to convince them he isn't the Phantom Flasher. They've been trying to catch that lunatic for years and this time they thought they'd got him.'

'What? Birkenshaw? They're out of their tinies, the man's a Town Councillor.'

'Was,' said Wilt. 'I doubt if he'll stand again. Not after what Emmeline told the policewoman. Said she knew his prick looked like that because he'd lured her into his back garden and waggled the thing at her.'

'Lured her?' said Braintree dubiously. 'With all due respect to your daughters, Henry, I wouldn't have said they were exactly lurable. Ingenious, perhaps, and . . .'

'Diabolical,' said Wilt. 'Don't think I mind what you say about them. I have to live with the hell-cats. Of course she wasn't lured. She's had a vendetta with his little pussy for months because it comes and knocks the stuffing out of ours. She was probably trying to poison the brute. Anyway, she was in his garden and according to her he waggled it. Not his version of course. Claimed he always pees on the compost heap and if little girls choose to lurk . . . Anyway, that didn't go down with the policewoman very well either. Said it was unhygienic.'

'Where was Eva while this was going on?'

'Oh, here and there,' said Wilt airily. 'Apart from practically accusing Mr Birkenshaw of being related to the Yorkshire Ripper ... I managed to stop that one going down in the police report by saying she was hysterical. Talk about drawing fire. At least I had the policewoman there to protect me and as far as I know the law of slander doesn't apply to ten-year-olds. If it does, we'll have to emigrate. As it is, I'm having to work nights to keep them at that blasted school for so-called gifted children. The cost is astronomic.'

'I thought Eva was getting something off by helping out there.'

'Helped out is more accurate. In fact, ordered off the premises,' said Wilt and asked for two more pints.

'What on earth for? I'd have thought they'd have been only too glad to have someone as energetic as Eva as an unpaid ancillary cleaning up and doing the cooking.'

'Not when the said ancillary takes it into her head to brighten up their micro-computers with metal polish. Anyway, she screwed the lot and it was a miracle we didn't have to replace them. Mind you, I wouldn't have minded handing over the ones we've got in the house. The place is a deathtrap of I triple E cables and floppy discs, and I can never get near the TV. And when I do, something called a dot matrix printer goes off somewhere and sounds like a hornets' nest in a hurry. And all for what? So that four girls of average if fiendish intelligence can steal a march on snotty-nosed small boys in the scholastic rat-race.'

'We're just old-fashioned,' said Braintree with a sigh. 'The fact is the computer's here to stay and children know how to use them and we don't. Even the language.'

'Don't talk to me about that gobbledygook. I used to think a poke was a crude form of sex. Instead it's something numerical in a programme and a programme's not what it was. Nothing is. Even bugs and bytes. And to pay for this electronic extravaganza, I spend Tuesday night at the prison teaching a bloody gangster what I don't know about E. M. Forster and Fridays at Baconheath Airbase giving lectures on British Culture and Institutions to a load of Yanks with time on their hands till Armageddon.'

'I shouldn't let the news of that leak out to Mavis Mottram,' said Braintree as they finished their beer and left the pub. 'She's taken up Banning the Bomb with a vengeance. She's been on to Betty about it and I'm surprised she hasn't roped Eva in.'

'She tried but it didn't work, for a change. Eva's too busy worrying about the quads to get involved in demonstrations.'

'All the same, I'd keep quiet about the airbase job. You don't want Mavis picketing your house.'

But Wilt wasn't sure. 'Oh, I don't know. It might make us slightly more popular with the neighbours. At the moment they've got it into their thick heads that I'm either a potential mass-murderer or a left-wing revolutionary because I teach at the Tech. Being picketed by Mavis on the wholly false grounds that I'm in favour of the Bomb might improve my image.' They walked back to the Tech by way of the cemetery.

At 45 Oakhurst Avenue, it was one of Eva Wilt's better days. There were days, better days and one of those days. Days were just days when nothing went wrong and she drove the quads to school without too much quarrelling, and came home to do the housework and went shopping and had a tuna-fish salad for lunch and did some mending afterwards and planted something in the garden and picked the children up from school and nothing particularly nasty happened. On one of those days everything went wrong. The quads quarrelled before, during and after breakfast, Henry lost his temper with them and she found herself having to defend them when she knew all the time he was right, the toast got stuck in the toaster and she was late getting the girls to school and something went wrong with the Hoover or the loo wouldn't flush and nothing seemed to be right with the world, so that she was tempted to have a glass of sherry before lunch and that was no good because then she'd want a nap afterwards and the rest of the day would be spent trying to catch up with what she had to do. But on one of her better days she did all the things she did on days and was somehow uplifted by the thought that the quads were doing wonderfully well at The School for The Mentally Gifted and would definitely get scholarships and go on to become doctors or scientists or something really creative, and that it was lovely to be alive in an age when all this was possible and not like it had been when she was a girl and had to do what she was told. It was on such days that she even considered having her mother to live with them instead of being in the old people's home in Luton and wasting all that money. Only considered it, of course, because Henry couldn't stand the old lady and had threatened to walk out and find himself digs if she ever stayed more than three days in the house.

'I'm not having that old bag polluting the atmosphere with her fags and her filthy habits,' he had shouted so loudly that even Mrs Hoggart, who had been in the bathroom at the time, didn't need her hearing aid to get the gist of the message. 'And another thing. The next time I come down to breakfast and find she's been lacing the teapot with brandy, and my brandy at that, I'll strangle the old bitch.'

'You've got no right to talk like that. After all, she is family—'

'Family?' yelled Wilt, 'I'll say she's family. Your fucking family, not mine. I don't foist my father on you—'

'Your father smells like an old badger,' Eva had retaliated, 'he's unhygienic. At least Mother washes.'

'And doesn't she need to, considering all the muck she smears on her beastly mug. Webster wasn't the only one to see the skull beneath the skin. I was trying to shave the other morning . . .'

'Who's Webster?' demanded Eva before Wilt could repeat the disgusting account of Mrs Hoggart's emergence from behind the shower curtain in the altogether.

'Nobody. It's from a poem, and talking about uncorseted breasts the old hag . . .'

'Don't you dare call her that. She's my mother and one day you'll be old and helpless and need—'

'Yes, well maybe, but I'm not helpless now and the last thing I need is that old Dracula in drag haunting the house and smoking in bed. It's a wonder she didn't burn the place down with that flaming duvet.'

It was the memory of that terrible outburst and the smouldering duvet that had prevented Eva from giving in to her better-day intentions. Besides, there had been truth in what Henry had said, even if he had put it quite horribly. Eva's feelings for her mother had always been ambiguous and part of her wish to have her in the house sprang from the desire for revenge. She'd show her what a really good mother was. And so on one of her better days, she telephoned her and told the old lady how wonderfully the quads were getting on and what a happy atmosphere there was in the home and how even Henry related to the children – Mrs Hoggart invariably broke into a hacking cough at this point – and on the best of days, invited her over for the weekend only to regret it almost as soon as she'd put the phone down. By then it had become one of those days.

But today she resisted the temptation and went round to Mavis Mottram's to have a heart-to-heart with her before lunch. She just hoped Mavis wouldn't try recruiting her for the Ban the Bomb demo.

Mavis did. 'It's no use your saying you have your hands full with the quads, Eva,' she said, when Eva had pointed out that she couldn't possibly leave the children with Henry, and what would happen if she were sent to prison. 'If there's a nuclear war you won't have any children. They'll all be dead in the first second. I mean Baconheath puts us in a first-strike situation. The Russians would be forced to take it out to protect themselves and we'd all go with it.'

Eva tried to puzzle this out. 'I don't see why we'd be a first-strike target if the Russians were being attacked,' she said finally, 'wouldn't it be a second strike?'

Mavis sighed. It was always so difficult to get things across to Eva. It always had been, and with the barrier of the quads behind which to retreat, it was practically impossible nowadays. 'Wars don't start like that. They start over trivial little things like the Archduke Ferdinand being assassinated at Sarajevo in 1914,' she said, putting it as simply as her work with the Open University allowed. But Eva was not impressed.

'I don't call assassinating people trivial,' she said. 'It's wicked and stupid.'

Mavis cursed herself. She ought to have remembered that Eva's experience with terrorists had prejudiced her against political murders. 'Of course it is. I'm not saying it isn't. What I'm—'

'It must have been terrible for his wife,' said Eva, pursuing her line of domestic consequences.

'Since she happened to be killed with him, I don't suppose she cared all that much,' said Mavis bitterly. There was something quite horribly anti-social about the whole Wilt family but she ploughed on. 'The whole point I'm trying to make is that the most terrible war in the history of mankind, up till then, happened because of an accident. A man and his wife were shot by a fanatic, and the result was that millions of ordinary people died. That sort of accident could happen again, and this time there'd be no one left. The human race would be extinct. You don't want that to happen, do you?'

Eva looked unhappily at a china figurine on the mantleshelf. She knew it had been a mistake to come anywhere near Mavis on one of her better days. 'It's just that I don't see what I can do to stop it,' she said and threw Wilt into the fray. 'And anyway, Henry says the Russians won't stop making the bomb and they've got nerve gas too, and Hitler had as well, and he'd have used it if he'd known we hadn't during the war.' Mavis took the bait.

'That's because he's got a vested interest in things staying the way they are,' she said. 'All men have. That's why they're against the women's peace movement. They feel threatened because we're taking the initiative and in a sense the bomb is symbolic of the male orgasm. It's potency on a mass destruction level.'

'I hadn't thought of it like that,' said Eva, who wasn't quite sure how a thing that killed everyone could be a symbol of an orgasm. 'And after all, he used to be a member of CND.'

' "Used to",' sniffed Mavis, 'but not any longer. Men just want us to be passive and stay in a subordinate sex role.'

'I'm sure Henry doesn't. I mean he's not very active sexually,' said Eva, still preoccupied with exploding bombs and orgasms.

'That's because you're a normal person,' said Mavis. 'If you hated sex he'd be pawing you all the time. Instead, he maintains his power by refusing you your rights.'

'I wouldn't say that.'

'Well, I would, and it's no use your claiming anything different.'

It was Eva's turn to look sceptical. Mavis had complained too often in the past about her husband's numerous affairs. 'But you're always saying Patrick's too sex-oriented.'

'Was,' said Mavis with rather sinister emphasis. 'His days of gadding about are over. He's learning what the male menopause is like. Prematurely.'

'Prematurely? I should think it must be. He's only forty-one, isn't he?'

'Forty,' said Mavis, 'but he's aged lately, thanks to Dr Kores.'

'Dr Kores? You don't mean to say Patrick went to her after that dreadful article she wrote in the *News*? Henry burnt the paper before the girls could read it.'

'Henry would. That's typical. He's anti freedom of information.'

'Well, it wasn't a very nice article, was it? I mean it's all very well to say that men are . . . well . . . only biological sperm banks but I don't think it's right to want them all neutered after they've had two children. Our cat sleeps all day and he's—'

'Honestly, Eva, you're so naïve. She didn't say anything about neutering them. She was simply pointing out that women have to suffer all the agonies of childbirth, not to mention the curse, and with the population explosion the world will face mass starvation unless something's done.'

'I can't see Henry being done. Not that way,' said Eva. 'He won't even let anyone talk about vasectomy. Says it has unwanted side-effects.'

Mavis snorted. 'As if the Pill didn't too, and far more dangerous ones. But the multi-national pharmaceutical corporations couldn't care less. All they are interested in is profits and they're controlled by men too.'

'I suppose so,' said Eva, who'd got used to hearing about multi-national companies though she still didn't know exactly what they were, and was completely at a loss with 'pharmaceutical'. 'All the same, I'm surprised Patrick agreed.'

'Agreed?'

'To have a vasectomy.'

'Who said anything about him having a vasectomy?'

'But you said he went to Dr Kores.'

'*I* went,' said Mavis grimly. 'I thought to myself, "I've had just about enough of you gallivanting about with other women, my boy, and Dr Kores may be able to help." And I was right. She gave me something to reduce his sex drive.'

'And he took it?' said Eva, genuinely astounded now.

'Oh, he takes it all right. He's always been keen on vitamins, especially Vitamin E. So I just swapped the capsules in the bottle. They're some sort of hormone or steroid and he takes one in the morning and two at night. Of course, they're still in the experimental stage but she told me they'd worked very well with pigs and they can't do any harm. I mean he's put on some weight and he's complained about his teats being a bit swollen, but he's certainly quietened down a lot. He never goes out in the evening. Just sits in front of the telly and dozes off. It's made quite a change.'

'I should think it has,' said Eva, remembering how randy Patrick Mottram had always been. 'But are you really sure it's safe?'

'Absolutely. Dr Kores assured me they're going to use it on gays and transvestites who are frightened of a sex-change operation. It shrinks the testicles or something.'

'That doesn't sound very nice. I wouldn't want Henry's shrinking.'

'I daresay not,' said Mavis, who had once made a pass at Wilt at a party, and still resented the fact that he hadn't responded. 'In his case she could probably give you something to stimulate him.'

'Do you really think so?'

'You can always try,' said Mavis. 'Dr Kores does understand women's problems and that's more than you can say for most doctors.'

'But I didn't think she was a proper doctor like Dr Buchman. Isn't she something in the University?'

Mavis Mottram stifled an impulse to say that, yes, she was a consultant in animal husbandry at that, which should suit Henry Wilt's needs even better than Patrick's.

'The two aren't mutually incompatible, Eva. I mean there is a medical school at the University, you know. Anyway, the point is, she's set up a clinic for women with problems, and I do think you'd find her very sympathetic and helpful.'

By the time Eva left and returned to 45 Oakhurst Avenue and a lunch of celery soup with bran magi-mixed into it, she was convinced. She would phone Dr Kores and go and see her about Henry. She was also rather pleased with herself. She had managed to divert Mavis from the depressing topic of the Bomb and on to alternative medicine and the need for women to determine the future because men had made such a mess of the past. Eva was all for that, and when she drove down to fetch the quads it was definitely one of her better days. New possibilities were burgeoning all over the place.

Chapter two

They were burgeoning all over the place for Wilt as well, but he wouldn't have put the day into the category of one of his better ones. He had returned to his office smelling of The Pig In A Poke's best bitter and hoping he could do some work on his lecture at the airbase without being disturbed, only to find the County Advisor on Communication Skills waiting for him with another man in a dark suit. 'This is Mr Scudd from the Ministry of Education,' said the Advisor. 'He's making a series of random visits to Colleges of Further Education on behalf of the Minister, to ascertain the degree of relevance of certain curricula.'

'How do you do,' said Wilt, and retreated behind his desk. He didn't like the County Advisor very much, but it was as nothing to his terror of men in dark grey suits, and three-piece ones at that, who acted on behalf of the Minister of Education. 'Do take a seat.'

Mr Scudd stood his ground. 'I don't think there's anything to be gained from sitting in your office discussing theoretical assumptions,' he said. 'My particular mandate is to report my observations, my personal observations, of what is acutally taking place on the classroom floor.'

'Quite,' said Wilt, hoping to hell nothing was actually taking place on any of his classroom floors. There had been a singularly nasty incident some years before when he'd had to stop what had the makings of a multiple rape of a rather too attractive student teacher by Tyres Two, who'd been inflamed by a passage in *By Love Possessed* which had been recommended by the Head of English.

'Then if you'll lead the way,' said Mr Scudd and opened the door. Behind him, even the County Advisor had assumed a hangdog look. Wilt led the way into the corridor.

'I wonder if you'd mind commenting on the ideological bias of your staff,' said Mr Scudd, promptly disrupting Wilt's desperate attempt to decide which class it would be safest to take the man into. 'I noticed you had a number of books on Marxism–Leninism in your office.'

'As a matter of fact, I do,' said Wilt and bided his time. If the sod had come on some sort of political witch-hunt, the emollient response seemed best. That way the bastard would land with his bum in the butter, but fast.

'And you consider them suitable reading matter for the working-class apprentices?'

'I can think of worse,' said Wilt.

'Really? So you admit to a left-wing tendency in your teaching.'

'Admit? I didn't admit to anything. You said I had books on Marxism–Leninism in my office. I don't see what that's got to do with what I teach.'

'But you also said you could think of worse reading material for your students,' said Mr Scudd.

'Yes,' said Wilt, 'that's exactly what I said.' The bloke was really getting on his wick now.

'Would you mind amplifying that statement?'

'Glad to. How about *Naked Lunch* for starters?'

'*Naked Lunch?*'

'Or *Last Exit From Brooklyn*. Nice healthy reading stuff for young minds, don't you think?'

'Dear God,' muttered the County Advisor, who had gone quite ashen.

Mr Scudd didn't look any too good either, though he inclined to puce rather than grey. 'Are you seriously telling me that you regard those two revolting books . . . that you encourage the reading of books like that?'

Wilt stopped outside a lecture room in which Mr Ridgeway was fighting a losing battle with a class of first-year A-level students who didn't want to hear what he thought about Bismark. 'Who said anything about encouraging students to read any particular books?' he asked above the din.

Mr Scudd's eyes narrowed. 'I don't think you quite understand the tenor of my questions,' he said, 'I am here . . .' He stopped. The noise coming from Ridgeway's class made conversation inaudible.

'So I've noticed,' shouted Wilt.

The County Advisor staggered to intervene. 'I really think, Mr Wilt,' he began, but Mr Scudd was staring maniacally through the glass pane at the class. At the back, a youth had just passed what looked suspiciously like a joint to a girl with yellow hair in Mohawk style who could have done with a bra.

'Would you say this was a typical class?' he demanded and turned back to Wilt to make himself heard.

'Typical of what?' said Wilt, who was beginning to enjoy the situation. Ridgeway's inability to interest or control supposedly high motivated A-level students would prepare Scudd nicely for the docility of Cake Two and Major Millfield.

'Typical of the way your students are allowed to behave.'

'My students? Nothing to do with me. That's History, not Communication Skills.' And before Mr Scudd could ask what the hell they were doing standing outside a classroom with bedlam going on inside, Wilt had walked on down the corridor. 'You still haven't answered my question,' said Mr Scudd when he had caught up.

'Which one?'

Mr Scudd tried to remember. The sight of that bloody girl had thrown his concentration. 'The one about the pornographic and revoltingly violent reading matter,' he said finally.

'Interesting,' said Wilt. 'Very interesting.'

'What's interesting?'

'That you read that sort of stuff. I certainly don't.'

They went up a staircase and Mr Scudd made use of the handkerchief he kept folded for decoration in his breast pocket. 'I don't read that filth,' he said breathlessly when they reached the top landing.

'Glad to hear it,' said Wilt.

'And I'd be glad to hear why you raised the issue.' Mr Scudd's patience was on a short leash.

'I didn't,' said Wilt, who, having reached the classroom in which Major Millfield was taking Cake Two, had reassured himself that the class was as orderly as he'd hoped. 'You raised it in connection with some historical literature you found in my office.'

'You call Lenin's *State and Revolution* historical literature? I most certainly don't. It's communist propaganda of a particularly virulent kind, and I find the notion that it's being fed to young minds in your department extremely sinister.'

Wilt permitted himself a smile. 'Do go on,' he said. 'There's nothing I enjoy more than listening to a highly trained intelligence leapfrogging common sense and coming to the wrong conclusions. It gives me renewed faith in parliamentary democracy.'

Mr Scudd took a deep breath. In a career spanning some thirty years of uninterrupted authority and bolstered by an inflation-linked pension in the near future, he had come to have a high regard for his own intelligence and he had no intention of having it disparaged now. 'Mr Wilt,' he said, 'I would be grateful to know what conclusions I am supposed to draw from the observations that the Head of Communication Skills at this College has a shelf full of works of Lenin in his office.'

'Personally, I'd be inclined not to draw any,' said Wilt, 'but if you press me . . .'

'I most certainly do,' said Mr Scudd.

'Well, one thing's for certain. I wouldn't suppose that the bloke was a raving Marxist.'

'Not a very positive answer.'

'Not a very positive question, come to that,' said Wilt. 'You asked me what conclusions I'd arrive at and when I tell you I wouldn't arrive at any, you're still not satisfied. I don't see what more I can do.'

But before Mr Scudd could reply, the County Advisor forced himself to intervene. 'I think Mr Scudd simply wants to know if there's any political bias in the teaching in your department.'

'Masses,' said Wilt.

'Masses?' said Mr Scudd.

'Masses?' echoed the County Advisor.

'Absolutely stuffed with it. In fact, if you were to ask me . . .'

'I am,' said Mr Scudd. 'That's precisely what I'm doing.'

'What?' said Wilt.

'Asking you how much political bias there is,' said Mr Scudd, having recourse to his handkerchief again.

'In the first place, I've told you, and in the second, I thought you said you didn't think there was anything to be gained from discussing theoretical assumptions and you'd come to see for yourself what went on on the classroom floor. Right?' Mr Scudd swallowed and looked desperately at the County Advisor, but Wilt went on. 'Right. Well you just take a shuftic in there where Major Millfield is having a class with Fulltime Caterers brackets Confectionery and Bakery close brackets Year Two, affectionately known as Cake Two, and then come and tell me how much political bias you've managed to squeeze out of the visit.' And without waiting for any further questions, Wilt went back down the stairs to his office.

'Squeeze out?' said the Principal two hours later. 'You have to ask the Minister of Education's Personal Private Secretary how much political bias he can squeeze out of Cake Two?'

'Oh, is that who he was, the Minister of Education's own Personal Private Secretary?' said Wilt. 'Well, what do you known about that? Now if he'd been an HMI . . .'

'Wilt,' said the Principal with some difficulty, 'if you think that bastard isn't going to lumber us with one of Her Majesty's Inspectors – in fact I shouldn't be surprised if the entire Inspectorate doesn't descend upon us – and all thanks to you, you'd better think again.'

Wilt looked round at the ad hoc committee that had been set up to deal with the crisis. It consisted of the Principal, the V-P, the County Advisor and, for no apparent reason, the Bursar. 'It's no skin off my nose how many Inspectors he rustles up. Only too glad to have them.'

'You may be but I rather doubt . . .' The Principal hesitated. The County Advisor's presence didn't make for a free flow of opinion on the deficiencies of other departments. 'I take it that any remarks I make will be treated as off the record and entirely confidential,' he said finally.

'Absolutely,' said the County Advisor, 'I'm only interested in Liberal Studies and . . .'

'How nice to hear that term used again. That's the second time this afternoon,' said Wilt.

'And you might have added the bloody studies,' snarled the Advisor, 'instead of leaving the wretched man with the impression that that other idiot lecturer was a fee-paying member of the Young Liberals and a personal friend of Peter Tatchell.'

'Mr Tatchell isn't a Young Liberal,' said Wilt. 'To the best of my knowledge he's a member of the Labour Party, left of centre of course, but . . .'

'And a fucking homosexual.'

'I've no idea. Anyway, I thought the compassionate word was "gay".'

'Shit,' muttered the Principal.

'Or that if you prefer,' said Wilt, 'though I'd hardly describe the term as compassionate. Anyway, as I was saying . . .'

'I am not interested in what you are saying. It's what you said in front of Mr Scudd that matters. You deliberately led him to believe that this College, instead of being devoted to Further Education . . .'

'I like that "devoted". I really do,' interrupted Wilt.

'Yes, devoted to Further Education, Wilt, and you led

him to think we employ nobody but paid-up members of the Communist Party and at the other extreme a bunch of lunatics from the National Front.'

'Major Millfield isn't a member of any party to the best of my knowledge,' said Wilt. 'The fact that he was discussing the social implications of immigration policies—'

'Immigration policies!' exploded the County Advisor. 'He was doing no such thing. He was talking about cannibalism among wogs in Africa and some swine who keeps heads in his fridge.'

'Idi Amin,' said Wilt.

'Never mind who. The fact remains that he was demonstrating a degree of racial bias that could get him prosecuted by the Race Relations Board and you had to tell Mr Scudd to go in and listen.'

'How the hell was I to know what the Major was on about? The class was quiet and I had to warn the other lecturers that the sod was on his way. I mean if you choose to pitch up out of the blue with a bloke who's got no official status . . .'

'Official status?' said the Principal. 'I've already told you Mr Scudd just happens to be—'

'Oh, I know all that and it still doesn't add up. The point is he walks into my office with Mr Reading here, noses his way through the books on the shelf, and promptly accuses me of being an agent of the bleeding Comintern.'

'And that's another thing,' said the Principal. 'You deliberately left him with the impression that you use Lenin's whatever it was called . . .'

'*The State and Revolution*,' said Wilt.

'As teaching material with day-release apprentices. Am I right, Mr Reading?'

The County Advisor nodded weakly. He still hadn't recovered from those heads in the fridge or the subsequent visit to Nursery Nurses who had been deep in a discussion on the impossible and utterly horrifying topic of post-natal abortion for the physically handicapped. The bloody woman had been in favour of it.

'And that's just the beginning,' continued the Principal, but Wilt had had enough.

'The end,' he said. 'If he'd bothered to be polite, it might have been different but he wasn't. And he wasn't even observant enough to see that those Lenin books belong to the History Department, were stamped to that effect, and were covered with dust. To the best of my knowledge, they've been on that shelf ever since my office was changed and they used to use them for the A-level special subject on the Russian Revolution.'

'Then why didn't you tell him that?'

'Because he didn't ask. I don't see why I should volunteer information to total strangers.'

'What about *Naked Lunch*? You volunteered that all right,' said the County Advisor.

'Only because he asked for worse reading material and I couldn't think of anything more foul.'

'Thank the Lord for small mercies,' murmured the Principal.

'But you definitely stated that the teaching in your department is stuffed – yes, you definitely used the word "stuffed" – with political bias. I heard you myself,' continued the County Advisor.

'Quite right too,' said Wilt. 'Considering I'm lumbered with forty-nine members of staff, including part-timers, and all the teaching they ever do is to natter away to classes and keep them quiet for an hour, I should think their political opinions must cover the entire spectrum, wouldn't you?'

'That isn't the impression you gave him.'

'I'm not here to give impressions,' said Wilt, 'I'm a teacher as a matter of unquestionable fact, not a damned public-relations expert. All right, now I've got to take a class of Electronics Engineers for Mr Stott who's away ill.'

'What's the matter with him?' asked the Principal inadvertently.

'Having another nervous breakdown. Understandably,' said Wilt and left the room.

Behind him the members of the Committee looked

wanly at the door. 'Do you really imagine this man Scudd will get the Minister to call for an enquiry?' asked the Vice-Principal.

'That's what he told me,' said the Advisor.'There are certain to be questions in the House after what he saw and heard. It wasn't simply the sex that got his goat, though that was bad enough in all conscience. The man's a Catholic and the emphasis on contraception—'

'Don't,' whispered the Principal.

'No, the thing that really upset him was being told to go and fuck himself by a drunken lout in Motor Mechanics Three. And Wilt, of course.'

'Isn't there something we can do about Wilt?' the Principal asked despairingly as he and the Vice-Principal returned to their offices.

'I don't see what,' said the V-P. 'He inherited half his staff and since he can't get rid of them, he has to do what he can.'

'What Wilt can do is land us with questions in Parliament, the total mobilization of Her Majesty's Inspectorate and a public enquiry into the way this place is run.'

'I shouldn't have thought they'd go to the lengths of a public enquiry. This man Scudd may have influence but I very much doubt . . .'

'I wouldn't. I saw the swine before he left and he was practically demented. What in God's name is post-natal abortion anyway?'

'Sounds rather like murder . . .' the Vice-Principal began, but the Principal was way ahead of him on a thought process that would lead to his forced retirement. 'Infanticide. That's it. Wanted to know if I was aware that we were running a course on Infanticide for future Nannies and asked if we had an evening class for Senior Citizens on Euthanasia or Do-It-Yourself Suicide. We haven't, have we?'

'Not to my knowledge.'

'If we had I'd ask Wilt to run it. That bloody man will be the end of me.'

*

At the Ipford Police Station, Inspector Flint shared his feelings. Wilt had already screwed his chances of becoming a Superintendent and Flint's misery had been compounded by the career of one of his sons, Ian, who had left school and home before taking his A-levels, and after graduating on marijuana and a suspended prison sentence had gone on to be seized by Customs and Excise loaded with cocaine at Dover. 'Bang goes any hope of promotion,' Flint had said morosely when his son was sent down for five years, and had brought down on his own head the wrath of Mrs Flint who blamed him for her son's delinquency. 'If you hadn't been so interested in your own blooming work and getting on and all, and had taken a proper father's interest in him, he wouldn't be where he is now,' she had shouted at him, 'but no, it had to be Yes Sir, No Sir, Oh certainly Sir, and any rotten night work you could get. And week-ends. And what did Ian ever see of his own father? Nothing. And when he did it was always this crime or that villain and how blooming clever you'd been to nick him. That's what your career's done for your family. B. all.'

And for once in his life, Flint wasn't sure she wasn't right. He couldn't bring himself to put it more positively than that. He'd always been right. Or in the right. You had to be to be a good copper, and he certainly hadn't been a bent one. And his career had had to come first.

'You can talk,' he'd said somewhat gratuitously, since it was about the only thing he'd ever allowed her to do apart from the shopping and washing up and cleaning the house and whining on about Ian, feeding the cat and the dog and generally skivvying for him. 'If I hadn't worked my backside off, we wouldn't have the house or the car and you wouldn't have been able to take the little bastard to the Costa . . .'

'Don't you dare call him that!' Mrs Flint had shouted, putting the hot iron on his shirt and scorching it in her anger.

'I'll call him what I bloody well like. He's a rotten villain like all the rest of them.'

'And you're a rotten father. About the only thing you ever did as a father was screw me, and I mean screw, because it wasn't anything else as far as I was concerned.' Flint had taken himself out of the house and back to the police station thinking dark thoughts about women and how their place was in the home, or ought to be, and he was going to be the laughing-stock of the Fenland Constabulary with cracks about him visiting the nick over in Bedford to see his own homegrown convict and a drug pusher at that, and what he'd do to the first sod who called him Snowy and harrying . . . And all the time there was, on the very edge of his mind, a sense of grievance against Henry fucking Wilt. It had always been there, but now it came back stronger than ever: Wilt had buggered his career with that doll of his and then the siege. Oh, yes, he'd almost admired Wilt at one stage but that was a long time ago, a very long time indeed. The little sod was sitting pretty in his house at Oakhurst Avenue and a good salary at the ruddy Tech, and one day he'd probably be the Principal of the stinking place. Whereas any hope Flint had ever had of rising to Super, and being posted to some place Wilt wasn't, had gone up in smoke. He was stuck with being Inspector Flint for the rest of his natural, and stuck with Ipford. As if to emphasize his lack of any hope, they'd brought Inspector Hodge in as Head of the Drug Squad and a right smart-arse he was too. Oh, they'd tried to butter over the crack, but the Super had called Flint in to tell him personally, and that had to mean something. That he was a dead-beat and they couldn't trust him in the drugs game, because his son was inside. Which had brought on another of his headaches which he'd always thought were migraines, only this time the police doctor had diagnosed hypertension and put him on pills.

'Of course I'm hypertense,' Flint had told the quack. 'With the number of brainy bastards round here who ought to be behind bars, any decent police officer's got to be tense. He wouldn't be any good at nailing the shits if he weren't. It's an occupational hazard.'

'It's whatever you like to call it, but I'm telling you you've got high blood pressure and . . .'

'That's not what you said a moment ago,' Flint had flashed back. 'You stated I had tension. Now then, which is it, hypertension or high blood pressure?'

'Inspector,' the doctor had said, 'you're not interrogating a suspect now.' (Flint had his reservations about that.) 'And I'm telling you as simply as I can that hypertension and high blood pressure are one and the same thing. I'm putting you on one diuretic a day—'

'One what?'

'It helps you pass water.'

'As if I needed anything to make me do that. I'm up twice in the blasted night as it is.'

'Then you'd better cut down on your drinking. That'll help your blood pressure, too.'

'How? You tell me not to be tense and the one thing that helps is a beer or two in the local.'

'Or eight,' said the doctor, who'd seen Flint in the pub. 'Anyway, it'll bring your weight down.'

'And make me piss less. So you give me a pill to make me piss more and tell me to drink less. Doesn't make sense.'

By the time Inspector Flint left the surgery, he still didn't know what the pills he had to take did for him. Even the doctor hadn't been able to explain how beta-blockers worked. Just said they did and Flint would have to stay on them until he died.

A month later the Inspector could tell the doctor how they worked. 'Can't even type any more,' he said, displaying a pair of large hands with white fingers. 'Look at them. Like bloody celery sticks that have been blanched.'

'Bound to have some side-effects. I'll give you something to relieve those symptoms.'

'I don't want any more of the piss pills,' said Flint. 'Those bleeding things are dehydrating me. I'm on the bloody trot all the time and it's obvious there's not enough blood left in me to get to my fingers. And that's not all. You want to try working some villain over and being taken short just when he's coming up with a confession. I tell you, it's affecting my work.'

The doctor looked at him suspiciously and thought wistfully of the days when his patients didn't answer back and police officers were of a different calibre to Flint. Besides, he didn't like the expression 'working some villain over'. 'We'll just have to try you out on some other medications,' he said, and was startled by the Inspector's reaction.

'Try me out on some other medicines?' he said belligerently. 'Who are you supposed to be treating, me or the bloody medicines? I'm the one with blood pressure, not them. And I don't like being experimented with. I'm not some bleeding dog, you know.'

'I suppose not,' said the doctor, and had doubled the Inspector's dose of beta-blockers but under a different trade name, added some pills to counter the effect on his fingers, and changed the name of the diuretics. Flint had gone back to his office from the chemist feeling like a walking medicine cabinet.

A week later, he was hard put to it to say what he felt like. 'Fucking awful is all I know,' he told Sergeant Yates who'd been unwise enough to enquire. 'I must have passed more bleeding water in the last six weeks than the Aswan Dam. And I've learnt one thing, this bloody town doesn't have enough public lavatories.'

'I should have thought there were enough to be going on with,' said Yates, who'd once had the unhappy experience of being arrested by a uniformed constable while loitering in the public toilets near the cinema in plain clothes trying to apprehend a genuine loo-lounger.

'Well, you can think again,' snapped Flint. 'I was caught short in Canton Street yesterday, and do you think I could find one? Not on your nelly. Had to use a lane between two houses and nearly got nabbed by a woman hanging her washing on the line. One of these days I'll be done for flashing.'

'Talking about flashing, we've had another report of a

case down by the river. Tried it out on a woman of fifty this time.'

'Makes a change from those Wilt bitches and Councillor Birkenshaw. Get a good look at the brute?'

'She said she couldn't see it very well because he was on the other side but she had the impression it wasn't very big.'

'It? It?' shouted Flint. 'I'm not interested in it. I'm talking about the bugger's mug. How the hell do you think we're going to identify the maniac. Have a prick parade and ask the victims to go along studying cocks? The next thing you'll be doing is issuing identikits of penises.'

'She couldn't see his face. He was looking down.'

'And peeing, I daresay. Probably on the same fucking tablets I'm doomed to. Anyway, I wouldn't take the evidence of a fifty-year-old blasted woman. They're all sex-mad at that age. I should know. My old woman's practically off her rocker about it and I keep telling her that the ruddy quack's lowered my blood pressure so much I couldn't get the fucking thing up even if I wanted to. Know what she said?'

'No,' said Sergeant Yates, who found the subject rather distasteful, and anyway it was obvious he didn't know what Mrs Flint had said and he didn't want to hear. The whole notion of anyone wanting the Inspector was beyond him. 'She had the gall to tell me to do it the other way.'

'The other way?' said Yates in spite of himself.

'The old soixante-neuf. Disgusting. And probably illegal. And if anyone thinks I'm going to go down at my age, and on my ruddy missus at that, they're clean off their fucking rockers.'

'I should think they'd have to be,' said the Sergeant almost pitifully. He'd always been relatively fond of old Flint, but there were limits. In a frantic attempt to change the topic to something less revolting, he mentioned the Head of the Drug Squad. He was just in time. The Inspector had just begun a repulsive description of Mrs Flint's attempts to stimulate him. 'Hodge? What's that bloody cock-sucker want now?' Flint bawled, still managing to combine the two subjects.

'Phone-tapping facilities,' said Yates. 'Reckons he's on to a heroin syndicate. And a big one.'

'Where?'

'Won't say, not to me any road.'

'What's he want my permission for? Got to ask the Super or the Chief Constable and I don't come into it. Or do I?' It had dawned on Flint that this might be a subtle dig at him about his son. 'If that bastard thinks he's going to take the piss out of me . . .' he muttered and stopped.

'I shouldn't think he could,' said Yates, getting his own back, 'not with those tablets you're on.'

But Flint hadn't heard. His mind had veered off along lines determined more than he knew by beta-blockers, vasodilators and all the other drugs he was on, but which combined with his natural hatred for Hodge and the accumulated worries of his job and his family to turn him into an exceedingly nasty man. If the Head of the Drug Squad thought he was going to put one over on him he'd got another think coming. 'There are more ways of stuffing a cat than filling it with cream,' he said with a gruesome smile.

Sergeant Yates looked at him doubtfully. 'Shouldn't it be the other way round?' he asked, and immediately regretted any reference to other way round. He'd had enough of Mrs Flint's thwarted sex life, and stuffing cats was definitely out. The old man must be off his rocker.

'Quite right,' said the Inspector. 'We'll fill the bugger with cream all right. Got any idea who he wants to tap?'

'He's not telling me that sort of thing. He reckons the uniform branch aren't to be trusted and he doesn't want any leaks.' The word was too much for Inspector Flint. He shot out of his chair and was presently finding temporary relief in the toilet.

By the time he returned to his office, his mood had changed to the almost dementedly cheerful. 'Tell him we'll give him all the co-operation he needs,' he told the Sergeant, 'only too pleased to help.'

'Are you sure?'

'Of course I'm sure. He's only got to come and see me. Tell him that.'

'If you say so,' said Yates and left the room a puzzled man. Flint sat on in a state of drug-induced bemusement. There was only one bright spot on his limited horizon. If that bastard Hodge wanted to foul up his career by making unauthorized phone taps, Flint would do all he could to encourage him. Fortified by this sudden surge of optimism, he absent-mindedly helped himself to another beta-blocker.

Chapter three

But already things were moving in a direction the Inspector would have found even more encouraging. Wilt had emerged from the meeting of the crisis committee rather too pleased with his performance. If Mr Scudd really had the influence with the Minister of Education he had claimed to, there might well be a full-scale inspection by the HMIs. Wilt welcomed the prospect. He had frequently thought about the advantages of such a confrontation. For one thing, he'd be able to demand an explicit statement on what the Ministry really thought Liberal Studies were about. Communication Skills and Expressive Attainment they weren't. Since the day some twenty years before when he'd joined the Tech staff, he'd never had a clear knowledge and nobody had been able to tell him. He'd started off with the peculiar dictum enunciated by Mr Morris, the then Head of Department, that what he was supposed to be doing was 'Exposing Day-Release

Apprentices to Culture', which had meant getting the poor devils to read *Lord Of The Flies* and *Candide,* and then discuss what they thought the books were about, and countering their opinions with his own. As far as Wilt could see, the whole thing had been counter-productive and as he had expressed it, if anyone was being exposed to anything, the lecturers were being exposed to the collective barbarism of the apprentices which accounted for the number who had nervous breakdowns or became milkmen with degrees. And his own attempt to change the curriculum to more practical matters, like how to fill in Income Tax forms, claim Unemployment Benefit, and generally move with some confidence through the maze of bureaucratic complications that had turned the Welfare State into a piggy-bank for the middle classes and literate skivers, and an incomprehensible and humiliating nightmare of forms and jargon for the provident poor, had been thwarted by the lunatic theories of so-called educationalists of the sixties like Dr Mayfield, and the equally irrational spending policies of the seventies. Wilt had persisted in his protestations that Liberal Studies didn't need video cameras and audio-visual aids galore, but could do with a clear statement from somebody about the purpose of Liberal Studies.

It had been an unwise request. Dr Mayfield and the County Advisor had both produced memoranda nobody could understand, there had been a dozen committee meetings at which nothing had been decided, except that since all the video cameras were available they might as well be used, and that Communication Skills and Expressive Attainment were more suited to the spirit of the times than Liberal Studies. In the event the education cuts had stymied the audio-visual aids and the fact that useless lecturers in more academic departments couldn't be sacked had meant that Wilt had been lumbered with even more deadbeats. If Her Majesty's Inspectors did descend, they might be able to clear the log jam and make some sense; Wilt would be only too pleased. Besides, he rather prided himself on his ability to hold his own in confrontations.

His optimism was premature. Having spent fifty minutes listening to Electronic Engineers explaining the meaning of cable television to him, he returned to his office to find his secretary, Mrs Bristol, in a flap. 'Oh, Mr Wilt,' she said as he came down the corridor. 'You've got to come quickly. She's there again and it's not the first time.'

'What isn't?' asked Wilt from behind a pile of *Shane* he had never used.

'That I've seen her there.'

'Seen whom where?'

'Her. In the loo.'

'Her in the loo?' said Wilt, hoping to hell Mrs Bristol wasn't having another of her 'turns'. She'd once gone all funny-peculiar when one of the girls in Cake Three had announced in all innocence, that she had five buns in the oven. 'I don't know what you're talking about.'

Nor, it appeared, did Mrs Bristol. 'She's got this needle thing and . . .' she petered out.

'Needle thing?'

'Syringe,' said Mrs Bristol, 'and it's in her arm and full of blood and . . .'

'Oh my God,' said Wilt, and headed past her to the door. 'Which loo?'

'The Ladies' staff one.'

Wilt halted in his tracks. 'Are you telling me one of the members of staff is shooting herself full of heroin in the Ladies' staff lavatory?'

Mrs Bristol *had* gone all funny now. 'I'd have recognized her if she'd been staff. It was a girl. Oh, do something Mr Wilt. She may do herself an injury.'

'You can say that again,' said Wilt, and bolted down the corridor and the flight of stairs to the toilet on the landing and went in. He was confronted by six cubicles, a row of washbasins, a long mirror and a paper-towel dispenser. There was no sign of any girl. On the other hand, the door of the third cubicle was shut and someone was making unpleasant sounds inside. Wilt hesitated. In less desperate circumstances, he might have supposed Mr Rusker, whose wife was a fibre freak, was having one of his problem days again. But Mr Rusker didn't use the Ladies' lavatory. Perhaps if he knelt down he might get a glimpse. Wilt decided against it. (A) He didn't want glimpses and (B) it had begun to dawn on him that he was, to put it mildly, in a delicate situation and bending down and peeping under doors in ladies' lavatories was open to misinterpretation. Better to wait outside. The girl, if there was a girl and not some peculiar figment of Mrs Bristol's imagination, would have to come out sometime.

With one last glance in the trash can for a hypodermic, Wilt tiptoed towards the door. He didn't reach it. Behind him a cubicle door opened. 'I thought so,' a voice shouted, 'a filthy Peeping Tom!' Wilt knew that voice. It belonged to Miss Hare, a senior lecturer in Physical Education, whom he had once likened rather too audibly in the staff-room to Myra Hindley in drag. A moment later, his arm had been wrenched up to the back of his neck and his face was in contact with the tiled wall.

'You little pervert,' Miss Hare continued, jumping to the nastiest, and, from Wilt's point of view, the least desirable conclusion. The last person he'd want to peep at was Miss Hare. Only a pervert would. It didn't seem the time to say so.

'I was just looking—' he began, but Miss Hare quite evidently had not forgotten the crack about Myra Hindley.

'You can keep your explanation for the police,' she screamed, and reinforced the remark by banging his face against the tiles. She was still enjoying the process, and Wilt wasn't, when the door opened and Mrs Stoley from Geography came in.

'Caught the voyeur in the act,' said Miss Hare. 'Call the police.' Against the wall, Wilt tried to offer his point of view and failed. Having Miss Hare's ample knee in the small of his back didn't help and his false tooth had come out.

'But that's Mr Wilt,' said Mrs Stoley uncertainly.

'Of course it's Wilt. It's just the sort of thing you'd expect from him.'

'Well . . .' began Mrs Stoley, who evidently hadn't.

'Oh for goodness' sake get a move on. I don't want the little runt to escape.'

'Am I trying to?' Wilt mumbled and had his nose rammed against the wall for his pains.

'If you say so,' said Mrs Stoley and left the room only to return five minutes later with the Principal and the V-P. By then, Miss Hare had transferred Wilt to the floor and was kneeling on him.

'What on earth's going on?' demanded the Principal. Miss Hare got up.

'Caught in the act of peeping at my private parts,' she said. 'He was trying to escape when I grabbed him.'

'Wasn't,' said Wilt groping for his false tooth and inadvisedly putting it back in his mouth. It tasted of some extremely strong disinfectant which hadn't been formulated as a mouthwash, and was doing things to his tongue. As he scrambled to his feet, and made a dash for the washbasins, Miss Hare applied a half-nelson.

'For God's sake let go,' yelled Wilt, by now convinced he was about to die of carbolic poisoning. 'This is all a terrible mistake.'

'Yours,' said Miss Hare and cut off his air supply.

The Principal looked dubiously at them. While he might have enjoyed Wilt's discomfiture in other circumstances, the sight of him being strangled by an athletically built woman like Miss Hare whose skirt had come down was more than he could stomach.

'I think it would be best if you let him go,' he said as Wilt's face darkened and his tongue stuck out. 'He seems to be bleeding rather badly.'

'Serves him right,' said Miss Hare, reluctantly letting Wilt breathe again. He stumbled to a basin and turned the tap on.

'Wilt,' said the Principal, 'what is the meaning of this?' But Wilt had his false tooth out again and was trying desperately to wash his mouth out under the tap.

'Hadn't we better wait for the police before he makes a statement?' asked Miss Hare.

'The police?' squawked the Principal and the V-P simultaneously. 'You're not seriously suggesting the police should be called in to deal with this . . . er. . . affair.'

'I am,' Wilt mumbled from the basin. Even Miss Hare looked startled.

'You are?' she said. 'You have the nerve to come in here and peer at . . .'

'Balls,' said Wilt, whose tongue seemed to be resuming its normal size, though it still tasted like a recently sterilized toilet bend.

'How dare you,' shouted Miss Hare, and was on the point of getting to grips with him again when the V-P intervened. 'I think we should hear Wilt's version before we do anything hasty, don't you?' Miss Hare obviously didn't, but she stopped in her tracks. 'I've already told you precisely what he was doing,' she said.

'Yes, well let me tell you what . . .'

'He was bending over and looking under the door,' continued Miss Hare remorselessly.

'Wasn't,' said Wilt.

'Don't you dare lie. I always knew you were a pervert. Remember that revolting incident with the doll?' she said, appealing to the Principal. The Principal didn't need reminding but it was Wilt who answered.

'Mrs Bristol,' he mumbled, dabbing his nose with a paper towel, 'Mrs Bristol's the one who started this.'

'Mrs Bristol?'

'Wilt's secretary,' explained the V-P.

'Are you suggesting you were looking for your secretary in here?' asked the Principal. 'Is that what you're saying?'

'No, I'm not. I'm saying Mrs Bristol will tell you why I was here and I want you to hear it from her before that damned bulldozer on anabolic steroids starts knocking hell out of me again.'

'I'm not standing here being insulted by a . . .'

'Then you'd better pull your skirt up,' said the V-P, whose sympathies were entirely with Wilt.

The little group made their way up the stairs, past a class of English A-level students who'd just ended an hour with Mr Gallen on The Pastoral Element in Wordsworth's *Prelude,* and were consequently unprepared for the urban element of Wilt's bleeding nose. Nor was Mrs Bristol. 'Oh dear, Mr Wilt, what have you done to yourself?' she asked. 'She didn't attack you?'

'Tell them,' said Wilt. 'You tell them.'

'Tell them what?'

'What you told me,' snapped Wilt, but Mrs Bristol was too concerned about his condition and the Principal and the V-P's presence had unnerved her. 'You mean about—'

'I mean . . . Never mind what I mean,' said Wilt lividly, 'just tell them what I was doing in the Ladies' lavatory, that's all.'

Mrs Bristol's face registered even more confusion. 'But I don't know,' she said, 'I wasn't there.'

'I know you weren't there, dammit. What they want to know is why I was.'

'Well . . .' Mrs Bristol began, and lost her nerve again, 'Haven't you told them?'

'Caesar's ghost,' said Wilt, 'can't you just spit it out. Here I am accused of being a Peeping Tom by Miss Burke and Hare over there . . .'

'You call me that again and your own mother wouldn't recognize you,' said Miss Hare.

'Since she's been dead for ten years, I don't suppose she would now,' said Wilt, retreating behind his desk. By the time the PE teacher had been restrained, the Principal was trying to make some sense out of an increasingly confused situation. 'Can someone please shed some light on this sordid business?' he asked.

'If anyone can, she can,' said Wilt, indicating his secretary. 'After all, she set me up.'

'Set you up, Mr Wilt? I never did anything of the sort. All I said was there was a girl in the staff toilet with a

hypodermic and I didn't know who she was and . . .'
Intimidated by the look of horror on the Principal's face,
she ground to a halt. 'Have I said something wrong?'

'You saw a girl with a hypodermic in the staff toilet?
And told Mr Wilt about it?'

Mrs Bristol nodded dumbly.

'When you say "girl" I presume you don't mean a
member of the staff?'

'I'm sure it wasn't. I didn't see her face but I'd have
known surely. And she had this awful syringe filled with
blood and . . .' She looked at Wilt for assistance.

'You said she was taking drugs.'

'There was no one in that toilet while I was there,' said
Miss Hare, 'I'd have heard them.'

'I suppose it could have been someone with diabetes,'
said the V-P, 'some adult student who wouldn't want to
use the student's toilet for obvious reasons.'

'Oh quite,' said Wilt, 'I mean we all know diabetics go
round with hypodermics full of blood. She was obviously
flushing back to get the maximum dose.'

'Flushing back?' said the Principal weakly.

'That's what the junkies do,' said the V-P. 'They inject
themselves and then—'

'I don't want to know,' said the Principal.

'Well, if she was taking heroin—'

'Heroin! That's all we need,' said the Principal, and sat
down miserably.

'If you ask me,' said Miss Hare, 'the whole thing's a
fabrication. I was in there ten minutes . . .'

'Doing what?' asked Wilt. 'Apart from attacking me.'

'Something feminine, if you must know.'

'Like taking steroids. Well, let me tell you that when I
went down there and I wasn't there more than . . .'

It was Mrs Bristol's turn to intervene. 'Down, did you
say down?'

'Of course I said down. What did you expect me to say?
Up?'

'But the toilet's on the fourth floor, not the second.
That's where she was.'

'Now you tell us. And where the hell do you think I went?'

'But I always go upstairs,' said Mrs Bristol. 'It keeps me in trim. You know that. I mean one's got to get some exercise and . . .'

'Oh, belt up,' said Wilt, and dabbed his nose with a bloodstained handkerchief.

'Right, let's get this straight,' said the Principal, deciding it was time to exercise some authority. 'Mrs Bristol tells Wilt here there is a girl upstairs injecting herself with something or other and instead of going upstairs, Wilt goes down to the toilet on the second floor and . . .'

'Gets beaten to a pulp by Ms Blackbelt Burke here,' said Wilt who was beginning to regain the initiative. 'And I don't suppose it's occurred to anyone to go up and see if that junkie's still there.'

But the Vice-Principal had already left.

'If that little turd calls me Burke again . . .' said Miss Hare menacingly. 'Anyway, I still think we should call the police. I mean, why did Wilt go downstairs instead of up? I find that peculiar.'

'Because I don't use the Ladies' or, in your case, the Bisexual Toilets, that's why.'

'Oh for God's sake,' said the Principal, 'there's obviously been some mistake and if we all keep calm . . .'

The Vice-Principal returned. 'No sign of her,' he said.

The Principal got to his feet. 'Well, that's that. Evidently there's been some mistake. Mrs Bristol may have imagined . . .' But any aspersions on Mrs Bristol's imagination he was about to make were stopped by the V-P's next words.

'But I did find this in the trash can,' he said, and produced a blood-stained lump of paper towel, which looked like Wilt's handkerchief.

The Principal regarded it with disgust. 'That hardly proves anything. Women do bleed occasionally.'

'Call it a jamrag and be done with it,' said Wilt

42

viciously. He was getting fed up with bleeding himself. Miss Hare turned on him.

'That's typical, you foulmouthed sexist,' she snapped.

'I was merely interpreting what the Principal was . . .'

'And more conclusively, this,' interrupted the V-P, this time producing a hypodermic needle.

It was Mrs Bristol's turn to bridle. 'There, what did I tell you. I wasn't imagining anything. There was a girl up there injecting herself and I did see her. Now what are you going to do?'

'Now we mustn't jump to conclusions just because . . .' the Principal began.

'Call the police. I demand that you call the police,' said Miss Hare, determined to take this opportunity for airing her opinions about Wilt and Peeping Toms as widely as possible.

'Miss Burke,' said the Principal, flustered into sharing Wilt's feelings about the PE lecturer, 'this is a matter that needs cool heads.'

'Miss Hare's my name and if you haven't the decency . . . And where do you think you're going?'

Wilt had taken the opportunity to sidle to the door. 'To the men's toilet to assess the damage you did, then the Blood Transfusion Unit for a refill and after that, if I can make it, to my doctor and the most litigious lawyer I can find to sue you for assault and battery.' And before Miss Hare could reach him, Wilt was off down the corridor and had closeted himself in the Men's toilet.

Behind him Miss Hare vented her fury on the Principal. 'Right, that does it,' she shouted. 'If you don't call the police, I will. I want the facts of this case spelt out loud and clear so that if that little sex-maniac goes anywhere near a lawyer, the public are going to learn the sort of people who teach here. I want this whole disgusting matter dealt with openly.'

It was the last thing the Principal wanted. 'I really don't think that's wise,' he said. 'After all, Wilt could have made a natural mistake.'

Miss Hare wasn't to be mollified. 'The mistake Wilt

made wasn't natural. And besides, Mrs Bristol did see a girl taking heroin.'

'We don't know that. There could be some quite ordinary explanation.'

'The police will find out soon enough once they've got that syringe,' said Miss Hare adamantly. 'Now then, are you going to phone them or am I?'

'If you put it like that, I suppose we'll have to,' said the Principal, eyeing her with loathing. He picked up the phone.

Chapter four

In the Men's toilet, Wilt surveyed his face in the mirror. It looked as unpleasant as it felt. His nose was swollen, there were streaks of blood on his chin and Miss Hare had managed to open an old cut above his right eye. Wilt washed his face in a basin and thought dismally about tetanus. Then he took his false tooth out and studied his tongue. It was not, as he had expected, twice its normal size, but it still tasted of disinfectant. He rinsed his mouth out under the tap with the slightly cheering thought that if his taste buds were anything to go by a tetanus germ wouldn't stand an earthly of surviving. After that, he put his tooth back and wondered yet again what it was about him that invited misunderstanding and catastrophe.

The face in the mirror told him nothing. It was a very ordinary face and Wilt had no illusions about it being handsome. And yet for all it ordinariness, it had to be the façade behind which lurked an extraordinary mind. In the past he had liked to think it was an original mind or, at the very least, an individual one. Not that that helped much. Every mind had to be individual and that didn't make everyone accident-prone, to put it mildly. No, the fact of the matter was that he lacked a sense of his own authority.

'You just let things happen to you,' he told the face in the mirror. 'It's about time you made them happen for you.' But as he said it, he knew it would never be like that. He would never be a dominating person, a man of power whose orders were obeyed without question. It wasn't his nature. To be more accurate, he lacked the stamina and drive to deal in details, to quibble over procedure and win allies and out-manoeuvre opponents, in short, to concentrate his attention on the means of gaining power. Worse still, he despised the people who had that drive. Invariably, they limited themselves to a view of the world in which they alone were important and to hell with what other people wanted. And they were everywhere, these committee Hitlers, especially at the Tech. It was about time they were challenged. Perhaps one day he would . . .

He was interrupted in this daydream by the entrance of the Vice-Principal. 'Ah, there you are, Henry,' he said, 'I thought I'd better let you know that we've had to call in the police.'

'About what?' asked Wilt, suddenly alarmed at the thought of Eva's reaction if Miss Hare accused him of being a voyeur.

'Drugs in the college.'

'Oh, that. A bit late in the day, isn't it? Been going on ever since I can remember.'

'You mean you knew about it?'

'I thought everyone did. It's common knowledge. Anyway, it's obvious we're bound to have a few junkies with all the students we've got,' said Wilt, and made good his escape while the Vice-Principal was still busy at the urinal. Five minutes later, he had left the Tech and was immersed once more in those speculative thoughts that seemed to occupy so much of his time when he was alone. Why was it, for instance, that he was so concerned with power when he wasn't really prepared to do anything about it? After all, he was earning a comfortable salary – it would have been a really good one if Eva hadn't spent so much of it on the quads' education – and objectively he had nothing to complain about. Objectively. And a fat lot that meant. What mattered was how one felt. On that score, Wilt came bottom even on days when he hadn't had his face mashed by Ms Hare.

Take Peter Braintree for example. He didn't have any sense of futility or lack of power. He had even refused promotion because it would have meant giving up teaching and taking on administrative duties. Instead, he was content to give his lectures on English literature and go home to Betty and the children and spend his evenings playing trains or making model aeroplanes when he'd finished marking essays. And at the weekends, he'd go off to watch a football match or play cricket. It was the same during the holidays. The Braintrees always went off camping and walking and came back cheerful, with none of the rows and catastrophes that seemed an inevitable part of the Wilt family excursions. In his own way, Wilt envied him, while having to admit that his envy was muted by a contempt he knew to be wholly unjustified. In the modern world, in any world, it wasn't enough just to be content and hope that everything would turn out for the best in the end. In Wilt's experience, they turned out for the worst, e.g. Miss Hare. On the other hand, when he did try to do something the result was catastrophic. There didn't seem to be any middle way.

He was still puzzling over the problem when he crossed Bilton Street and walked up Hillbrow Avenue. Here too, the signs told him that almost everyone was content with his lot. The cherry trees were in bloom, and pink and white petals littered the pavement like confetti. Wilt noted each front garden, most of them neat and bright with wallflowers, but some, where academics from the University lived, unkempt and overgrown with weeds. On the corner of Pritchard Street, Mr Sands was busy among his heathers and azaleas, proving to an uninterested world that it was possible for a retired bank manager to find satisfaction by growing acid-loving plants on an alkaline soil. Mr Sands had explained the difficulties to Wilt one day, and the need to replace all the topsoil with peat to lower the pH. Since Wilt had no idea what pH stood for, he hadn't a clue what Mr Sands had been talking about, and in any case, he had been more interested in Mr Sands' character and the enigma of his contentment. The man had spent forty years presumably fascinated by the movement of money from one account to the other, fluctuations in the interest rate and the granting of loans and overdrafts, and now all he seemed prepared to talk about were the needs of his camellias and miniature conifers. It didn't make sense and was just as unfathomable as the character of Mrs Cranley who had once figured so spectacularly in a trial to do with a brothel in Mayfair, but who now sang in the choir at St Stephens and wrote children's stories filled with remorseless whimsy and an appalling innocence. It was beyond him. He could only deduce one fact from his observations. People could and did change their lives from one moment to the next, and quite fundamentally at that. And if they could, there was no reason why he shouldn't. Fortified with the knowledge, he strode on more confidently and with the determination not to put up with any nonsense from the quads tonight.

As usual he was proved wrong. He had no sooner opened the front door, than he was under siege. 'Ooh, Daddy, what have you done to your face?' demanded Josephine.

'Nothing,' said Wilt, and tried to escape upstairs before the real inquisition could begin. He needed a bath and his clothes stank of disinfectant. He was stopped by Emmeline who was playing with her hamster halfway up.

'Don't step on Percival,' she said, 'she's pregnant.'

'Pregnant?' said Wilt, momentarily nonplussed. 'He can't be. It's impossible.'

'Percival's a she, so it is.'

'A she? But the man at the petshop guaranteed the thing was a male. I asked him specifically.'

'And she's not a thing,' said Emmeline. 'She's an expectant mummy.'

'Better not be,' said Wilt. 'I'm not having the house overrun by an exploding population of hamsters. Anyway, how do you know?'

'Because we put her in with Julian's to see if they'd fight to the death like the book said, and Pervical went into a trance and didn't do anything.'

'Sensible fellow,' said Wilt, immediately identifying with Pervical in such horrid circumstances.

'She's not a fellow. Mummy hamsters always go into a trance when they want to be done.'

'Done?' said Wilt inadvisedly.

'What you do to Mummy on Sunday mornings and Mummy goes all funny afterwards.'

'Christ,' said Wilt, cursing Eva for not shutting the bedroom door. Besides, the mixture of accuracy and baby-talk was getting to him. 'Anyway, never mind what we do. I want to . . .'

'Does Mummy go into a trance, too?' asked Penelope, who was coming down the stairs with a doll in a pram.

'It's not something I'm prepared to discuss,' said Wilt. 'I need a bath and I'm going to have one. And now.'

'Can't,' said Josephine. 'Sammy's having her hair washed. She's got nits. You smell funny too. What's that on your collar?'

'And all down the front of your shirt.' This from Penelope.

'Blood,' said Wilt, endowing the word with as much threat as he could. He pushed past the pram and went into the bedroom, wondering what it was about the quads that gave them some awful sort of collective authority. Four separate daughters wouldn't have had the same degree of assertiveness and the quads had definitely inherited Eva's capacity for making the worst of things. As he undressed, he could hear Penelope bearing the glad tidings of his misfortune to Eva through the bathroom door.

'Daddy's come home smelling of disinfectant and he's cut his face.'

'He's taking off his trousers and there's blood all down his shirt,' Josephine chimed in.

'Oh, great,' said Wilt. 'That ought to bring her out like a scalded cat.'

But it was Emmeline's announcement that Daddy had said Mummy went into a trance when she wanted a fuck that caused the trouble.

'Don't use that word,' yelled Wilt. 'If I've told you once I've told you a thousand times and I never said anything about your bleeding mother going into a trance. I said—'

'What did you call me?' Eva shouted, storming out of the bathroom. Wilt pulled up his Y-fronts again and sighed. On the landing, Emmeline was describing with clinical accuracy the mating habits of female hamsters, and attributing the description to Wilt.

'I didn't call you a bloody hamster. That's a downright lie. I don't know the first thing about the fucking things and I certainly never wanted them in—'

'There you go,' shouted Eva. 'One moment you're telling the children not to use filthy language and the next you're using it youself. You can't expect them to—'

'I don't expect them to lie. That's far worse than the sort of language they use and anyway Penelope used it first. I—'

'And you've absolutely no right to discuss our sex life with them.'

'I don't and I wasn't,' said Wilt. 'All I said was I didn't want the house overrun by blasted hamsters. The man in the shop sold me that mentally deficient rat as a male, not a bloody breeding machine.'

'Now you're being disgustingly sexist as well,' yelled Eva.

Wilt stared wildly round the bedroom. 'I am not being sexist,' he said finally. 'It just happens to be a well-known fact that hamsters—'

But Eva had seized on his inconsistency. 'Oh yes you are. The way you talk anyone would think women were the only ones who wanted you-know-what.'

'You-know-what my foot. Those four little bints out there know what without you-know-whating—'

'How dare you call your own daughters bints? That's a disgusting word.'

'Fits,' said Wilt, 'and as for their being my own daughters, I can tell you it's—'

'I shouldn't,' said Eva.

Wilt didn't. Push Eva too far and there was no knowing what would happen. Besides, he'd enough of women's power in action for one day. 'All right, I apologize,' he said. 'It was a stupid thing to say.'

'I should think it was,' said Eva, coming off the boil and picking his shirt off the floor. 'How on earth did you get all this blood on your new shirt?'

'Slipped and fell in the gents,' said Wilt, deciding the time was hardly appropriate for a more accurate account. 'That's why it smells like that.'

'In the gents?' said Eva suspiciously. 'You fell over in the gents?'

Wilt gritted his teeth. He could see any number of awful consequences developing if the truth leaked out but he'd already committed himself.

'On a bar of soap,' he said. 'Some idiot had left it on the floor.'

'And another idiot stepped on it,' said Eva, scooping up Wilt's jacket and trousers and depositing them in a plastic basket. 'You can take these to the dry-cleaners on the way to work tomorrow.'

'Right,' said Wilt, and headed for the bathroom.

'You can't go in there yet. I'm still washing Samantha's hair and I'm not having you prancing around in the altogether . . .'

'Then I'll wear my pants in the shower,' said Wilt and was presently hidden behind the shower curtain listening to Penelope telling the world that female hamsters frequently bit the male's testicles after copulating.

'I wonder they bother to wait. Talk about having your

50

cake and eating it,' muttered Wilt, and absentmindedly soaped his Y-fronts.

'I heard that,' said Eva and promptly turned the hot tap on in the bath. Behind the shower curtain Wilt juddered under a stream of cold water. With a grunt of despair, he wrenched at the cold tap and stepped from the shower.

'Daddy's foaming at his panties,' squealed the quads delightedly.

Wilt lurched at them rabidly. 'Not the only fucking place he'll be foaming if you don't get the hell out of here,' he shouted.

Eva turned the hot tap in the bath off. 'That's no way to set an example,' she said, 'talking like that. You should be ashamed of yourself.'

'Like hell I should. I've had a bloody awful day at the Tech and I've got to go out to the prison to teach that ghastly creature McCullum, and I no sooner step into the bosom of my menagerie than I—'

The front doorbell rang loudly downstairs. 'That's bound to be Mr Leach next door come to complain again,' said Eva.

'Sod Mr Leach,' said Wilt and stepped back under the shower.

This time he learnt what it felt like to be scalded.

Chapter five

Things were hotting up for other people in Ipford as well. The Principal for one. He had just arrived home and was opening the drinks cabinet in the hope of dulling his memory of a disastrous day, when the phone rang. It was the Vice-Principal. 'I'm afraid I've got some rather disturbing news,' he said with a lugubrious satisfaction the Principal recognized. He connected it with funerals.

'It's about that girl we were looking for . . .' The Principal reached for the gin bottle and missed the rest of the sentence. He got back in time to hear something about the boiler-room. 'Say that again,' he said, holding the bottle between his knees and trying to open it with one hand.

'I said the caretaker found her in the boiler-room.'

'In the boiler-room? What on earth was she doing there?'

'Dying,' said the Vice-Principal, affecting an even more sombre tone.

'Dying?' The Principal had the bottle open now and poured himself a large gin. This was even more awful than he expected.

'I'm afraid so.'

'Where is she now?' asked the Principal, trying to stave off the worst.

'Still in the boiler-room.'

'Still in the . . . But good God man, if she's in that condition, why the devil haven't you got her to hospital?'

'She isn't in that condition,' said the Vice-Principal and paused. He too had had a hard day. 'What I said was that she was dying. The fact of the matter is that she's dead.'

'Oh, my God,' said the Principal and swigged neat gin. It was better than nothing. 'You mean she died of an overdose?'

'Presumably. I suppose the police will find out.'

The Principal finished the rest of the gin. 'When did this happen?'

'About an hour ago.'

'An hour ago? I was still in my office an hour ago. Why the hell wasn't I told?'

'The caretaker thought she was drunk first of all and fetched Mrs Ruckner. She was taking an ethnic needle-work class with Home Economics in the Morris block and—'

'Never mind about that now,' snapped the Principal. 'A girl's dead on the premises and you have to go on about Mrs Ruckner and ethnic needlework.'

'I'm not going on about Mrs Ruckner,' said the Vice-Principal, driven to some defiance, 'I'm merely trying to explain.'

'Oh, all right, I've heard you. So what have you done with her?'

'Who? Mrs Ruckner?'

'No, the damned girl, for God's sake. There's no need to be flippant.'

'If you're going to adopt that tone of voice, you'd better come here and see for yourself,' said the Vice-Principal and put the phone down.

'You bloody shit,' said the Principal, unintentionally addressing his wife who had just entered the room.

At Ipford Police Station the atmosphere was fairly acrimonious too. 'Don't give me that,' said Flint who had returned from a fruitless visit to the Mental Hospital to interview a patient who had confessed (quite falsely) to being the Phantom Flasher. 'Give it to Hodge. He's drugs and I've had my fill of the bloody Tech.'

'Inspector Hodge is out,' said the Sergeant, 'and they specially asked for you. Personally.'

'Pull the other one,' said Flint. 'Someone's hoaxing you. The last person they want to see is me. And it's mutual.'

'No hoax, sir. It was the Vice-Principal himself. Name of Avon. My lad goes there so I know.'

Flint stared at him incredulously. 'Your son goes to that hell-hole? And you let him? You must be out of your mind. I wouldn't let a son of mine within a mile of the place.'

'Possibly not,' said the Sergeant, tactfully avoiding the observation that since Flint's son was doing a five-year stretch, he wasn't likely to be going any place. 'All the same, he's an apprentice plumber. Got day-release classes and he can't opt out of them. There's a law about it.'

'You want my opinion, there ought to be a law stopping youngsters having anything to do with the sods who teach there. When I think of Wilt . . .' He shook his head in despair.

'Mr Avon said something about your discreet approach being needed,' the Sergeant went on, 'and anyway, they don't know how she died. I mean, it doesn't have to be an overdose.'

Flint perked up. 'Discreet approach my arse,' he muttered. 'Still, a genuine murder there makes a change.' He lumbered to his feet and went down to the car pool and drove down to Nott Road and the Tech. A patrol car was parked outside the gates. Flint swept past it and parked deliberately in the space reserved for the Bursar. Then with the diminished confidence he always felt when returning to the Tech, he entered the building. The Vice-Principal was waiting for him by the Enquiries Desk. 'Ah, Inspector, I'm so glad you could come.'

Flint regarded him suspiciously. His previous visits hadn't been welcomed. 'All right, where's the body?' he said abruptly and was pleased to see the Vice-Principal wince.

'Er . . . in the boiler-room,' he said. 'But first there's the question of discretion. If we can avoid a great deal of publicity it would really be most helpful.'

Inspector Flint cheered up. When the sods started squealing about publicity and the need for discretion, things had got to be bad. On the other hand, he'd had enough lousy publicity from the Tech himself. 'If it's anything to do with Wilt . . .' he began, but the Vice-Principal shook his head.

'Nothing like that, I assure you,' he said. 'At least, not directly.'

'What's that mean, not directly?' said Flint warily. With Wilt, nothing was ever direct.

'Well, he was the first to be told that Miss Lynchknowle had taken an overdose but he went to the wrong loo.'

'Went to the wrong loo?' said Flint and bared his teeth in a mock smile. A second later the smile had gone. He'd smelt trouble. 'Miss who?'

'Lynchknowle. That's what I mean about . . . well, the need for discretion. I mean . . .'

'You don't have to tell me. I know, don't I just,' said

Flint rather more coarsely than the Vice-Principal liked. 'The Lord Lieutenant's daughter gets knocked off here and you don't want him to . . .' He stopped and looked hard at the V-P. 'How come she was here in the first place? Don't tell me she was shacked up with one of your so-called students.'

'She was one of our students,' said the Vice-Principal, trying to maintain some dignity in the face of Flint's patent scepticism. 'She was Senior Secs Three and . . .'

'Senior Sex Three? What sort of course is that, for hell's sake? Meat One was sick enough considering they were a load of butcher's boys, but if you're telling me you've been running a class for prostitutes and one of them's Lord Lynchknowle's ruddy daughter . . .'

'Senior Secretarics,' spluttered the Vice-Principal, 'a very respectable course. We've always had excellent results.'

'Like deaths,' said Flint. 'All right, let's have a look at your latest victim.'

With the certainty now that he'd done the wrong thing in asking for Flint, the Vice-Principal led the way across the quad.

But the Inspector hadn't finished. 'I hear you've been putting it out as a self-administered OD. Right?'

'OD?'

'Overdose.'

'Of course. You're not seriously suggesting it could have been anything else?'

Inspector Flint fingered his moustache. 'I'm not in a position to suggest anything. Yet. I'm asking why you say she died of drugs.'

'Well, Mrs Bristol saw a girl injecting herself in the staff toilet and went to fetch Wilt . . .'

'Why Wilt of all people? Last person I'd fetch.'

'Mrs Bristol is Wilt's secretary,' said the V-P and went on to explain the confused course of events. Flint listened grimly. The only part he enjoyed was hearing how Wilt had been dealt with by Miss Hare. She sounded like a woman after his own heart. The rest fitted in with his preconceptions of the Tech.

'One thing's certain,' he said when the Vice-Principal had finished, 'I'm not drawing any conclusions until I've made a thorough examination. And I do mean thorough. The way you've told it doesn't make sense. One unidentified girl takes a fix in a toilet and the next thing you know Miss Lynchknowle is found dead in the boiler-room. How come you assume it's the same girl?'

The Vice-Principal said it just seemed logical. 'Not to me it doesn't,' said Flint. 'And what was she doing in the boiler-room?'

The Vice-Principal looked miserably down the steps at the door and resisted the temptation to say she'd been dying. That might work with the Principal but Inspector Flint's manner didn't suggest he'd respond kindly to statements of the obvious. 'I've no idea. Perhaps she just felt like going somewhere dark and warm.'

'And perhaps she didn't,' said Flint. 'Anyway, I'll soon find out.'

'I just hope you will be discreet,' said the V-P, 'I mean it's a very sensitive . . .'

'Bugger discretion,' said Flint, 'all I'm interested in is the truth.'

Twenty minutes later, when the Principal arrived, it was all too obvious that the Inspector's search for the truth had assumed quite alarming dimensions. The fact was that Mrs Ruckner, more accustomed to the niceties of ethnic needlework than resuscitation, had allowed the body to slip behind the boiler: that the boiler hadn't been turned off added a macabre element to the scene. Flint had refused to allow it to be moved until it had been photographed from every possible angle, and he had summoned fingerprint and forensic experts from the Murder Squad along with the police surgeon. The Tech car park was lined with squad cars and an ambulance and the buildings themselves seemed to be infested with policemen. And all this in full view of students arriving for evening classes. To the Principal, it appeared as if the

Inspector was intent on attracting the maximum adverse publicity.

'Is the man mad?' he demanded of the Vice-Principal, stepping over a white tape that had been laid on the ground outside the steps to the boiler-room.

'He says he's treating it as a murder case until he's proved it isn't,' said the Vice-Principal weakly, 'and I wouldn't go down there if I were you.'

'Why the hell not?'

'Well, for one thing there's a dead body and . . .'

'Of course there's a dead body,' said the Principal, who had been in the War and frequently mentioned the fact. 'Nothing to be squeamish about.'

'If you say so. All the same . . .'

But the principal had already gone down the steps into the boiler-room. He was escorted out a moment later looking decidedly unwell. 'Jesus wept! You could have told me they were holding an autopsy on the spot,' he muttered. 'How the hell did she get in that state?'

'I rather think Mrs Ruckner . . .'

'Mrs Ruckner? Mrs Ruckner?' gurgled the Principal, trying to equate what he had just seen in some way with the tenuous figure of the part-time lecturer in ethnic needlework and finding it impossible. 'What the hell has Mrs Ruckner got to do with that . . . that . . .'

But before he could express himself at all clearly, they were joined by Inspector Flint. 'Well, at least we've got a real dead corpse this time,' he said, timing his cheerfulness nicely. 'Makes a change for the Tech, doesn't it?'

The Principal eyed him with loathing. Whatever Flint might feel about the desirability of real dead corpses littering the Tech he didn't share Flint's opinions. 'Now look here, Inspector . . .' he began in an attempt to assert some authority.

But Flint had opened a cardboard box. 'I think you had better look in here first,' he said. 'Is this the sort of printed matter you encourage your students to read?'

The Principal stared down into the box with a horrid fascination. If the cover of the top magazine was anything to go by – it depicted two women, a rack and a revoltingly androgynous man clad in chains and a . . . the Principal preferred not to think what it looked like – the entire box was filled with printed matter he wouldn't have wanted his students to know about, let alone read.

'Certainly not,' he said, 'that's downright pornography.'

'Hard core,' said Flint, 'and there's more where this little lot came from. Puts a new complexion on things, doesn't it?'

'Dear God,' muttered the Principal, as Flint trotted off across the quad, 'are we to be spared nothing? That bloody man seems to find the whole horrible business positively enjoyable.'

'It's probably because of that terrible incident with Wilt some years back,' said the V-P. 'I don't think he's ever forgotten it.'

'Nor have I,' said the Principal, looking gloomily round at the buildings in which he had once hoped to make a name for himself. And in a sense it seemed he had. Thanks to so many things that were connected, in his mind, with Wilt. It was the one topic on which he would have agreed with the Inspector. The little bastard ought to be locked up.

And in a sense Wilt was. To prevent Eva from learning that he spent Friday evenings at Baconheath Airbase he devoted himself on Mondays to tutoring a Mr McCullum at Ipford Prison and then led her to suppose he had another tutorial with him four evenings later. He felt rather guilty about this subterfuge but excused himself with the thought that if Eva wanted to buy an expensive education plus computers for four daughters, she couldn't seriously expect his salary, however augmented by HM Prison Service, to pay for it. The airbase lectures did that and anyway Mr McCullum's company constituted a form of penance. It also had the effect of assuaging Wilt's sense of guilt. Not that his pupil didn't do his damnedest to instil one. A sociology lecturer from the Open University had given him a solid grounding in that subject and Wilt's attempts to further Mr McCullum's interest in E. M. Foster and *Howards End* were constantly interrupted by the convict's comments on the socio-economically disadvantaged environment which had led him to end up where and what he was. He was also fairly fluent on the class war, the need for a preferably bloody revolution and the total redistribution of wealth. Since he had spent his entire life pursuing riches by highly illegal and unpleasant means, ones which involved the deaths of four people and the use of a blowtorch as a persuader on several gentlemen in his debt, thus earning himself the soubriquet 'Fireworks Harry' and 25 years from a socially prejudiced judge, Wilt found the argument somewhat suspect.

He didn't much like Mr McCullum's changes of mood either. They varied from whining self-pity, and the claim that he was deliberately being turned into a cabbage, through bouts of religious fervour during which the name Longford came up rather too often, and finally to a bloody-minded belligerence when he threatened to roast the fucking narks who'd shopped him. On the whole, Wilt preferred McCullum the cabbage and was glad that the tutorials were conducted through a grill of substantial wire mesh and in the presence of an even more substantial warder. After Miss Hare and the verbal battering he'd had from Eva, he could do with some protection and this evening Mr McCullum's mood had nothing to do with vegetables. 'Listen,' he told Wilt thickly, 'you don't have a clue, do you? Think you know everything but you haven't done time. Same with this E. M. Forster. He was a middle-class scrubber too.'

'Possibly,' said Wilt, recognizing that this was not one of the nights on which to press Mr McCullum too frankly on the need to stick to the subject. 'He was certainly middle-class. On the other hand, this may have endowed him with the sensitivity needed to—'

'Fuck sensitivity. Lived with a pig, that's how sensitive he was, dirty sod.'

Wilt considered this estimation of the private life of the great author dubious. So, evidently, did the warder. 'Pig?' said Wilt, 'I don't think he did you know. Are you sure?'

'Course I'm sure. Fucking pig by the name of Buckingham.'

'Oh, him,' said Wilt, cursing himself for having encouraged the beastly man to read Forster's biography as background material to the novels. He should have realized that any mention of policemen was calculated to put 'Fireworks Harry' in a foul mood. 'Anyway, if we look at his work as a writer, as an observer of the social scene and . . .'

McCullum wasn't having any of that. 'The social scene my eye and Betty Martin. Spent more time looking up his own arsehole.'

'Well, metaphorically I suppose you could . . .'

'Literally,' snarled McCullum, and turned the pages of the book. 'How about this? January second ". . . have the illusion I am charming and beautiful . . . blah, blah . . . but would powder my nose if I wasn't found out . . . blah, blah . . . The anus is clotted with hairs . . ." And that's in your blooming Forster's diary. A self-confessed narcissistic fairy.'

'Must have used a mirror, I suppose,' said Wilt, temporarily thrown by this revelation. 'All the same his novels reflect . . .'

'I know what you're going to say,' interrupted McCullum. 'They have social relevance for their time. Balls. He could have got nicked for what he did, slumming it with one of the State's sodding hatchet men. His books have got about as much social relevance as Barbara bloody Cartland's. And we all know what they are, don't we? Literary asparagus.'

'Literary asparagus?'

'Chambermaid's delight,' said Mr McCullum with peculiar relish.

'It's an interesting theory,' said Wilt, who had no idea what the beastly man was talking about, 'though personally I'd have thought Barbara Cartland's work was pure escapism whereas . . .'

'That's enough of that,' interrupted the warder, 'I don't want to hear that word again. You're supposed to be talking about books.'

'Listen to Wilberforce,' said McCullum, still looking fixedly at Wilt, 'bloody marvellous vocabulary he's got, hasn't he?'

Behind him the warder bridled. 'My name's not Wilberforce and you know it,' he snapped.

'Well then, I wasn't talking about you, was I?' said McCullum. 'I mean everyone knows you're Mr Gerard, not some fucking idiot who has to get someone literate to read the racing results for him. Now as Mr Wilt here was saying . . .'

Wilt tried to remember. 'About Barbara Cartland being moron fodder,' prompted McCullum.

'Oh yes, well according to your theories, reading romantic novels is even more detrimental to working-class consciousness than . . . What's the matter?'

Mr McCullum was smiling horribly at him through the mesh. 'Screw's pissed off,' he hissed. 'Knew he would. Got him on my payroll and his wife reads Barbara Cartland so he couldn't stand to listen. Here, take this.'

Wilt looked at the rolled-up piece of paper McCullum was thrusting through the wire. 'What is it?'

'My weekly essay.'

'But you write that in your notebook.'

'Think of it like that,' said McCullum, 'and stash it fast.'

'I'll do no . . .'

Mr McCullum's ferocious expression had returned. 'You will,' he said.

Wilt put the roll in his pocket and 'Fireworks' relaxed. 'Don't make much of a living, do you?' he asked. 'Live in a semi and drive an Escort. No big house with a Jag on the forecourt, eh?'

'Not exactly,' said Wilt, whose taste had never been drawn to Jaguars. Eva was dangerous enough in a small car.

'Right. Well now's your chance to earn 50K.'

'50K?'

'Grand. Cash,' said McCullum and glanced at the door behind him. So did Wilt, hopefully, but there was no sign of the warder. 'Cash?'

'Old notes. Small denominations and no traceability. Right?'

'Wrong,' said Wilt firmly. 'If you think you can bribe me into . . .'

'Gob it,' said McCullum with a nasty grunt. 'You've got a wife and four daughters and you live in a brick and mortar, address 45 Oakhurst Avenue. You drive an Escort, pale dog-turd, number-plate HPR 791 N. Bank at Lloyds, account number 0737 . . . want me to go on?' Wilt didn't. He got to his feet but Mr McCullum hadn't finished. 'Sit down while you've still got knees,' he hissed. 'And daughters.'

Wilt sat down. He was suddenly feeling rather weak. 'What do you want?' he asked.

Mr McCullum smiled. 'Nothing. Nothing at all. You just go off home and check that piece of paper and everything's going to be just jake.'

'And if I don't?' asked Wilt feeling weaker still.

'Sudden bereavement is a sad affair,' said McCullum, 'very sad. Specially for cripples.'

Wilt gazed through the wire mesh and wondered, not for the first time in his life, though by the sound of things it might be the last, what it was about him that attracted the horrible. And McCullum was horrible, horrible and evilly efficient. And why should the evil be so efficient? 'I still want to know what's on that paper,' he said.

'Nothing,' said McCullum, 'it's just a sign. Now as I see it Forster was the typical product of a middle-class background. Lots of lolly and lived with his old Ma . . .'

'Bugger E. M. Forster's mother,' said Wilt. 'What I want to know is why you think I'm going to . . .'

But any hope he had of discussing his future was ended by the return of the warder. 'You can cut the lecture, we're shutting up shop.'

'See you next week, Mr Wilt,' said McCullum with a leer as he was led back to his cell. Wilt doubted it. If there was one thing on which he was determined, it was that he would never see the swine again. Twenty-five years was far too short a sentence for a murdering gangster. Life should mean life and nothing less. He wandered miserably down the passage towards the main gates, conscious of the paper in his pocket and the awful alternatives before him. The obvious thing to do was to report McCullum's threats to the warder on the gate. But the bastard had said he had one warder on his payroll and if one, why not more? In fact, looking back over the months, Wilt could remember several occasions when McCullum had indicated that he had a great deal of influence in the prison. And outside too, because he'd even known the number of Wilt's bank account. No, he'd have to report to someone in authority, not an ordinary screw.

'Had a nice little session with "Fireworks"?' enquired the warder at the end of the corridor with what Wilt considered to be sinister emphasis. Yes, definitely he'd have to speak to someone in authority.

At the main gate it was even worse. 'Anything to declare, Mr Wilt?' said the warder there with a grin, 'I mean we can't tempt you to stay inside, can we?'

'Certainly not,' said Wilt hurriedly.

'You could do worse than join us, you know. All mod cons and telly and the grub's not at all bad nowadays. A nice little cell with a couple of friendly mates. And they do say it's a healthy life. None of the stress you get outside . . .'

But Wilt didn't wait to hear any more. He stepped out into what he had previously regarded as freedom. It didn't seem so free now. Even the houses across the road, bathed in the evening sunshine, had lost their moderate attraction; instead, their windows were empty and menacing. He got into his car and drove a mile along Gill Road before pulling into a side street and stopping. Then making sure no one was watching him, he took the piece of paper out of his pocket and unrolled it. The paper was blank. Blank? That didn't make sense. He held it up to the light and stared at it but the paper was unlined and as far as he could see, had absolutely nothing written on it. Even when he held it horizontally and squinted along it he could make out no indentations on the surface to suggest that a message had been written on it with a matchstick or the blunt end of a pencil. A man was coming towards him along the pavement. With a sense of guilt, Wilt put the paper on the floor and took a road map from the dashboard and pretended to be looking at it until the man had passed. Even then he checked in the rear-view mirror before picking up the paper again. It remained what it had been before, a blank piece of notepaper with a ragged edge as though it had been torn very roughly from a pad. Perhaps the swine had used invisible ink. Invisible ink? How the hell would he get invisible ink in prison? He couldn't unless . . . Something in Wilt's literary memories stirred. Hadn't Graham Greene or Muggeridge mentioned using bird-shit as ink when he was a spy in the Second World War? Or was it lemon juice? Not that it mattered much. Invisible ink was meant to be invisible and if that bastard had intended him to read it, he'd have told him how. Unless, of course, the swine was clear round the bend and in Wilt's opinion, anyone who'd murdered four people and tortured others with a blowtorch as part of the process of earning a living had to be bloody well demented. Not that that let McCullum off the hook in the least. The bugger was a murderer whether he was sane or not, and the sooner he fulfilled his own predictions and became a cabbage the better. Pity he hadn't been born one.

With a fresh sense of desperation, Wilt drove on to The Glassblowers' Arms to think things out over a drink.

Chapter six

'All right, call it off,' said Inspector Flint, helping himself to a plastic cup of coffee from the dispenser and stumping into his office.

'Call it off?' said Sergeant Yates, following him in.

'That's what I said. I knew it was an OD from the start. Obvious. Gave those old windbags a nasty turn all the same, and they could do with a bit of reality. Live in a bloody dream world where everything's nice and hygienic because it's been put into words. That way they don't happen, do they?'

'I hadn't thought of it like that,' said Yates.

The Inspector took a magazine out of the cardboard box and studied a photograph of a threesome grotesquely intertwined. 'Bloody disgusting,' he said.

Sergeant Yates peered over his shoulder. 'You wouldn't think anyone would have the nerve to be shot doing that, would you?'

'Anyone who does that ought to be shot, if you ask me,' said Flint. 'Though mind you they're not really doing it. Can't be. You'd get ruptured or something. Found this little lot in that boiler-room and it didn't do that murky Principal a bit of good. Turned a very queer colour, he did.'

'Not his, are they?' asked Yates.

Flint shut the magazine and dumped it back in the box. 'You never know, my son, you never know. Not with so-called educated people you don't. It's all hidden behind words with them. They look all right from the outside, but it's what goes on in here that's really weird.' Flint tapped his forehead significantly. 'And that's something else again.'

'I suppose it must be,' said Yates. 'Specially when it's hygienic into the bargain.'

Flint looked at him suspiciously. He never knew if Sergeant Yates was as stupid as he made out. 'You trying to be funny or something?'

'Of course not. Only first you said they lived in a hygienic dream world of words; and then you say they're kinky in the head. I was just putting the two together.'

'Well, don't,' said Flint. 'Don't even try. Just get me Hodge. The Drug Squad can take this mess over, and good luck to them.' The Sergeant went out, leaving Flint studying his pale fingers and thinking weird thoughts of his own about Hodge, the Tech and the possibilities that might result from bringing the Head of the Drug Squad and that infernal institution together. And Wilt. It was an interesting prospect, particularly when he remembered Hodge's request for phone-tapping facilities and his generally conspiratorial air. Kept his cards close to his chest, did Inspector Hodge, and a fat lot of good it had done him so far. Well, two could play at that game, and if ever there was a quicksand of misinformation and inconsequentiality, it had to be the Tech and Wilt. Flint reversed the order. Wilt and the Tech. And Wilt had been vaguely connected with the dead girl, if only by going to the wrong toilet. The word alerted Flint to his own immediate needs. Those bloody pills had struck again.

He hurried down the passage for a pee and as he stood there, standing and staring at the tiled wall and a notice which said, 'Don't drop your cigarette ends in the urinal. It makes them soggy and difficult to light', his disgust changed to inspiration. There was a lesson to be learned from that notice if he could only see it. It had to do with the connection between a reasonable request and an utterly revolting supposition. The word 'inconsequential' came to mind again. Sticking Inspector Bloody Hodge onto Wilt would be like tying two cats together by their tails and seeing which one came out on top. And if Wilt didn't, Flint had sorely misjudged the little shit. And behind Wilt there was Eva and those foul quads and if that frightful combination didn't foul Hodge's career up as effectively as it had wrecked Flint's, the Inspector deserved promotion. With the delightful thought that he'd be getting his own back on Wilt too, he returned to his office and was presently doodling figures of infinite confusion which was exactly what he hoped to initiate.

He was still happily immersed in this daydream of revenge when Yates returned. 'Hodge is out,' he reported. 'Left a message he'd be back shortly.'

'Typical,' said Flint. 'The sod's probably lurking in some coffee bar trying to make up his mind which dolly bird he's going to nail.'

Yates sighed. Ever since Flint had been on those ruddy penis-blockers or whatever they were called, he'd had girls on his mind. 'Why shouldn't he be doing that?' he asked.

'Because that's the way the sod works. A right shoddy copper. Pulls some babe in arms in for smoking pot and then tries to turn her into a supergrass. Been watching too much TV.'

He was interrupted by the preliminary report from the Lab. 'Massive heroin dose,' the technician told him, 'that's for starters. She'd used something else we haven't identified yet. Could be a new product. It's certainly not the usual. Might be "Embalming Fluid" though.'

'Embalming Fluid? What the hell would she be doing with that?' said Flint with a genuine and justified revulsion.

'It's a name for another of these hallucinogens like LSD only worse. Anyway, we'll let you know.'

'Don't,' said Flint. 'Deal direct with Hodge. It's his pigeon now.'

He put the phone down and shook his head sorrowfully. 'Says she fixed herself with heroin and some filth called Embalming Fluid,' he told Yates. 'You wouldn't credit it, would you? Embalming Fluid! I don't know what the world's coming to.'

Fifty miles away, Lord Lynchknowle's dinner had been interrupted by the arrival of a police car and the news of his daughter's death. The fact that it had come between the mackerel pâté and the game pie, and on the wine side, an excellent Montrachet and a Chateau Lafite 1962, several bottles of which he'd opened to impress the Home

Secretary and two old friends from the Foreign Office, particularly annoyed him. Not that he intended to let the news spoil his meal by announcing it before he'd finished, but he could foresee an ugly episode with his wife afterwards for no better reason than that he had come back to the table with the rather unfortunate remark that it was nothing important. Of course, he could always excuse himself on the grounds that hospitality came first, and old Freddie was the Home Secretary after all, and he wasn't going to let that Lafite '62 go to waste, but somehow he knew Hilary was going to kick up the devil of a fuss about it afterwards. He sat on over the Stilton in a pensive mood wishing to God he'd never married her. Looking back over the years, he could see that his mother had been right when she'd warned him that there was bad blood in 'that family', the Puckertons.

'You can't breed bad blood out, you know,' she'd said, and as a breeder of bull terriers, she'd known what she was talking about. 'It'll come out in the end, mark my words.'

And it had, in that damned girl Penny. Silly bitch should have stuck to showjumping instead of getting it into her head she was going to be some sort of intellectual and skiving off to that rotten Tech in Ipford and mixing with the scum there. All Hilary's fault, too, for encouraging the girl. Not that she'd see it that way. All the blame would be on his side. Oh well, he'd have to do something to pacify her. Phone the Chief Constable perhaps and get Charles to put the boot in. His eyes wandered round the table and rested moodily on the Home Secretary. That was it, have a word with Freddie before he left and see that the police got their marching orders from the top.

By the time he was able to get the Home Secretary alone, a process that required him to lurk in the darkness outside the cloakroom and listen to some frank observations about himself by the hired waitresses in the kitchen, Lord Lynchknowle had worked himself up into a state of indignation that was positively public-spirited. 'It's not simply a personal matter, Freddie,' he told the Home

68

Secretary, when the latter was finally convinced Lynch-knowle's daughter was dead and that he wasn't indulging that curious taste for which he'd been renowned at school. 'There she was at this bloody awful Tech at the mercy of all these drug pedlars. You've got to put a stop to it.'

'Of course, of course,' said the Home Secretary, backing into a hatstand and a collection of shooting sticks and umbrellas. 'I'm deeply sorry—'

'It's no use you damned politicians being sorry,' continued Lynchknowle, forcing him back against a clutter of raincoats, 'I begin to understand the man-in-the-street's disenchantment with the parliamentary process.' (The Home Secretary doubted it.) 'What's more, words'll mend no fences' (the Home Secretary didn't doubt that) 'and I want action.'

'And you'll have it, Percy,' the Home Secretary assured him, 'I guarantee that. I'll get the top men at Scotland Yard onto it tomorrow first thing and no mistake.' He reached for the little notebook he used to appease influential supporters. 'What did you say the name of the place was?'

'Ipford,' said Lord Lynchknowle, still glowering at him.

'And she was at the University there?'

'At the Tech.'

'Really?' said the Home Secretary, with just enough inflexion in his voice to lower Lord Lynchknowle's resolve.

'All her mother's fault,' he said defensively.

'Quite. All the same, if you will allow your daughters to go to Technical Colleges, not that I'm against them you understand, but a man in your position can't be too careful . . .'

In the hall, Lady Lynchknowle caught the phrase.

'What are you two men doing down there?' she asked shrilly.

'Nothing, dear, nothing,' said Lord Lynchknowle. It was a remark he was to regret an hour later when the guests had gone.

'Nothing?' shrieked Lady Lynchknowle, who had by then recovered from the condolences the Home Secretary had offered so unexpectedly. 'You dare to stand there and call Penny's death nothing?'

'I am not actually standing, my dear,' said Lynch-knowle from the depths of an armchair. But his wife was not to be deflected so easily.

'And you sat through dinner knowing she was lying there on a marble slab? I knew you were a callous swine but . . .'

'What the hell else was I supposed to do?' yelled Lynch-knowle, before she could get into her stride. 'Come back to the table and announce that your daughter was a damned junkie? You'd have loved that, wouldn't you? I can just hear you now . . .'

'You can't,' shrieked his wife, making her fury heard in the servants' quarters. Lynchknowle lumbered to his feet and slammed the door. 'And don't think you're going to—'

'Shut up,' he bawled. 'I've spoken to Freddie and he's putting Scotland Yard onto the case and now I'm going to call Charles. As Chief Constable he can—'

'And what good is that going to do? He can't bring her back to me!'

'Nobody can, dammit. And if you hadn't put the idea into her empty head that she was capable of earning her own living when it was as clear as daylight she was as thick as two short planks, none of this would have happened.' Lord Lynchknowle picked up the phone and dialled the Chief Constable.

At The Glassblowers' Arms, Wilt was on the phone too. He had spent the time trying to think of some way to circumvent whatever ghastly plans McCullum had in mind for him without revealing his own identity to the prison authorities. It wasn't easy.

After two large whiskies, Wilt had plucked up enough courage to phone the prison, had refused to give his name and had asked for the Governor's home number. It wasn't in the phone book. 'It's ex-directory,' said the warder in the office.

'Quite,' said Wilt. 'That's why I'm asking.'

'And that's why I can't give it to you. If the Governor wanted every criminal in the district to know where he could be subjected to threats, he'd put it there wouldn't he?'

'Yes,' said Wilt. 'On the other hand, when a member of the public is being threatened by some of your inmates, how on earth is he supposed to inform the Governor that there's going to be a mass breakout?'

'Mass breakout? What do you know about plans for a mass breakout?'

'Enough to want to speak to the Governor.' There was a pause while the warder considered this and Wilt fed the phone with another coin.

'Why can't you tell me?' the warder asked finally.

Wilt ignored the question. 'Listen,' he said with a desperate earnestness that sprang from the knowledge that having come so far he couldn't back down, and that if he didn't convince the man that this was a genuine crisis, McCullum's accomplices would shortly be doing something ghastly to his knees, 'I assure you that this is a deeply serious matter. I wish to speak to the Governor privately. I will call back in ten minutes. All right?'

'It may not be possible to reach him in that time, sir,' said the warder, recognizing the voice of genuine desperation. 'If you can give me your number, I'll get him to call you.'

'It's Ipford 23194,' he said, 'and I'm not joking.'

'No, sir,' said the warder. 'I'll be back to you as soon as I can.'

Wilt put the phone down and wandered back to his whisky at the bar uncomfortably aware that he was now committed to a course of action that could have horrendous consequences. He finished his whisky and ordered another to dull the thought that he'd given the warder the phone number of the pub where he was well-known. 'At least it proved to him that I was being serious,' he thought and wondered what it was about the bureaucratic mentality that made communication so difficult. The main thing was to get in touch with the Governor as soon as possible and explain the situation to him. Once McCullum had been transferred to another prison, he'd be off the hook.

At HM Prison Ipford, the information that a mass escape was imminent was already causing repercussions. The Chief Warder, summoned from his bed, had tried to telephone the Governor. 'The blasted man must be out to dinner somewhere,' he said when the phone had rung for several minutes without being answered. 'Are you certain it wasn't a hoax call?'

The warder on duty shook his head. 'Sounded genuine to me,' he said. 'Educated voice and obviously frightened. In fact, I have an idea I recognized it.'

'Recognized it?'

'Couldn't put a name to it but he sounded familiar somehow. Anyway, if it wasn't genuine, why did he give me his phone number so quick?' The Chief Warder looked at the number and dialled it. The line was engaged. A girl at The Glassblowers' Arms was talking to her boyfriend. 'Why didn't he give his name?'

'Sounded frightened to death like I told you. Said something about being threatened. And with some of the swine we've got in here . . .'

The Chief Warder didn't need telling. 'Right. We're not taking any chances. Put the emergency plan into action pronto. And keep trying to contact the bloody Governor.'

Half an hour later, the Governor returned home to find the phone in his study ringing. 'Yes, what is it?'

'Mass breakout threatened,' the warder told him, 'a man . . . ' But the Governor wasn't waiting. He'd been living in terror for years that something of this sort was going to happen. 'I'll be right over,' he shouted and dashed for his car. By the time he reached the prison his fears had been turned to panic by the wail of police sirens and the presence on the road of several fire engines travelling at high speed in front of him. As he ran towards the gate, he was stopped by three policemen.

'Where do you think you're going?' a sergeant demanded. The Governor looked at him lividly.

'Since I happen to be the Governor,' he said, 'the Governor of this prison, you understand, I'm going inside. Now if you'll kindly stand aside.'

'Any means of identification, sir?' asked the Sergeant. 'My orders require me to prevent anyone leaving or entering.'

The Governor rummaged through the pockets of his suit and produced a five-pound note and a comb. 'Now look here, officer . . .' he began, but the Sergeant was already looking. At the five-pound note. He ignored the comb.

'I shouldn't try that one if I were you,' he said.

'Try what one! I don't seem to have anything else on me.' 'You heard that one, Constable,' said the sergeant, 'Attempting to offer a bribe to—'

'A bribe . . . offer a bribe? Who said anything about offering a bribe?' exploded the Governor. 'You asked me for means of identification and when I try to produce some, you start talking about bribes. Ask the warder on the gate to identify me, dammit.' It took another five minutes of protest to get inside the prison and by then his nerves were in no state to deal at all adequately with the situation. 'You've done what?' he screamed at the Chief Warder.

'Moved all the men from the top floors to the cells below, sir. Thought it better in case they got onto the roof. Of course, they're a bit cramped but . . .'

'Cramped? They were four to a one-man cell already. You mean to say they're eight now? It's a wonder they haven't started rioting already.' He was interrupted by the sound of screams from C Block. As Prison Officer Blaggs hurried away, the Governor tried to find out what was happening. It was almost as difficult as getting into the prison had been. A battle was apparently raging on the third floor of A Wing. 'That'll be due to putting Fidley and Gosling in with Stanforth and Haydow,' the warder in the office said.

'Fidley and . . . Put two child murderers in with a couple of decent honest-to-God armed bank robbers? Blaggs must be mad. How long did it take them to die?'

'I don't think they're dead yet,' said the warder with rather more disappointment in his voice than the Governor approved. 'Last I heard, they'd managed to stop Haydow from castrating Fidley. That was when Mr Blaggs decided to intervene.'

'You mean the lunatic waited?' asked the Governor.

'Not exactly, sir. You see, there was this fire in D Block—'

'Fire in D Block? What fire in D Block?'

'Moore set fire to his mattress, sir, and by the time—' But the Governor was no longer listening. He knew now that his career was at stake. All it needed to finish him was for that lunatic Blaggs to have acted as an accessory to murder by packing all the swine in the Top Security Block into one cell. He was just on his way to make quite certain when Chief Warder Blaggs returned. 'Everything's under control, sir,' he said cheerfully.

'Under control?' spluttered the Governor. 'Under control? If you think the Home Secretary's going to think "under control" means having child killers castrated by other prisoners, I can assure you you're not up-to-date with contemporary regulations. Now then, about Top Security.'

'Nothing to worry about there, sir. They're all sleeping like babes.'

'Odd,' said the Governor. 'If there was going to be an attempted breakout you'd think they were bound to be involved. You're sure they're not shamming?'

'Positive, sir,' said Blaggs proudly. 'The first thing I did, sir, by way of a precaution, was to lace their cocoa with that double-strength sleeping stuff.'

'Sweet Jesus,' moaned the Governor, trying to imagine the consequences of the Chief Warder's experiment in preventive sedation if news leaked out to the Howard League for Penal Reform. 'Did you say "double strength"?'

The Chief Warder nodded. 'Same stuff we had to use on Fidley that time he saw the Shirley Temple film and went bananas. Mind you, he's not going to get a hard-on after tonight, not if he's wise.'

'But that was double-strength phenobarb,' squawked the Governor.

'That's right, sir. So I gave them double strength like it said. Went out like lights they did.'

The Governor could well believe it. 'You've gone and given four times the proper dose to those men,' he moaned, 'probably killed the brutes. That stuff's lethal. I never told you to do that.'

Chief Warder Blaggs looked crestfallen. 'I was only doing what I thought best, sir. I mean those swine are a menace to society. Half of them are psychopathic killers.'

'Not the only psychopaths round here,' muttered the Governor. He was about to order a medical team into the prison to stomach-pump the villains Blaggs had sedated, when the warder by the phone intervened. 'We could always say Wilson poisoned them,' he said, 'I mean, that's what they're terrified of. Remember that time they went on dirty strike and Mr Blaggs here let Wilson do some washing up in the kitchen?'

The Governor did, and would have preferred to forget it. Putting a mass poisoner anywhere near a kitchen had always struck him as insane.

'Did the trick, sir. They came off dirtying their cells double quick.'

'And went on hunger strike instead,' said the Governor.

'And Wilson didn't like it much either, come to that,' said the warder, for whom the incident evidently had pleasant memories. 'Said we'd no right making him wash up in boxing gloves. Proper peeved he was—'

'Shut up,' yelled the Governor, trying to get back to a world of comparative sanity, but he was interrupted by the phone.

'It's for you, sir,' said the Chief Warder significantly.

The Governor grabbed it. 'I understand you have some information to give me about an escape plan,' he said, and realized he was talking to the buzz of a pay phone. But before he could ask the Chief Warder how he knew it was for him, the coin dropped. The Governor repeated his statement.

'That's what I'm phoning about,' said the caller. 'Is there any truth in the rumour?'

'Any truth in the . . .' said the Governor. 'How the devil would I know? You were the one to bring the matter up.'

'News to me,' said the man. 'That is Ipford Prison, isn't it?'

'Of course it's Ipford Prison and what's more, I'm the Governor. Who the hell did you think I was?'

'Nobody,' said the man, now sounding decidely perplexed, 'nobody at all. Well, not nobody exactly but . . . well . . . you don't sound like a Prison Governor. Anyway, all I'm trying to find out is if there's been an escape or not.'

'Listen,' said the Governor, beginning to share the caller's doubts about his own identity, 'you phoned earlier in the evening with information about an escape plot and—'

'I did? You off your rocker or something? I've been out covering a burst bloody bulkloader on Bliston Road for the last three bloody hours and if you think I've had time to call you, you're bleeding barmy.'

The Governor struggled with the alliteration before realizing something else was wrong. 'And who am I speaking to?' he asked, mustering what little patience he still retained.

'The name's Nailtes,' said the man, 'and I'm from the *Ipford Evening News* and—'

The Governor slammed the phone down and turned on Blaggs. 'A bloody fine mess you've landed us in,' he shouted. 'That was the *Evening News* wanting to know if there's been an escape.'

Chief Warder Blaggs looked dutifully abashed. 'I'm

sorry if there's been some mistake . . .' he began and brought a fresh torrent of abuse on his head.

'Mistake? Mistake?' yelled the Governor.'Some maniac rings up with some fucking cock-and-bull story about an escape and you have to poison . . .' But further discussion was interrupted by news of a fresh crisis. Three safe-breakers, who had been transferred from a cell designed to hold one Victorian convict to another occupied by four Grievous Bodily Harm merchants from Glasgow, known as the Gay Gorbals, had begun to fulfil Wilt's prophesy by escaping and demanding to be closeted with some het-erosexual murderers for protection.

The Governor found them arguing their case with warders in B Block. 'We're not going in with a load of arse-bandits and that's a fact,' said the spokesman.

'It's only a temporary move,' said the Governor, him-self temporizing. 'In the morning—'

'We'll be suffering from AIDS,' said the safebreaker.

'Aids?'

'Acquired Immune Deficiency Syndrome. We want some good, clean murderer, not those filthy swine with anal herpes. A stretch is one thing and so's a bang to rights but not the sort of stretch those Scotch sods would give us and we're fucked if we're going to be banged to wrong. This is supposed to be a prison, not Dotheboys Hall.'

By the time the Governor had pacified them and sent them back to their own cell, he was beginning to have his doubts about the place himself. In his opinion, the prison felt more like a mad-house. His next visit, this time to Top Security, made an even worse impression. A sepulchral silence hung over the floodlit building and, as the Gover-nor passed from cell to cell, he had the illusion of being in a charnel-house. Wherever he looked, men who in other circumstances he would happily have seen dead, looked as though they were. Only the occasional ghastly snore suggested otherwise. For the rest, the inmates hung over the sides of their beds or lay grotesquely supine on the floor in attitudes that seemed to indicate that rigor mortis had already set in.

'Just let me find the swine who started this little lot,' he muttered. 'I'll . . . I'll . . . I'll . . .' He gave up. There was nothing in the book of legal punishments that would fit the crime.

Chapter seven

By the time Wilt left The Glassblowers' Arms, his desperation had been alleviated by beer and his inability to get anywhere near the phone. He'd moved onto beer after three whiskies, and the change had made it difficult for him to be in two places at the same time, a prerequisite, it seemed, for finding the phone unoccupied. For the first half hour, a girl had been engaged in an intense conversation on reversed charges, and when Wilt had returned from the toilet, her place had been taken by an aggressive youth who had told him to bugger off. After that, there seemed to be some conspiracy to keep him away from the phone. A succession of people had used it and Wilt had ended up sitting at the bar and drinking, and generally arriving at the conclusion that things weren't so bad after all, even if he did have to walk home instead of driving.

'The bastard's in prison,' he told himself as he left the pub. 'And what's more, he's not coming out for twenty years, so what have I got to worry about? Can't hurt me, can he?'

All the same, as he made his way along the narrow streets towards the river, he kept glancing over his shoulder and wondering if he was being followed. But apart from a man with a small dog and a couple who passed him on bicycles, he was alone and could find no evidence of menace. Doubtless that would come later. Wilt tried to figure out a scenario. Presumably, McCullum had given him the piece of paper as a token message, an indication that he was to be some sort of link-man. Well, there was an easy way out of that one; he wouldn't go near the bloody prison again. Might make things awkward as far as Eva was concerned though. He'd just have to make himself scarce on Monday nights and pretend he was still teaching the loathsome McCullum. Shouldn't be too difficult and anyway, Eva was so engrossed in the quads and their so-called development, she hardly noticed what he was doing. The main thing was that he still had the airbase job and that brought the real money in.

But in the meantime, he had more immediate problems to deal with. Like what to tell Eva when he got home. He looked at his watch and saw that it was midnight. After midnight and without the car. Eva would certainly demand an explanation. What a bloody world it was, where he spent his days dealing with idiotic bureaucrats who interfered at the Tech, and was threatened by maniacs in prison, and after all that, came home to be bullied into lying by a wife who didn't believe he'd done a stroke of work all day. And in a bloody world, only the bloody-minded made any mark. The bloody-minded and the cunning. People with drive and determination. Wilt stopped under a street light and looked at the heathers and azaleas in Mr Sands' garden for the second time that day, but this time with a resurgence of those dangerous drives and determinations which beer and the world's irrationality induced in him. He would assert himself. He would do something to distinguish himself from the mass of dull, stupid people who accepted what life handed out to him and then passed on probably into oblivion (Wilt was never sure about that) without leaving more than the fallacious memories of their children and the fading snapshots in the family album. Wilt would be . . . well, anyway, Wilt would be Wilt, whatever that was. He'd have to give the matter some thought in the morning.

In the meantime, he'd deal with Eva. He wasn't going to stand any nonsense about where have you been? or what have you been up to this time? He'd tell her to mind her own . . . No, that wouldn't do. It was the sort of challenge the damned woman was waiting for and would only provoke her into keeping him awake half the night discussing what was wrong with their marriage. Wilt knew what was wrong with their marriage; it had been going on for twenty years and Eva had had quads instead of having one at a time. Which was typical of her. Talk about never doing things by halves. But that was beside the point. Or was it? Perhaps she'd had quads to compensate in some ghastly deterministic and genetical way for marrying only half a man. Wilt's mind shot off on a tangent once again as he considered the fact, if it was one, that after wars the birthrate of males shot up as if nature with a capital N was automatically compensating for their shortage. If Nature was that intelligent, it ought to have known better than to make him attractive to Eva, and vice versa. He was driven from this line of thought by another attribute of Nature. This time its call. Well, he wasn't peeing in a rose bush again. Once was enough.

He hurried up the street and was presently letting himself surreptitiously into 45 Oakhurst Avenue with the resolve that if Eva was awake he would say the car had broken down and he'd taken it to a garage. It was better to be cunning than bloody-minded after all. In the event, there was no need to be anything more than quiet. Eva, who had spent the evening mending the quads' clothes and who had discovered that they had cut imitation flies in their knickers as a blow for sexual equality, was fast asleep. Wilt climbed carefully into bed beside her and lay in the darkness thinking about drive and determination.

Drive and determination were very much in the air at the police station. Lord Lynchknowle's phone call to the Chief Constable, and the news that the Home Secretary had promised Scotland Yard's assistance, had put the skids under the Superintendent and had jerked him from his chair in front of the telly and back to the station for an urgent conference.

'I want results and I don't care how you get them,' he

told the meeting of senior officers inadvisedly. 'I'm not having us known as the Fenland equivalent of Soho or Piccadilly Circus or wherever they push this muck. Is that clear? I want action.'

Flint smirked. For once he was glad of Inspector Hodge's presence. Besides, he could honestly claim that he had gone straight to the Tech and had made a very thorough investigation of the cause of death. 'I think you'll find all the preliminary details in my report, sir,' he said. 'Death was due to a massive overdose of heroin and something called Embalming Fluid. Hodge might know.'

'It's Phencyclidine or PCP,' he said. 'Comes under a whole series of names like Super Grass, Hog, Angel Dust and Killer Weed.'

The Superintendent didn't want a catalogue of names. 'What's the filth do, apart from kill kids, of course?'

'It's like LSD only a hell of a sight worse,' said Hodge. 'Puts them into psychosis if they smoke the stuff too much and generally blows their minds. It's bloody murder.'

'So we've gathered,' said the Superintendent. 'Where'd she get it is what I want to know. Me and the Chief Constable *and* the Home Secretary.'

'Hard to say,' said Hodge. 'It's a Yankee habit. Haven't seen it over here before.'

'So she went to the States and bought it there on holiday? Is that what you're saying?'

'She wouldn't have fixed herself with the stuff if she had,' said Hodge, 'she'd have known better. Could have got it from someone in the University, I suppose.'

'Well, wherever she got it,' said the Superintendent grimly, 'I want that source traced, and fast. In fact, I want this town clean of heroin and every other drug before we have Scotland Yard descending on us like a ton of bricks and proving we're nothing but a bunch of country hicks. Those aren't my words, they're the Chief Constable's. Now then, we're quite certain she took this stuff herself? She could have been . . . well, given it against her will?'

'Not according to my information,' said Flint, recognizing the attempt to shift the investigation in his direction and clear Lord Lynchknowle's name from any connection with the drug scene. 'She was seen shooting herself with it in one of the Staff toilets at the Tech. If shooting's the right word,' said Flint, and looked across at Hodge, hoping to shift onto him the burden of keeping Scotland Yard at bay while screening the Lynchknowles.

The Superintendent wasn't interested. 'Whatever,' he said. 'So there's no question of foul play?'

Flint shook his head. The whole beastly business of drugs was foul play but now didn't seem the time to discuss the question. What was important from Flint's point of view was to land Hodge with the problem up to his eyebrows. Let him foul this case up and his head really would be on the chopping-block. 'Mind you,' he said, 'I did find it suspicious she was using the Staff toilet. Could be that's the connection.'

'What is?' demanded the Superintendent.

'Well, I'm not saying they are and I'm not saying they're not,' said Flint, with what he liked to think was subtle equivocation. 'All I'm saying is some of the staff could be.'

'Could be what, for Christ's sake?'

'Involved in pushing,' said Flint. 'I mean, that's why it's been so difficult to get a lead on where the stuff's coming from. Nobody'd suspect lecturers to be pushing the muck, would they?' He paused before putting the boot in. 'Take Wilt for example, Mr Henry Wilt. Now there's a bloke I wouldn't trust further than I could throw him and even then I wouldn't turn my back. This isn't the first time we've had trouble over there, you know. I've got a file on that sod as thick as a telephone directory and then some. And he's Head of the Liberal Studies Department at that. You should see some of the drop-outs he's got working for him. Beats me why Lord Lynchknowle let his daughter go to the Tech in the first place.' He paused again. Out of the corner of his eye he could see Inspector Hodge making notes. The bastard was taking the bait. So was the Superintendent.

'You may have something there, Inspector,' he said. 'A

lot of teachers are hangovers from the sixties and seventies and that rotten scene. And the fact that she was spotted in the Staff toilet . . .' It was this that did it. By the time the meeting broke up, Hodge was committed to a thorough investigation of the Tech and had been given permission to send in undercover agents.

'Let me have a list of the names and I'll forward it to the Chief Constable,' said the Superintendent. 'With the Home Secretary involved, there shouldn't be any difficulty, but for God's sake, get some results.'

'Yes, sir,' said Inspector Hodge, and went off to his office a happy man.

So did Flint. Before leaving the station, he called in on the Head of the Drug Squad with Wilt's file. 'If this is any use . . .' he said and dropped it on the desk with apparent reluctance. 'And any other help I can give you, you've only to ask.'

'I will,' said Inspector Hodge, with the opposite intention. If one thing was certain, it was that Flint would get no credit for breaking the case. And so, while Flint drove home and unwisely helped himself to a brown ale before going to bed, Hodge sat on in his office planning the campaign that would lead to his promotion.

He was still there two hours later. Outside, the street lamps had gone off and Ipford slept, but Hodge sat on, his mind already infected with the virus of ambition and hope. He had gone carefully through Flint's report on the discovery of the body and for once he could find no fault with the Inspector's conclusions. They were confirmed by the preliminary report from Forensic. The victim had died from an overdose of heroin mixed with Embalming Fluid. It was this last which interested Hodge.

'American,' he muttered yet again, and checked with the Police National Computer on the incidence of its use. Negligible, as he had thought. All the same, the drug was extremely dangerous and its spread in the States had been so rapid that it had been described as the syphilis of drug abuse. Crack this case and Hodge's name would be known, not simply in Ipford, but through the Lord Lieutenant to the Home Secretary and . . . Hodge's dreams pursued his name before returning to the present. He picked up Wilt's file doubtfully. He hadn't been in Ipford at the time of the Great Doll Case and its ghastly effects on Flint's career, but he'd heard about it in the canteen, where it was generally acknowledged that Mr Henry Wilt had outfoxed Inspector Flint. Made him look a damned fool was the usual verdict, but it had never been clear what Wilt had really been up to. No one in his right mind went round burying inflatable dolls dressed in his wife's clothes at the bottom of piling-holes with twenty tons of concrete on top of them. And Wilt had. It followed that either Wilt hadn't been in his right mind, or that he'd been covering some other crime. Diverting suspicion. Anyway, the sod had got away with whatever he'd been up to and had screwed Flint into the bargain. So Flint had a grudge against the bastard. That was generally acknowledged too.

It was therefore with justified suspicion that Hodge turned to Wilt's file and began to read in detail the transcript of his interrogation. And as he read, a certain grim respect for Wilt grew in his mind. The sod hadn't budged from his story, in spite of being kept awake and deluged with questions. And he had made Flint look the idiot he was. Hodge could see that, just as he could see why Flint had a grudge against him. But above all his own intuition told him that Wilt had to have been guilty of something. Just had to be. And he'd been too clever for the old bugger. Which explained why Flint had been prepared to hand the file over to him. He wanted this Wilt nailed. Only natural. All the same, knowing Flint's attitude to him, Hodge was amazed he had given him the file. Not with all that stuff showing what a moron he was. Must be something else there. Like the old man knew when he was beaten? And certainly he looked it lately. Sounded it too, so maybe giving him the file was tacitly acknowledging the fact. Hodge smiled to himself. He'd always known he was the better man and that his chance to prove it would come. Well, now it bloody well had.

He turned to Flint's report on Miss Lynchknowle again and read it through carefully. There was nothing wrong with Flint's methods and it was only when he came to the bit about Wilt having gone to the wrong toilet that Inspector Hodge saw where the old man had made a mistake. He read through it again.

'Principal reported Wilt went to toilet on the second floor when he should have gone to the one on the fourth floor.' And later 'Wilt's secretary, Mrs Bristol, said she told Wilt to go to Ladies' staff toilet on the fourth floor. Claimed she'd seen girl there before.' It fitted. Another of clever Mr Wilt's little moves, to go to the wrong toilet. But Flint hadn't spotted that or he'd have interviewed the sod. Hodge made a mental note to check Mr Wilt's movements. But surreptitiously. There was no point in putting him on his guard. Hodge made more notes. 'Tech laboratory facilities provide means of making Embalming Fluid. Check', was one. 'Source heroin', another. And all the time while he concentrated, part of his mind ran on different lines, involving romantic-sounding places like the 'Golden Triangle' and the 'Golden Crescent', those jungle areas of Thailand and Burma and Laos, or in the case of the 'Golden Crescent', the laboratories of Pakistan from which heroin came into Europe. In Hodge's mind, small dark men, Pakis, Turks, Iranians and Arabs, converged on Britain by donkey or container truck or the occasional ship: always at night, a black and sinister movement of the deadly opiates financed by men who lived in large houses and belonged to country clubs and had yachts. And then there was the Sicilian Connection with Mafia murders almost daily on the streets of Palermo. And finally the 'pushers' in England, little runts like Flint's son doing his time in Bedford. That again could be an explanation for Flint's change of attitude, his ruddy son. But the romantic picture of distant lands and evil men was the dominant one, and Hodge himself the dominant figure in it, a lone ranger in the war against the most insidious of all crimes.

Reality was different of course, and converged with Hodge's mental geography only in the fact that heroin did come from Asia and Sicily and that an epidemic of terrible addiction had come to Europe, and only the most determined and intelligent police action and international cooperation would bring it to a halt. Which, since the Inspector in spite of his rank was neither intelligent nor possessed of more than a vivid imagination, was where he came unstuck. In place of intelligence, there was only determination, the determination of a man without a family and with few friends, but with a mission. And so Inspector Hodge worked on through the night planning the action he intended to take. It was four in the morning when he finally left the station and walked round the corner to his flat for a few hours' sleep. Even then, he lay in the darkness gloating over Flint's discomfiture. 'The sod's getting his comeuppance,' he thought before falling asleep.

On the other side of Ipford, in a small house with a neat garden distinguished by a nicely symmetrical goldfish pond with a stone cherub in the middle, Inspector Flint would have agreed, though the cause of his problem had rather more to do with brown ale and those bloody piss pills than with Hodge's future. On the latter score, he was quietly confident. He went back to bed wondering if it wouldn't be a wise move to take some leave. He had a fortnight due to him, and anyway he could justifiably claim his doctor had told him to take it easy. A trip to the Costa Brava, or maybe Malta? The only trouble there was that Mrs Flint tended to get randy in the heat. It was about the only time she did these days, thank God. Perhaps Cornwall would be a better bet. On the other hand, it would be a pity to miss watching Hodge come unstuck and if Wilt didn't run rings round the shit, Flint wasn't the man he thought he was. Talk about tying two cats together by their tails!

And so the night wore on. At the Prison, the activities Wilt had initiated went on. At two, another prisoner in D Block set fire to his mattress, only to have it extinguished by an enterprising burglar using the slop bucket. But it was in Top Security that matters were more serious. The Governor had been disconcerted to find two prisoners wide awake in McCullum's cell, and because it was McCullum's cell, he had been wary of entering without at least six warders to ensure his safety, and six warders were hard to find, partly because they shared the Governor's apprehension and partly because they were busy elsewhere. Lacking their support, the Governor was forced to conduct a dialogue with McCullum's companions through the cell door. Known as the Bull and the Bear, they acted as McCullum's bodyguards.

'Why aren't you men asleep?' demanded the Governor.

'Might be if you hadn't turned the ruddy light on,' said the Bull, who had once made the mistake of falling madly in love with a bank manager's wife, only to be betrayed when he had fulfilled her hopes by murdering her husband and robbing the bank of fifty thousand pounds. She had gone on to marry a stockbroker.

'That's no way to speak to me,' said the Governor, peering suspiciously through the peep-hole. Unlike the other two prisoners, McCullum appeared to be fast asleep. One hand hung limply over the side of his bunk, and his face was unnaturally pallid. Considering that the swine was usually a nasty ruddy colour, the Governor was perturbed. If anyone was likely to be involved in an escape plot, he'd have sworn McCullum was. In which case, he'd have been . . . The Governor wasn't sure what he'd have been, but he certainly wouldn't have been fast asleep, with his face that ghastly grey colour, while the Bull and the Bear were wide awake. There was something distinctly fishy about his being asleep.

'McCullum,' shouted the Governor, 'McCullum, wake up.'

McCullum didn't move. 'Blimey,' said the Bear, sitting up. 'What the fuck's going on?'

'McCullum,' yelled the Governor, 'I am ordering you to wake up.'

'What the fuck's up with you?' yelled the Bull. 'Middle

of the bleeding night and some screw has to go off his nut and go round fucking waking people up. We got fucking rights, you know, even if we are in nick, and Mac isn't going to like this.'

The Governor clenched his teeth and counted to ten. Being called a screw wasn't what he liked either. 'I am simply trying to ascertain that Mr McCullum is all right,' he said. 'Now will you kindly wake him up.'

'All right? All right? Why shouldn't he be all right?' asked the Bear.

The Governor didn't say. 'It's merely a precautionary measure,' he answered. McCullum's refusal to show any sign of life – and in fact his attitude and complexion to show just the opposite – was getting to him. If it had been anyone else, he'd have opened the cell door and gone in. But the swine could well be shamming, and with the Bull and the Bear to help him, might be planning to over-power a warder going in to see what was wrong. With a silent curse on the Chief Warder for making his life so difficult, the Governor hurried off to get assistance. Behind him, the Bull and the Bear expressed their feel-ings about fucking screws who left the fucking light on all fucking night, when it occurred to them that there might be something to be said for checking McCullum after all. The next moment, Top Security was made hellish by their shouts.

'He's fucking dead,' screamed the Bear, while the Bull made a rudimentary attempt to resuscitate McCullum by applying what he thought was artificial respiration, and which in fact meant hurling himself on the body and expelling what remained of breath from his victim's lungs.

'Give him the fucking kiss of life,' ordered the Bear, but the Bull had reservations. If McCullum wasn't dead, he had no intention of bringing him back to consciousness to find he was being kissed, and if he had coughed it, he didn't fancy kissing a corpse.

'Squeamish sod,' yelled the Bear, when the Bull stated his views on the question. 'Here, let me get at him.' But even then he was put off by McCullum's coldness. 'You bloody murderers,' he shouted through the cell door.

'You've done it this time,' said the Governor. He had found the Chief Warder in the office enjoying a cup of coffee. 'You and your infernal sedatives.'

'Me?' said the Chief Warder.

The Governor took a deep breath. 'Either McCullum's dead or he's shamming very convincingly. Get me ten warders and the doctor. If we hurry, we may be in time to save him.'

They rushed down the passage, but the Chief Warder had yet to be convinced. 'I gave him the same dose as everyone else. He's having you on.'

Even when they had secured the ten warders and were outside the cell door, he delayed matters. 'I suggest you leave this to us, sir,' he said. 'If they take hostages, you ought to be on the outside to conduct negotiations. We're dealing with three extremely dangerous men, you know.' The Governor doubted it. Two seemed more probable.

Chief Warder Blaggs peered into the cell. 'Could have painted his face with chalk or something,' he said. 'He's a right crafty devil.'

'And pissed himself into the bargain?'

'Never does things by halves, does our Mac,' said the Chief Warder. 'All right, stand clear of the door in there. We're coming in.' A moment later the cell was filled with prison officers and in the mêlée that followed, the late McCullum received some post mortem injuries which did nothing to improve his appearance. But there was no doubt he was dead. It hardly needed the prison doctor to diagnose death as due to acute barbiturate poisoning.

'Well, how was I to know that the Bull and the Bear were going to give him their cups of cocoa?' said the Chief Warder plaintively, at a meeting held in the Governor's office to discuss the crisis.

'That's something you're going to have to explain to the Home Office enquiry,' said the Governor.

They were interrupted by a prison officer who

announced that a cache of drugs had been found in McCullum's sodden mattress. The Governor looked out at the dawn sky and groaned.

'Oh, and one other thing, sir,' said the warder. 'Mr Coven in the office has remembered where he heard that voice on the telephone. He thought he recognized it at the time. Says it was Mr Wilt.'

'Mr Wilt?' said the Governor. 'Who the hell's Mr Wilt?'

'A lecturer from the Tech or something who's been teaching McCullum English. Comes every Monday.'

'McCullum? Teaching McCullum English? And Coven's certain he was the one who phoned?' In spite of his fatigue, the Governor was wide awake now.

'Definitely, sir. Says he thought it was familiar and naturally when he heard "Fireworks" Harry'd snuffed it, he made the connection.'

So had the Governor. With his career in jeopardy he was prepared to act decisively. 'Right,' he said, casting discretion to the draught that blew under the door. 'McCullum died of food poisoning. That's the official line. Next . . .'

'What do you mean, "food poisoning"?' asked the prison doctor. 'Death was due to an overdose of pheno-barbitone and I'm not going on record as saying—'

'And where was the poison? In his cocoa, of course,' snapped the Governor. 'And if cocoa isn't food, I don't know what is. So we put it out as food poisoning.' He paused and looked at the doctor. 'Unless you want to go down as the doctor who nearly poisoned thirty-six prisoners.'

'Me? I didn't have anything to do with it. That goon went and dosed the sods.' He pointed at Chief Warder Blaggs, but the Chief Warder had spotted the out.

'On your instructions,' he said with a meaningful glance at the Governor. 'I mean I couldn't have laid my hands on that stuff if you hadn't authorized it, could I now? You always keep the drugs cupboard in the dispensary locked, don't you? Be irresponsible not to, I'd have thought.'

'But I never did . . .' the doctor began, but the Governor stopped him.

'I'm afraid Mr Blaggs has a point there,' he said. 'Of course if you want to dispute the facts with the Board of Enquiry, that is your privilege. And doubtless the Press would make something of it. PRISON DOCTOR INVOLVED IN POISONING CONVICT would look well in the *Sun*, don't you think?'

'If he had drugs in his cell, I suppose we could say he died of an overdose,' said the doctor.

Chapter eight

'There's no use in saying you didn't come home late last night because you did,' said Eva. It was breakfast, and, as usual, Wilt was being cross-examined by his nearest and dearest. On her other days, Eva left it to the quads to make the meal a misery for him by asking questions about computers or biochemistry about which he knew absolutely nothing. But this morning the absence of the car had given her the opportunity to get her own questions in.

'I didn't say I didn't come in late,' said Wilt through a mouthful of muesli. Eva was still into organic foods and her home-made muesli, designed to guarantee an adequate supply of roughage, did just that and more.

'That's a double negative,' said Emmeline.

Wilt looked at her balefully. 'I know it is,' he said, and spat out the husk of a sunflower seed.

'Then you weren't telling the truth,' Emmeline continued. 'Two negatives make a positive and you didn't say you had come in late.'

'And I didn't say I hadn't,' said Wilt, struggling with his daughter's logic and trying to use his tongue to get the bran off the top of his dentures. The damned stuff seemed to get everywhere.

'There's no need to mumble,' said Eva. 'What I want to know is where the car is.'

'I've already told you. I left it in a car park. I'll get a mechanic to go round and see what's wrong with the thing.'

'You could have done that last night. How do you expect me to take the girls to school?'

'I suppose they could always walk,' said Wilt, extracting a raisin from his mouth with his fingers and examining it offensively. 'It's an organic form of transportation, you know. Unlike this junior prune which would appear to have led a sedentary life and a sedimentary death. I wonder why it is that health foods so frequently contain objects calculated to kill. Now take this—'

'I am not interested in your comments,' said Eva. 'You're just trying to wriggle out of it and if you expect me to . . .'

'Walk?' interrupted Wilt. 'God forbid. The adipose tissue with which you—'

'Don't you adipose me, Henry Wilt,' Eva began, only to be interrupted by Penelope.

'What's adipose?'

'Mummy is,' said Wilt. 'As to the meaning, it means fat, fatty deposits and appertaining to fat.'

'I am not fat,' said Eva firmly, 'and if you think I'm spending my precious time walking three miles there and three miles back twice a day you're wrong.'

'As usual,' said Wilt. 'Of course. I was forgetting that the gender arrangements of this household leave me in a minority of one.'

'What are gender arrangements?' demanded Samantha.

'Sex,' said Wilt bitterly and got up from the table.

Behind him Eva snorted. She was never prepared to discuss sex in front of the quads. 'It's all very well for you,' she said, reverting to the question of the car which provided a genuine grievance. 'All you have to do is—'

'Catch a bus,' said Wilt, and hurried out of the house before Eva could think of a suitable reply. In fact there was no need. He caught a lift with Chesterton from the Electronics Department and listened to his gripes about financial cuts and why they didn't make them in Communication Skills and get rid of some of those Liberal Studies deadbeats.

'Oh well, you know how it is,' said Wilt as he got out of the car at the Tech. 'We have to make good the inexactitudes of science.'

'I didn't know there were any,' said Chesterton.

'The human element,' said Wilt enigmatically, and went through the library to the lift and his office. The human element was waiting for him.

'You're late, Henry,' said the Vice-Principal.

Wilt looked at him closely. He usually got on rather well with the V-P. 'You're looking pretty late youself,' he said. 'In fact, if I hadn't heard you speak, I'd say you were a standing corpse. Been whooping it up with the wife?'

The Vice-Principal shuddered. He still hadn't got over the horror of seeing his first dead body in the flesh, rather than on the box, and trying to drown the memory in brandy hadn't helped. 'Where the hell did you get to last night?'

'Oh, here and there, don't you know,' said Wilt. He had no intention of telling the V-P he did extra-mural teaching.

'No, I don't,' said the V-P. 'I tried calling your house and all I got was some infernal answering service.'

'That'd be one of the computers,' said Wilt. 'The quads have this programme. It runs on tape, I think. Quite useful really. Did it tell you to fuck off?'

'Several times,' said the Vice-Principal.

'The wonders of science. I've just been listening to Chesterton praising—'

'And I've just been listening to the Police Inspector,' cut in the V-P, 'on the subject of Miss Lynchknowle. He wants to see you.'

Wilt swallowed. Miss Lynchknowle hadn't anything to

do with the prison. It didn't make sense. In any case, they couldn't have got on to him so quickly. Or could they? 'Miss Lynchknowle? What about her?'

'You mean you haven't heard?'

'Heard what?' said Wilt.

'She's the girl who was in the toilet,' said the V-P. 'She was found dead in the boiler-room last night.'

'Oh God,' said Wilt. 'How awful.'

'Quite. Anyway, we had the police swarming all over the place last night and this morning there's a new man here. He wants a word with you.'

They walked down the corridor to the Principal's office. Inspector Hodge was waiting there with another policeman. 'Just a matter of routine, Mr Wilt,' he said when the Vice-Principal had shut the door. 'We've already interviewed Mrs Bristol and several other members of the staff. Now I understand you taught the late Miss Lynchknowle?'

Wilt nodded. His previous experience with the police didn't dispose him to say more than he had to. The sods always chose the most damning interpretation.

'You taught her English?' continued the Inspector.

'I teach Senior Secretaries Three English, yes,' said Wilt.

'On Thursday afternoons at 2.15 p.m.?'

Wilt nodded again.

'And did you notice anything odd about her?'

'Odd?'

'Anything to suggest that she might be an addict, sir.'

Wilt tried to think. Senior Secretaries were all odd as far as he was concerned. Certainly in the context of the Tech. For one thing, they came from 'better families' than most of his other students and seemed to have stepped out of the fifties with their perms and their talk about Mummies and Daddies who were all wealthy farmers or something in the Army. 'I suppose she was a bit different from the other girls in the class,' he said finally. 'There was this duck, for instance.'

'Duck?' said Hodge.

'Yes, she used to bring a duck she called Humphrey with her to class. Bloody nuisance having a duck in a lesson but I suppose it was a comfort to her having a furry thing like that.'

'Furry?' said Hodge. 'Ducks aren't furry. They have feathers.'

'Not this one,' said Wilt. 'Like a teddy bear. You know, stuffed. You don't think I'd have a live duck shitting all over the place in my class, do you?'

Inspector Hodge said nothing. He was beginning to dislike Wilt.

'Apart from that particular addiction, I can't think of anything else remarkable about her. I mean, she didn't twitch or seem unduly pale or even go in for those sudden changes of mood you tend to find with junkies.'

'I see,' said Hodge, holding back the comment that Mr Wilt seemed exceedingly well-informed on the matter of symptoms. 'And would you say there was much drug-taking at the College?'

'Not to my knowledge,' said Wilt. 'Though, come to think of it, I suppose there must be some with the numbers we've got. I wouldn't know. Not my scene.'

'Quite, sir,' said the Inspector, simulating respect.

'And now, if you don't mind,' said Wilt, 'I have work to do.' The Inspector didn't mind.

'Not much there,' said the Sergeant when he'd left.

'Never is with the really clever sods,' said Hodge.

'I still don't understand why you didn't ask him about going to the wrong toilet and what the secretary said.'

Hodge smiled. 'If you really want to know, it's because I don't intend to raise his suspicions one little iota. That's why. I've been checking on Mr Wilt and he's a canny fellow, he is. Scuppered old Flint, didn't he? And why? I'll tell you. Because Flint was fool enough to do what Wilt wanted. He pulled him in and put him through the wringer and Mr Wilt got away with bloody murder. I'm not getting caught the same way.'

'But he never did commit any murder. It was only a fucking inflatable doll he'd buried,' said the Sergeant.

'Oh, come off it. You don't think the bugger did that without he had a reason? That's a load of bull. No, he was pulling some other job and he wanted a cover, him and his missus, so they fly a kite and Flint falls for it. That old fart wouldn't know a decoy if it was shoved under his bloody snout. He was so busy grilling Wilt about that doll he couldn't see the wood for the trees.'

Sergeant Runk fought his way through the mixed metaphors and came out none the wiser. 'All the same,' he said finally, 'I can't see a lecturer here being into drugs, not pushing anyway. Where's the lifestyle? No big house and car. No country-club set. He doesn't fit the bill.'

'And no big salary here either,' said Hodge. 'So maybe he's saving up for his old age. Anyway, we'll check him out and he won't ever know.'

'I should have thought there were more likely prospects round about,' said the Sergeant. 'What about that Greek restaurant bloke Macropolis or something you've been bugging? We know he's been into heroin. And there's that fly boy down the Siltown Road with the garage we had for GBH. He was on the needle himself.'

'Yeah, well he's inside, isn't he? And Mr Macropolis is out of the country right now. Anyway, I'm not saying it is Wilt. She could have been down in London getting it for all we know. In which case, it's off our patch. All I'm saying is, I'm keeping an open mind and Mr Wilt interests me, that's all.'

And Wilt was to interest him still further when they returned to the police station an hour later. 'Super wants to see you,' said the Duty Sergeant. 'He's got the Prison Governor with him.'

'Prison Governor?' said Hodge. 'What's he want?'

'You,' said the Sergeant, 'hopefully.'

Inspector Hodge ignored the crack and went down the passage to the Superintendent's office. When he came out half an hour later, his mind was alive with circumstantial evidence, all of which pointed most peculiarly to Wilt. Wilt had been teaching one of the most notorious gangsters in Britain, now thankfully dead of an overdose of one of his own drugs. (The prison authorities had decided to use the presence of so much heroin in McCullum's mattress as the cause of death, rather than the phenobarb one, much to Chief Warder Blaggs' relief.) Wilt had been closeted with McCullum at the very time Miss Lynchknowle's body had been discovered. And, most significantly of all, Wilt, within an hour of leaving the prison and presumably on learning that the police were busy at the Tech, had rung the prison anonymously with a phoney message about a mass break-out and McCullum had promptly taken an overdose.

If that little lot didn't add up to something approaching a certainty that Wilt was involved, Hodge didn't know one. Anyway, add it to what he already knew of Wilt's past and it was certain. On the other hand, there was still the awkward little matter of proof. It was one of the disadvantages of the English legal system, and one Hodge would happily have dispensed with in his crusade against the underworld, that you had first to persuade the Director of Public Prosecutions that there was a case to be answered, and then go on to present evidence that would convince a senile judge and a jury of do-gooders, half of whom had already been nobbled, that an obvious villain was guilty. And Wilt wasn't an obvious villain. The bastard was as subtle as hell and to send the sod down would require evidence that was as hard as ferro-concrete.

'Listen,' Hodge said to Sergeant Runk and the small team of plain-clothes policemen who constituted his private crime squad, 'I don't want any balls-ups so this has got to be strictly covert and I mean covert. No one, not even the Super, is to know it's going on, so we'll code-name it Flint. That way, no one will suspect. Anyone can say Flint round this station and it doesn't register. That's one. Two is, I want Mr Wilt tailed twenty-four hours continuous. And another tail on his missus. No messing. I want to know what those people do every moment of the day and night from now on in.'

'Isn't that going to be a bit difficult?' asked Sergeant

Runk. 'Day *and* night. There's no way we can put a tail in the house and . . .'

'Bug it is what we'll do,' said Hodge. 'Later. First off we're going to patternize their lives on a time-schedule basis. Right?'

'Right,' echoed the team. In their time, they had patternized the lives of a fish-and-chip merchant and his family who Hodge had suspected were into hard-core porn; a retired choirmaster – this time for boys; and a Mr and Mrs Pateli for nothing better than their name.In each case the patternizing had failed to confirm the Inspector's suspicions, which were in fact wholly groundless, but had established as incontrovertible facts that the fish-and-chip merchant opened his shop at 6 p.m. except Sundays, that the choirmaster was having a happy and vigorous love affair with a wrestler's wife, and in any case had an aversion amounting almost to an allergy for small boys, and that the Patelis went to the Public Library every Tuesday, that Mr Pateli did full-time unpaid work with the Mentally Handicapped, while Mrs Pateli did Meals on Wheels. Hodge had justified the time and expense by arguing that these were training sessions in preparation for the real thing.

'And this is it,' continued Hodge. 'If we can nail this one down before Scotland Yard takes over we'll be quids in. We're also going into a surveillance mode at the Tech. I'm going over to see the Principal about it now. In the meantime, Pete and Reg can move into the canteen and the Student's Common Room and make out they're mature students chucked out for dope at Essex or some other University.'

Within an hour, Operation Flint was underway. Pete and Reg, suitably dressed in leather garments that would have alarmed the most hardened Hell's Angels, had already emptied the Students' Common Room at the Tech by their language and their ready assumption that everyone there was on heroin. In the Principal's office, Inspector Hodge was having more or less the same effect on the Principal and the V-P, who found the notion that the Tech was the centre for drug distribution in Fenland particularly horrifying. They didn't much like the idea of being lumbered with fifteen educationally subnormal coppers as mature students.

'At this time of year?' said the Principal. 'Dammit, it's April. We don't enrol mature students this term. We don't enrol any, come to that. They come in September. And anyway, where the hell would we put them?'

'I suppose we could always call them "Student Teachers",' said the V-P. 'That way they could sit in on any classes they wanted to without having to say very much.'

'Still going to look bloody peculiar,' said the Principal. 'And frankly, I don't like it at all.'

But it was the Inspector's assertion that the Lord Lieutenant, the Chief Constable and, worst of all, the Home Secretary didn't like what had been going on at the Tech that turned the scales.

'God, what a ghastly man,' said the Principal, when Hodge had left. 'I thought Flint was foul enough, but this one's even bloodier. What is it about policemen that is so unpleasant? When I was a boy, they were quite different.'

'I suppose the criminals were, too,' said the V-P. 'I mean, it can't be much fun with sawn-off shotguns and hooligans hurling Molotov cocktails at you. Enough to turn any man bloody.'

'Odd,' said the Principal, and left it at that.

Meanwhile Hodge had put the Wilts under surveillance. 'What's been happening?' he asked Sergeant Runk.

'Wilt's still at the Tech so we haven't been able to pick him up yet, and his missus hasn't done anything much except the shopping.'

But even as he spoke, Eva was already acting in a manner calculated to heighten suspicion. She had been inspired to phone Dr Kores for an appointment. Where the inspiration came from she couldn't have said, but it had partly to do with an article she had read in her

supermarket magazine on sex and the menopause entitled 'No Pause In The Pause, The Importance of Foreplay
In The Forties', and partly with the glimpse she'd had of
Patrick Mottram at the check-out counter where he
usually chatted up the prettiest girl. On this occasion, he
had ogled the chocolate bars instead and had ambled off
with the glazed eyes of a man for whom the secret
consumption of half a pound of Cadbury's Fruit and Nut
was the height of sensual experience. If Dr Kores could
reduce the randiest man in Ipford to such an awful
condition, there was every possibility she could produce
the opposite effect in Henry.

Over lunch, Eva had read the article again and, as
always on the subject of sex, she was puzzled. All her
friends seemed to have so much of it, either with their
husbands or with someone, and obviously it was important, otherwise people wouldn't write and talk so much
about it. All the same, Eva still had difficulty reconciling it
with the way she'd been brought up. Mind you, her
mother had been quite wrong going on about remaining
a virgin until she was married. Eva could see that now.
She certainly wasn't going to do the same with the quads.
Not that she'd have them turn into little tarts like the
Hatten girls, wearing make-up at fourteen and going
around with rough boys on motorbikes. But later on,
when they were eighteen and at university, then it would
be all right. They'd need experience before they got
married instead of getting married to get . . . Eva stopped
herself. That wasn't true, she hadn't married Henry just
for sex. They'd been genuinely in love. Of course, Henry
had groped and fiddled but never nastily like some of the
boys she'd gone out with. If anything, he'd been rather
shy and embarrassed and she'd had to encourage him.
Mavis was right to call her a full-blooded woman. She did
like sex but only with Henry. She wasn't going to have
affairs, especially not with the quads in the house. You
had to set an example and broken homes were bad. On
the other hand, so were homes where both parents were
always quarrelling and hated one another. So divorce was

a good thing too. Not that anything like that threatened her marriage. It was just that she had a right to a more fulfilling love life and if Henry was too shy to ask for help, and he certainly was, she'd have to do it for him. So she had phoned Dr Kores and had been surprised to learn that she could come at half-past two.

Eva had set off with an unnoticed escort of two cars and four policemen and had caught the bus at the bottom of Perry Road to Silton and Dr Kores' shambolic herb farm. 'I don't suppose she has time to keep it tidy,' Eva thought as she made her way past a number of old frames and a rusty cultivator to the house. All the same, she was slightly dismayed by the lack of organization. If it had been her garden, it wouldn't have looked like that. But then anything organic tended to go its own way, and Dr Kores did have a reputation as an eccentric. In fact, she had prepared herself to be confronted by some wizened old creature with a plaid shawl when the door opened and a severe woman in a white coat stood looking at her through strangely tinted dark glasses.

'Ms Wilt?' she said. Was there just the hint of a V for the W? But before Eva could consider this question, she was being ushered down the hallway and into a consulting-room. Eva looked round apprehensively as the doctor took a seat behind the desk. 'You are having problems?' she asked.

Eva sat down. 'Yes,' she said, fiddling with the clasp of her handbag and wishing she hadn't made the appointment.

'With your husband I think you said, yes?'

'Well, not with him exactly,' said Eva, coming to Henry's defence. After all, it wasn't his fault he wasn't as energetic as some other men. 'It's just that he's . . . well . . . not as active as he might be.'

'Sexually active?' Eva nodded.

'How old?' continued Dr Kores.

'You mean Henry? Forty-three. He'll be forty-four next March. He's a—'

But Dr Kores was clearly uninterested in Wilt's

astrological sign. 'And the sexual gradient has been steep?'

'I suppose so,' said Eva, wondering what a sexual gradient was.

'Maximum weekly activity please.'

Eva looked anxiously at an Anglepoise lamp and tried to think. 'Well, when we were first married . . .' she paused.

'Go on,' Dr Kores ordered.

'Well, Henry did it three times one night I remember,' said Eva, blurting the statement out. 'He only did it once of course.'

The doctor's ballpen stopped. 'Please explain,' she said. 'First you said he was sexually active three times in one night. And second you said he was only once. Are you saying there was seminal ejaculation only on the first occasion?'

'I don't really know,' said Eva. 'It's not easy to tell, is it?'

Dr Kores eyed her doubtfully. 'Let me put it another way. Was there a penile spasm at the climax of each episode?'

'I suppose so,' said Eva. 'It's so long ago now and all I remember is that he was ever so tired next day.'

'In which year did this take place?' asked the doctor, having written down 'Penile spasm uncertain.'

'1963. In July,' said Eva. 'I remember that because we were on a walking holiday in the Peak District and Henry said he's peaked out.'

'Very amusing,' said Dr Kores dryly. 'And that is his maximum sexual attainment?'

'He did it twice in 1970 on his birthday . . .'

'And the plateau was how many times a week?' asked Dr Kores, evidently determined to prevent Eva from intruding anything remotely human into the discussion.

'The plateau? Oh, well it used to be once or twice but now I'm lucky if it's once a month and sometimes we go even longer.'

Dr Kores licked her thin lips and put the pen down. 'Mrs Wilt,' she said, leaning on the desk and forming a triangle with her fingertips and thumbs. 'I deal exclusively with the problems of the female in a male-dominated social context, and to speak frankly, I find your attitude to your relationship with your husband unduly submissive.'

'Do you really?' said Eva, beginning to perk up. 'Henry always says I'm too bossy.'

'Please,' said the doctor with something approaching a shudder, 'I'm not in the least interested in your husband's opinions or in his person. If you choose to be, that is your business. Mine is to help you as an entirely independent being and, to be truthful, I find your self-objectivization highly distasteful.'

'I'm sorry,' said Eva, wondering what on earth self-objectivization was.

'For instance, you have repeatedly stated that and I quote "He did it three times" and again "He did it twice . . ." '

'But he did,' Eva protested.

'And who was the "It"? You?' said the doctor vehemently.

'I didn't mean it that way . . .' Eva began but Dr Kores was not to be stopped. 'And the very word "did" or "done" is a tacit acceptance of marital rape. What would your husband say if you were to do him?'

'Oh, I don't think Henry'd like that,' said Eva, 'I mean, he's not very big and . . .'

'If you don't mind,' said the doctor, 'size does not come into it. The question of attitude is predominant. I am only prepared to help you if you make a determined effort to see yourself as the leader in the relationship.' Behind the blue tinted spectacles her eyes narrowed.

'I'll certainly try,' said Eva.

'You will succeed,' said the doctor sibilantly. 'It is of the essence. Repeat after me "I will succeed." '

'I will succeed,' said Eva.

'I am superior,' said Dr Kores.

'Yes,' said Eva.

'Not "Yes",' hissed the doctor, gazing even more

103

peculiarly into Eva's eyes, 'but "I am superior".'

'I am superior,' said Eva obediently.

'Now both.'

'Both,' said Eva.

'Not that. I want you to repeat both remarks. First . . .'

'I will succeed,' said Eva, finally getting the message, 'I am superior.'

'Again.'

'I will succeed. I am superior.'

'Good,' said the doctor. 'It is vital that you establish the correct psychic attitude if I am to help you. You will repeat those auto-instructs three hundred times a day. Do you understand?'

'Yes,' said Eva. 'I am superior. I will succeed.'

'Again,' said the doctor.

For the next five minutes Eva sat fixed in her chair and repeated the assertions while Dr Kores stared unblinking into her eyes. 'Enough,' she said finally. 'You understand what this means, of course?'

'Sort of,' said Eva. 'It's to do with what Mavis Mottram says about women taking the leading rôle in the world, isn't it?'

Dr Kores sat back in her chair with a thin smile. 'Ms Wilt,' she said, 'for thirty-five years I have made a continuous study of the sexual superiority of the feminine in the mammalian world. Even as a child I was inspired by the mating habits of arachnida – my mother was something of an expert in the field before so unfortunately marrying my father, you understand.'

Eva nodded. Fortunately for her she had missed the reference to spiders but she was too fascinated not to understand that whatever Dr Kores was saying was somehow important. She had the future of the quads in mind.

'But,' continued the doctor, 'my own work has been concentrated upon the higher forms of life and, in particular, the infinitely superior talents of the feminine in the sphere of survival. At every level of development, the rôle of the male is subordinate and the female demonstrates an adaptability which preserves the species. Only in the human world, and then solely in the social context rather than the purely biological, has this process been reversed. This reversal has been achieved by the competitive and militaristic nature of society in which the brute force of the masculine has found justification for the suppression of the feminine. Would you agree?'

'Yes, I suppose so,' said Eva, who had found the argument difficult to follow but could see that it made some sort of sense.

'Good,' said Dr Kores. 'And now we have arrived at a world crisis in which the extermination of life on earth has been made probable by the masculine distortion of scientific development for military purposes. Only we women can save the future.' She paused and let Eva savour the prospect. 'Fortunately, science has also put into our hands the means of so doing. The purely physical strength of the male has lost its advantage in the automated society of the present. Man is redundant and with the age of the computer, it is women who will have power. You have, of course, read of the work done at St Andrew's. It is proven that women have the larger corpus collossum than men.'

'Corpus collossum?' said Eva.

'One hundred million brain cells, neural fibre connecting the hemispheres of the brain and essential in the transfer of information. In working with the computer, this interchange has the highest significance. It could well be to the electronic age what the muscle was to the age of the physical . . .'

For another twenty minutes, Dr Kores talked on, swinging between an almost demented fervour for the feminine, rational argument and the statement of fact. To Eva, ever prone to accept enthusiasm uncritically, the doctor seemed to embody all that was most admirable about the intellectual world to which she had never belonged. It was only when the doctor seemed to sag in her chair that Eva remembered the reason she had come. 'About Henry . . .' she said hesitantly.

For a moment, Dr Kores continued to focus on a future in which there were probably no men, before dragging herself back to the present. 'Oh yes, your husband,' she said almost absently. 'You wish for something to stimulate him sexually, yes?'

'If it's possible,' said Eva. 'He's never been . . .'

But Dr Kores interrupted her with a harsh laugh.

'Ms Wilt,' she said, 'have you considered the possibility that your husband's lack of sexual activity may be only apparent?'

'I don't quite understand.'

'Another woman perhaps?'

'Oh, no,' said Eva. 'Henry isn't like that. He really isn't.'

'Or latent homosexuality?'

'He wouldn't have married me if he'd been like that, would he?' said Eva, now genuinely shocked.

Dr Kores looked at her critically. It was at moments like this that her faith in the innate superiority of the feminine was put to the test. 'It has been known,' she said through clenched teeth and was about to enter into a discussion of the family life of Oscar Wilde when the bell rang in the hall.

'Excuse me a moment,' she said and hurried out. When she returned it was through another door. 'My dispensary,' she explained. 'I have there a tincture which may prove beneficial. The dose is, however, critical. Like many medications, it contains elements that taken in excess will produce definite contraindication. I must warn you not to exceed the stated dose by as much as five millilitres. I have supplied a syringe for the utmost accuracy in measurement. Within those limits, the tincture will produce the desired result. Beyond them, I cannot be held responsible. You will naturally treat the matter with the utmost confidentiality. As a scientist, I cannot be held responsible for the misapplication of proven formulae.'

Eva put the plastic bottle in her bag and went down the hall. As she passed the rusty cultivator and the broken frames, her mind was in a maelstrom of contradictory impressions. There had been something weird about Dr Kores. It wasn't what she said that was wrong, Eva could see her words made good sense. It was rather in the way she said them and how she behaved. She'd have to discuss it with Mavis. All the same, as she stood at the bus stop she found herself repeating 'I am superior. I will succeed' almost involuntarily.

A hundred yards away, two of Inspector Hodge's plain-clothes men watched her and made notes of the time and place. The patternizing of the Wilts' lives had begun in earnest.

Chapter nine

And it continued. For two days, teams of detectives kept watch on the Wilts and reported back to Inspector Hodge who found the signals unambiguous. Eva's visit to Dr Kores was particularly damning.

'Herb farm? She went to a herb farm in Silton?' said the Inspector incredulously. After forty-eight almost sleepless hours and as many cups of black coffee, he could have done with some alternative medicine himself. 'And she came out with a large plastic bottle?'

'Apparently,' said the detective. Trying to keep up with Eva had taken its toll. So had the quads. 'For all I know, she went in with one. All we saw was her taking the bottle out of her bag when she was waiting for the bus.'

Hodge ignored the logic. As far as he was concerned, suspects who visited herb farms, and had bottles in their bags afterwards, were definitely guilty.

But it was Mavis Mottram's arrival at 45 Oakhurst Avenue later that afternoon that interested him most. 'Subject collects children from school at 3.30,' he read from the written report, 'gets home and a woman drives up in a mini.'

'Correct.'

'What's she look like?'

'Forty, if she's a day. Dark hair. Five foot four. Blue anorak and khaki trousers with leg-warmers. Goes in at 3.55, leaving at 4.20.'

'So she could have collected the bottle?'

'Could have, I suppose, but she hadn't got a bag and there was no sign of it.'

'Then what?'

'Nothing till the nextdoor neighbour comes home at 5.30. Look, it's all there in my report.'

'I know it is,' said Hodge, 'I'm just trying to get the picture. How did you know his name was Gamer?'

'Blimey, I'd have to be stone deaf not to, the way she gave it to him, not to mention his wife carrying on something chronic.'

'So what happened?'

'This bloke Gamer goes in the door of 43,' said the detective, 'and five minutes later he's out again like a scalded cat with his wife trying to stop him. Dashes round to the Wilts' and tries to go in the side gate round the back of the house. Grabs the latch on the gate and the next moment he's flat on his back in the flower bed, twitching like he's got St Vitus' dance and his missus is yelling like they've killed him.'

'So what you're saying is the back gate was electrified?' said Hodge.

'I'm not saying it. He did. As soon as he could speak, that is, and had stopped twitching. Mrs Wilt comes out and wants to know what he's doing in her wallflowers. By that time he's got to his feet, just, and is yelling that her fucking hellcats — his words, not mine — have tried to murder him by stealing some statuette he's got in his back garden, and they've put it in theirs, and wired up the back gate to the fucking mains. And Mrs Wilt tells him not to be so silly and kindly not to use filthy language in front of her daughters. After that, things got a bit confusing with him wanting his statue and her saying she hadn't got it, and wouldn't have it if he gave it to her because it's dirty.'

'Dirty?' muttered Hodge. 'What's dirty about it?'

'It's one of those ones of a small boy peeing. Got it on his pond. She practically called him a pervert. And all the time his wife is pleading with him to come on home and never mind the ruddy statue, they can always get another one when they've sold the house. That got to him. "Sell the house?" he yells, "Who to? Even a raving lunatic wouldn't buy a house next to the bloody Wilts." Probably right at that.'

'And what happened in the end?' asked Hodge, making a mental note that he'd have an ally in Mr Gamer.

'She insists he come through the house and see if his statue's there, because she's not going to have her girls called thieves.'

'And he went?' said Hodge incredulously.

'Hesitantly,' said the detective. 'Came out shaken and swearing he'd definitely seen it there and if she didn't believe those kids had tried to kill him, why were all the lights in the house on the blink. That had her, and he pointed out there was a piece of wire still tied to the bootscraper outside the back gate.'

'Interesting,' said Hodge. 'And was there?'

'Must have been, because she got all flustered then, especially when he said it was evidence to show the police.'

'Naturally, with that bottle of dope still in the house,' said Hodge. 'No wonder they'd fixed the back door.' A new theory had been formulated in his mind. 'I tell you we're on to something, this time.'

Even the Superintendent, who shared Flint's view that Inspector Hodge was a greater menace to the public than half the petty crooks he arrested and would gladly have put the sod on traffic duty, had to admit that for once the Inspector seemed to be on the right track. 'This fellow Wilt's got to be guilty of something,' he muttered as he studied the report of Wilt's extraordinary movements during his lunch break.

In fact, Wilt had been on the look-out for McCullum's associates and had almost immediately spotted the two detectives in an unmarked car when he'd walked out of the Tech to pick up the Escort at the back of The Glassblowers' Arms, and had promptly taken evasive action with an expertise he'd learnt from watching old thrillers on TV. As a result, he'd doubled back down side roads, had disappeared up alleyways, had bought a number of wholly unnecessary items in crowded shops and had even bolted in the front doors of Boots and out the back before heading for the pub.

'Returned to the Tech car park at 2.15,' said the Superintendent. 'Where'd he been?'

'I'm afraid we lost him,' said Hodge. 'The man's an expert. All we know is he came back driving fast and practically ran for the building.'

Nor had Wilt's behaviour on leaving the Tech that evening been calculated to inspire confidence in his innocence. Anyone who walked out of the front gate wearing dark glasses, a coat with the collar turned up and a wig (Wilt had borrowed one from the Drama Department) and spent half an hour sitting on a bench by the bowling green on Midway Park, scrutinizing the passing traffic before sneaking back to the Tech car park, had definitely put himself into the category of a prime suspect.

'Think he was waiting for someone?' the Superintendent asked.

'More likely trying to warn them off,' said Hodge. 'They've probably got a system of signalling. His accomplices drive past and see him sitting there and get the message.'

'I suppose so,' said the Superintendent, who couldn't think of anything else that made sense. 'So we can expect an early arrest. I'll tell the Chief Constable.'

'I wouldn't say that, sir,' said Hodge, 'just that we've got a definite lead. If I'm right, this is obviously a highly organized syndicate. I don't want to rush into an early arrest when this man could lead us to the main source.'

'There is that,' said the Superintendent gloomily. He

110

had been hoping that Hodge's handling of the case would prove so inept that he could call in the Regional Crime Squad. Instead the confounded man seemed to be making a success of it. And after that he'd doubtless apply for promotion and get it. Hopefully somewhere else. If not, the Superintendent would apply for a transfer himself. And there was still a chance Hodge would foul things up.

At the Tech, Hodge had. His insistence on putting plain-clothes detectives in, masquerading as apprentices or even more unsatisfactorily as Trainee Teachers, was playing havoc with staff morale.

'I can't stand it,' Dr Cox, Head of Science, told the Principal. 'It's bad enough trying to teach some of the students we get, without having a man poking about who doesn't know the difference between a Bunsen burner and a flamethrower. He practically burnt down the lab. on the third floor. And as for being any sort of teacher . . .'

'He doesn't have to say anything. After all, they're only here to observe.'

'In theory,' said Dr Cox. 'In practice, he keeps taking my students into corners and asking them if they can get him some Embalming Fluid. Anyone would think I was running a funeral home.'

The Principal explained the term. 'God Almighty, no wonder the wretched fellow asked to stay behind last night to check the chemical inventory.'

It was the same in botany. 'How was I to know she was a policewoman?' Miss Ryfield complained. 'And anyway I had no idea students were growing marijuana as pot plants in the greenhouses. She seems to hold me responsible.' Only Dr Board viewed the situation at all philosophically. Thanks to the fact that none of the policemen spoke French, his department had been spared intrusion.

'After all, it is 1984,' he announced to an ad hoc committee in the staff room, 'and as far as I can tell, discipline has improved enormously.'

'Not in my department,' said Mr Spirey of Building. 'I've had five punch-ups in Plasterers and Bricklayers and Mr Gilders is in hospital with bicyle-chain wounds.'

'Bicycle-chain wounds?'

'Someone called the young thug from the police station a fucking pig and Mr Gilders tried to intervene.'

'And I suppose the apprentices were arrested for carrying offensive weapons?' said Dr Mayfield.

The Head of Building shook his head. 'No, it was the policeman who had the bicycle chain. Mind you, they made a right mess of him afterwards,' he added with some satisfaction.

But it was among Senior Secretaries that Hodge's investigations had been carried out most vigorously. 'If this goes on much longer, our exam results will be appalling,' said Miss Dill. 'You have no idea the effect of having girls taken out of class and interrogated is having on their typing performance. The impression seems to be that the College is a hotbed of vice.'

'Would that it were,' said Dr Board. 'But, as usual, the papers have got it all wrong. Still, page 3 is something.' And he produced a copy of the *Sun* and a photograph of Miss Lynchknowle in the nude, taken in Barbados the previous summer. The caption read DRUG HEIRESS DEAD AT TECH.

'Of course I've seen the papers and the publicity is disgraceful,' said the Principal to the members of the Education Committee. Originally called to discuss the impending visitation of HMIs, it was now more concerned with the new crisis. 'The point I am trying to make is that this is an isolated incident and . . .'

'It isn't,' said Councillor Blighte-Smythe. 'I have here a list of catastrophes which have bedevilled the College since your appointment. First there was that awful business with the Liberal Studies lecturer who . . .'

Mrs Chatterway, whose views were indefatigably progressive, intervened. 'I hardly think there's anything to be gained by dwelling on the past,' she said.

'Why not?' demanded Mr Squidley. 'It's time someone

was held accountable for what goes on there. As tax- and rate-payers, we have a right to a decent practical education for our children and . . .'

'How many children do you have at the Tech?' snapped Mrs Chatterway.

Mr Squidley looked at her in disgust. 'None, thank God,' he said. 'I wouldn't let one of my kids anywhere near the place.'

'If we could just keep to the point,' said the Chief Education Officer.

'I am,' said Mr Squidley, 'very much to the point, and the point is that as an employer, I'm not paying good money to have apprentices turned into junkies by a lot of fifth-rate academic drop-outs.'

'I resent that,' said the Principal. 'In the first place, Miss Lynchknowle wasn't an apprentice, and in the second we have some extremely dedicated—'

'Dangerous nutters,' said Councillor Blighte-Smythe.

'I was going to say "dedicated teachers".'

'Which doubtless accounts for the fact that the Minister of Education's secretary is pushing for the appointment of a board of enquiry to investigate the teaching of Marxism-Leninism in the Liberal Studies Department. If that isn't a clear indication something's wrong, I don't know what is.'

'I object. I object most strongly,' said Mrs Chatterway. 'The real cause of the problem lies in spending cuts. If we are to give our young people a proper sense of social responsibility and care and concern—'

'Oh God, not that again,' muttered Mr Squidley. 'If half the louts I have to employ could even read and bloody write . . .'

The Principal glanced significantly at the Chief Education Officer and felt more comfortable. The Education Committee would come to no sensible conclusions. It never did.

At 45 Oakhurst Avenue, Wilt glanced nervously out of the window. Ever since his lunch break and the discovery that he was being followed, he'd been on edge. In fact, he had driven home with his eyes so firmly fixed on the rear-view mirror that he had failed to notice the traffic lights on Nott Road and had banged into the back of the police car which had taken the precaution of tailing him from the front. The resulting exchange with the two plain-clothes men who were fortunately unarmed had done a lot to confirm his view that his life was in danger.

And Eva had hardly been sympathetic. 'You never do look where you're going,' she said, when he explained why the car had a crumpled bumper and radiator. 'You're just hopeless.'

'You'd feel fairly hopeless if you'd had the sort of day I've had,' said Wilt and helped himself to a bottle of homebrew. He took a swig of the stuff and looked at his glass dubiously.

'Must have left the bloody sugar out, or something,' he muttered, but Eva quickly switched the conversation to the incident with Mr Gamer. Wilt listened half-heartedly. His beer didn't usually taste like that and anyway it wasn't always quite so flat.

'As if girls their age could lift a horrid statue like that over the fence,' said Eva, concluding a singularly biased account of the incident.

Wilt dragged his attention away from his beer. 'Oh, I don't know. That probably explains what they were doing with Mr Boykins' block and tackle the other day. I wondered why they'd become so interested in physics.'

'But to say they'd tried to electrocute him,' said Eva indignantly.

'You tell me why the whole damned house was out,' said Wilt. 'The main fuse was blown, that's why. Don't tell me a mouse got into the toaster again either, because I checked. Anyway, that mouse didn't blow all the fuses and if I hadn't objected to having putrefying mouse savoury for breakfast instead of toast and marmalade, you'd never have noticed.'

'That was quite different,' said Eva. 'The poor thing got in there looking for crumbs. That's why it died.'

'And Mr Gamer damn near died because he was

looking for his ruddy garden ornament,' said Wilt. 'And I can tell you who gave your brood that idea, the blooming mouse, that's who. One of these days they'll get the hang of the electric chair and I'll come home and find the Radleys' boy with a saucepan on his head and a damned great cable running to the cooker plug, as dead as a dodo.'

'They'd never do anything like that,' said Eva. 'They know better. You always look on the worst side of things.'

'Reality,' said Wilt, 'that's what I look at and what I see is four lethal girls who make Myra Hindley seem like a suitable candidate for a kindergarten teacher.'

'You're just being horrid,' said Eva.

'So's this bloody beer,' said Wilt as he opened another bottle. He took a mouthful and swore, but his words were drowned by the Magimix which Eva had switched on, in part to make an apple and carrot slaw because it was so good for the quads, but also to express her irritation. Henry could never admit the girls were bright and intelligent and good. They were always bad to him.

So was the beer. Eva's addition of five millilitres of Dr Kores' sexual stimulant to each bottle of Wilt's Best Bitter had given the stuff a new edge to it and, besides, it was flat. 'Must have left the screw top loose on this batch.' Wilt muttered as the Magimix came to a halt.

'What did you say?' Eva asked unpleasantly. She always suspected Wilt of using the cover of the Magimix, or the coffee-grinder to express his true thoughts.

'Nothing at all,' said Wilt, preferring to keep off the topic of beer. Eva was always going on about what it did to his liver and for once he believed her. On the other hand, if McCullum's thugs were going to duff him up, he intended to be drunk when they started, even if the muck did taste peculiar. It was better than nothing.

On the other side of Ipford, Inspector Flint sat in front of the telly and gazed abstractedly at a film on the life-cycle of the giant turtle. He didn't give a damn about turtles or their sex life. About the only thing he found in their favour was that they had the sense not to worry about their offspring and left the little buggers to hatch out on a distant beach or, better still, to get eaten by predators. Anyway, the sods lived two hundred years and presumably didn't have high blood pressure.

Instead, his thoughts reverted to Hodge and the Lynchknowle girl. Having pointed the Head of the Drug Squad towards the morass of inconsequentiality that was Wilt's particular forte, it had begun to dawn on him that he might gain some kudos by solving the case himself. For one thing, Wilt wasn't into drugs. Flint was certain of that. He knew Wilt was up to something – stood to reason – but his copper's instinct told him that drugs didn't fit.

So someone else had supplied the girl with the muck that had killed her. With all the slow persistence of a giant turtle swimming in the depths of the Pacific, Flint went over the facts. The girl dead on heroin and PCP: a definite fact. Wilt teaching that bastard McCullum (also dead from drugs): another fact. Wilt making a phone call to the prison: not a fact, merely a probability. An interesting probability for all that, and if you subtracted Wilt from the case there was absolutely nothing to go on. Flint picked up the paper and looked at the dead girl's photo. Taken in Barbados. Smart set and half of them on drugs. If she'd got the stuff in that circle Hodge hadn't got a hope in hell. They kept their secrets. Anyway, it might be worth checking up on his findings so far. Flint switched off the TV and went into the hall. 'I'm just going out to stretch my legs,' he called out to his wife and was answered by a grim silence. Mrs Flint didn't give a damn what he did with his legs.

Twenty minutes later, he was in his office with the report on the interview with Lord and Lady Lynch-knowle in front of him. Naturally, it had never dawned on them that Linda was on drugs. Flint recognized the symptoms and the desire to clear themselves of all blame. 'About as much parental care as those bloody turtles,' he muttered and turned to the interview with the girl who'd shared a flat with Miss Lynchknowle. This time there was something more positive. No, Penny hadn't been to London for ages. Never went anywhere, in fact, not even home at weekends. Discos occasionally, but generally a loner and had given up her boyfriend at the University before Christmas etcetera. No recent visitors either. Occasionally, she'd go out of an evening to a coffee bar or just wander along by the river. She'd seen her down there twice on her way back from the cinema. Whereabouts exactly? Near the marina. Flint made a note of that, and also of the fact that the Sergeant who'd visited her had asked the right questions. Flint noted the names of some of the coffee bars. There was no point in visiting them, they'd be covered by Hodge and, besides, Flint had no intention of being seen to be interested in the case. Above all, though, he knew he was acting on intuition, the 'smell' of the case which came from his long experience and his knowledge that whatever else Wilt was – and the Inspector had his own views on the matter – he wasn't pushing drugs. All the same, it would be interesting to know if he had made that phone call to the prison on the night McCullum took an overdose. There was something strangely coincidental about that incident, too. It was easy enough to hear the story from Mr Blaggs. Flint had known the Chief Warder for years and had frequently had the pleasure of consigning prisoners to his dubious care.

And so presently he was standing in the pub near the prison discussing Wilt with the Chief Warder with a frankness Wilt would have found only partly reassuring. 'If you want my opinion,' said Mr Blaggs, 'educating villains is anti-social. Only gives them more brains than they need. Makes your job more difficult when they come out, doesn't it?'

Flint had to agree that it didn't make it any easier. 'But you don't reckon Wilt had anything to do with Mac's having a cache of junk in his cell?' he asked.

'Wilt? Never. A bloody do-gooder, that's what he is. Mind you, I'm not saying they're not daft enough, because I know for a fact they are. What I'm saying is, a nick ought to be a prison, not a fucking finishing-school for turning half-witted petty thieves into first-rate bank robbers with degrees in law.'

'That's not what Mac was studying for, is it?' asked Flint.

Mr Blaggs laughed. 'Didn't need to,' he said. 'He had enough cash on the outside, he had a fistful of legal beavers on his payroll.'

'So how come Wilt's supposed to have made this phone call?' asked Flint.

'Just what Bill Coven thought, he took the call,' said Blaggs, and looked significantly at his glass. Flint ordered two more pints. 'He just thought he recognized Wilt's voice,' Blaggs continued, satisfied that he was getting his money's worth for information. 'Could have been anyone.'

Flint paid for the beer and tried to think what to ask next. 'And you've got no idea how Mac got his dope then?' he asked finally.

'Know exactly,' said Blaggs proudly. 'Another bloody do-gooder only this time a fucking prison visitor. If you ask me, they should ban all vi—'

'A prison visitor?' interrupted Flint, before the Chief Warder could express his views on a proper prison regime, which involved perpetual solitary confinement for all convicts and mandatory hanging for murderers, rapists and anyone insulting a prison officer. 'You mean a visitor to the prison?'

'I don't. I mean an authorized prison visitor, a bloody licensed busybody. They come in and treat us officers like we've committed the ruddy crimes and the villains are all bloody orphans who didn't get enough teat when they were toddlers. Right, well, this bitch of a PV, name of Jardin, was the one McCullum got to bring his stuff in.'

'Christ,' said Flint. 'What did she do that for?'

'Scared,' said Blaggs. 'Some of Mac's nastier mates on the outside paid her a visit with razors and a bottle of nitric acid and threatened to leave her looking like a

cross between a dog's dinner and a leper with acne unless
. . . You get the message?'

'Yes,' said Flint, who'd begun to sympathize with the
prison visitor, though for the life of him he couldn't
visualize what a leper with acne looked like. 'And you
mean she walked in and announced the fact?'

'Oh dear me, no,' said Blaggs. 'Starts off we've done for
Mr – I ask you, *Mister*? – fucking McCullum ourselves.
Practically said I'd hanged the sod myself, not that I'd
have minded. So we took her down the morgue – of
course it just happened the prison quack was doing an
autopsy at the time and didn't much like the look of
things by the sound of it, using a saw he was, too – and he
wasn't having any crap about anyone doing anything to
the bugger. Right, well when she'd come to, like, and he's
saying the swine died of drug overdose and anyone who
said different'd end up in court for slander, she cracked.
Tears all over the place and practically down on her
knees in front of the Governor. And it all comes out how
she's been running heroin into the prison for months.
Ever so bleeding sorry and all.'

'I should bloody well think so,' said Flint. 'When's she
going to be charged?'

Mr Blaggs drank his beer mournfully. 'Never,' he
grunted.

'Never? But smuggling anything, let alone drugs, into a
prison is an indictable offence.'

'Don't tell me,' said Blaggs. 'On the other hand, the
Governor don't want no scandal, can't afford one with his
job up for grabs and anyway, she'd done a social service in
a way by shoving the bugger where he belongs.'

'There is that,' said Flint. 'Does Hodge know this?'

The Chief Warder shook his head. 'Like I said, the
Governor don't want no publicity. Anyway, she claimed
she thought the stuff was talcum powder. Like hell, but
you know what a Rumpole would do with a defence like
that. Prison authorities entirely to blame, and so on.
Negligence, the lot.'

'Did she say where she got the heroin?' asked Flint.

'Picked it up back of a telephone box on the London Road at night. Never saw the blokes who delivered it.'

'And it won't have been any of the lot who'd threatened her either.'

By the time the Inspector left the pub, he was a happy man. Hodge was way off line, and Flint had a conscience-stricken prison visitor to question. He wasn't even worried about the effect of four pints of the best bitter being flushed through his system by those bloody piss-pills. He'd already charted his route home by way of three relatively clean public lavatories.

Chapter ten

But if Flint's mood had changed for the better, Inspector Hodge's hadn't. His interpretation of Wilt's behaviour had been coloured by the accident at the end of Nott Road. 'The bastard's got to know we're onto him, ramming a police car like that,' he told Sergeant Runk, 'so what's he do?'

'Buggered if I know,' said the Sergeant, who preferred early nights and couldn't think at all clearly at one in the morning.

'He goes for an early arrest, knowing we've got no hard evidence and will have to let him go.'

'What's he want us to do that for?'

'Because if we pull him in again he can start squealing about harassment and civil bloody liberties,' said Hodge.

'Seems an odd way of going about things,' said Runk.

'And what about sending your wife out to a herb farm to pick up a load of drugs on the very day after a girl dies of the filth? Isn't that a bit odd too?' Hodge demanded.

'Definitely,' said Runk. 'In fact, I can't think of anything odder. Any normal criminal would lie bloody low.'

Inspector Hodge smiled unpleasantly. 'Exactly. But we're not dealing with any ordinary criminal. That's the point I'm trying to make. We've got one of the cleverest monkeys I've ever had to catch on our hands.'

Sergeant Runk couldn't see it. 'Not if he sends his missus out to get a bottle of the stuff when we're watching her, he's not clever. Downright stupid.'

Hodge shook his head sadly. It was always difficult to get the Sergeant to understand the complexities of the criminal mind. 'Suppose there was nothing remotely like drugs in that bottle she was seen carrying?' he asked.

Sergeant Runk dragged his thoughts back from beds and tried to concentrate. 'Seem a bit of a wasted journey,' was all he could find to say.

'It's also intended to lead us up the garden path,' said Hodge. 'And that's his tactics. You've only to look at Wilt's record to see that. Take that doll caper for instance. He had old Flint by the short and curlies there, and why? Because the stupid fool pulled him in for questioning when all the evidence he had to go on was a blown-up doll of Mrs Wilt down a piling-hole with twenty tons of concrete on top of her. And where was the real Mrs Wilt all that week? Out on a boat with a couple of hippie Yanks who were into drugs up to their eyeballs and Flint lets them flee the country without grilling them about what they'd really been doing down the coast. Sticks out a mile they were smuggling and Wilt had set himself up for a decoy and kept Flint busy digging up a plastic doll. That's how cunning Wilt is.'

'I suppose when you put it like that it makes sense,' said Runk. 'And you reckon he's using the same tactics now.'

'Leopards,' said Hodge.

'Leopards?'

'Don't change their bleeding spots.'

'Oh, them,' said the Sergeant, who could have done without ellipses at that time of night.

'Only this time he's not dealing with some old-fashioned dead-beat copper like Flint,' said Hodge, now thoroughly convinced by the persuasiveness of his argument. 'He's dealing with me.'

'Makes a change. And talking about changes, I'd like to go . . .'

'To 45 Oakhurst Avenue,' said Hodge decisively, 'that's where you're going. I want Mr Smart-Arse Wilt's car wired for sound and we're calling off the physical observation. This time it's going to be electronic all the way.'

'Not if I have anything to do with it,' said Runk defiantly, 'I've enough sense to know better than start tinkering with a sod like Wilt's car. Besides, I've got a wife and three kids to—'

'What the hell's your family got to do with it?' said Hodge. 'All I'm saying is, we'll go round there while they're asleep—'

'Asleep? A bloke who electrifies his back gate, you think he takes chances with his bloody car? You can do what you like, but I'm buggered if I'm going to meet my Maker charred to a fucking cinder by a maniac who's linked his car to the national grid. Not for you or anyone else.'

But Hodge was not to be stopped. 'We can check it's safe,' he insisted.

'How?' asked Runk, who was wide awake now. 'Let a police dog pee against the thing and see if he gets 32,000 volts up his prick? You've got to be joking.'

'I'm not,' said Hodge. 'I'm telling. Go and get the equipment.'

Half an hour later, a desperately nervous Sergeant wearing gum boots and electrically safe rubber gloves eased the door of Wilt's car open. He'd already been round it four times to check there were no wires running from the house and had earthed it with a copper rod. Even so, he was taking no chances and was a trifle surprised that the thing didn't explode.

'All right, now where do you want the tape recorder?' he asked when the Inspector finally joined him.

'Somewhere where we can get at the tape easily,' Hodge whispered.

Runk groped under the dash and tried to find a space.

'Too bloody obvious,' said Hodge. 'Stick it under his seat.'

'Anything you say,' said Runk and stuffed the recorder into the springs. The sooner he was out of the damned car, the better. 'And what about the transmitter?'

'One in the boot and the other . . .'

'Other?' said Runk. 'You're going to get him picked up by the TV licence-detector vans at this rate. One of these sets has a radius of five miles.'

'I'm not taking chances,' said Hodge. 'If he finds one, he won't look for the other.'

'Not unless he has his car serviced.'

'Put it where no one looks.'

In the end, and then only after a lot of disagreement, the Sergeant attached one radio magnetically in a corner of the boot and was lying under the car searching for a hiding-place for the second when the lights came on in the Wilts' bedroom. 'I told you the swine wouldn't take any chances,' he whispered frantically as the Inspector fought his way in beside him. 'Now we're for it.'

Hodge said nothing. With his face pressed against an oily patch of tarmac and something that smelt disgustingly of cats, he was incapable of speech.

So was Wilt. The effect of Dr Kores' sexual stimulant added to his homebrew – Wilt had surreptitiously finished six bottles in an effort to find one that didn't taste peculiar – had been to leave him mentally befuddled and with the distinct impression that something like a battalion of army ants had taken possession of his penis and were busily digging in. Either that, or one of the quads had dementedly shoved the electric toothbrush up it while he was asleep. It didn't seem likely. But then again the sensation he was experiencing didn't seem in the least likely either. As he switched on the bedside lamp and hurled the sheet back to see what on earth was wrong, he glimpsed an expanse of red panties beside him. Eva in red panties? Or was she on fire too?

Wilt stumbled out of bed and fought a losing battle with his pyjama cord for dragging the damned things down without bothering to undo them and pointed the Anglepoise at the offending organ in an effort to identify the cause of his agony. The beastly creature (Wilt had always granted his penis a certain degree of autonomy or, more accurately, had never wholly associated himself with its activities) looked normal enough but it certainly didn't feel normal, not by a long chalk. Perhaps if he put some cold cream on it . . .

He hobbled across to Eva's dressing-table and searched among the jars. Where the hell did she keep the cold cream? In the end, he chose one that called itself a moisturizer. That'd do. It didn't. By the time he'd smeared half the jar on himself and a good deal on the pillow, the burning sensation seemed to have got worse. And whatever was going on was taking place *inside*. The army ants weren't digging in, the sods were digging out. For one insane moment he considered using an aerosol of Flykil to flush them out, but decided against it. God alone knew what a load of pressurized insecticide would do to his bladder and anyway the bloody thing was full enough already. Perhaps if he had a pee . . . Still clutching the moisturizer, he hobbled through to the bathroom. 'Must have been a fucking lunatic who first called it relieving oneself,' he thought when he'd finished. About the only relief he'd found was that he hadn't peed blood and there didn't appear to be any ants in the pan afterwards. And peeing hadn't helped. If anything, it had made things even worse. 'The bloody thing'll ignite in a minute,' Wilt muttered, and was considering using the shower hose as a fire extinguisher when a better idea occurred to him. There was no point in smearing moisturizer on the outside. The stuff was needed internally. But how the hell to get it there? A tube of toothpaste caught his eye. That was what he needed. Oh no, it wasn't. Not with toothpaste. With moisturizer. Why didn't they pack the muck in tubes?

Wilt opened the medicine cupboard and groped among the old razors, the bottles of aspirin and cough mixture for a tube of something vaguely suitable for squeezing up his penis but apart from Eva's hair remover . . . 'Sod that for a lark,' said Wilt, who had once accidentally brushed his teeth with the stuff, 'I'm not shoving that defoliant up any place.' It would have to be the moisturizing cream or nothing. And it wasn't going to be nothing. With a fresh and frenzied sense of desperation, he lurched from the bathroom clutching the jar and stumbled downstairs to the kitchen and was presently scrabbling in the drawer by the sink. A moment later he had found what he was looking for.

Upstairs, Eva turned over. For some time she had been vaguely aware that her back was cold but too vaguely to do anything about it. Now she was also aware that the light was on and that the bed beside her was empty and the bedclothes had been flung back. Which explained why she'd been freezing. Henry had evidently gone to the lavatory. Eva pulled the blankets back and lay awake waiting for him to return. Perhaps he'd be in the mood to make love. After all, he'd had two bottles of his beer and Dr Kores' aphrodisiac and she'd put on her red panties and it was much nicer to make love in the middle of the night when the quads were fast asleep than on Sunday mornings when they weren't, and she had to get up and shut the door in case they came in. Even that wasn't guaranteed to work. Eva would always remember one awful occasion when Henry had almost made it and she had suddenly smelt smoke and there'd been a series of screams from the quads. 'Fire! Fire!' they'd yelled, and she and Henry had hurled themselves from the bed and onto the landing in the altogether only to find the quads there with her jam-making pan filled with burning newspaper. It had been one of those rare occasions when she'd had to agree with Henry about the need for a thorough thrashing. Not that the quads had had one. They'd been down the stairs and out of the front door before Wilt could catch them and he'd been unable to pursue them down the street without a stitch of clothing on. No, it was much nicer at night and she was just wondering if she ought to take her panties off now and not wait, when a crash from downstairs put the thought out of her mind.

Eva climbed out of bed and putting a dressing-gown on, went down to investigate. The next moment all thoughts of making love had gone. Wilt was standing in the middle of the kitchen with her cake-icing syringe in one hand and his penis in the other. In fact, the two seemed to be joined together.

Eva groped for words. 'And what do you think you're doing?' she demanded when she could speak.

Wilt turned a crimson face towards her. 'Doing?' he asked, conscious that the situation was one that was open to any number of interpretations and none of them nice.

'That's what I said, doing,' said Eva.

Wilt looked down at the syringe. 'As a matter of fact . . .' he began, but Eva was ahead of him.

'That's my icing syringe.'

'I know it is. And this is my John Thomas,' said Wilt. Eva regarded the two objects with equal disgust. She would never be able to ice a cake with the syringe again and how she could ever have found anything faintly attractive about Wilt's John Thomas was beyond her. 'And for your information,' he continued, 'that is your moisturizing cream on the floor.'

Eva stared down at the jar. Even by the peculiar standards of 45 Oakhurst Avenue there was something disorientating about the conjunction – and conjunction was the right word – of Wilt's thingamajig and the icing syringe and the presence on the kitchen floor of a jar of her moisturizing cream. She sat down on a stool.

'And for your further information,' Wilt went on, but Eva stopped him. 'I don't want to hear,' she said.

Wilt glared at her lividly. 'And I don't want to feel,' he snarled. 'If you think I find any satisfaction in squirting whatever's in that emulsifier you use for your face up my whatsit at three o'clock in the morning, I can assure you I don't.'

'I don't see why you're doing it then,' said Eva, beginning to have an awful feeling herself.

'Because, if I didn't know better, I'd think some

bloody sadist had larded my waterworks with pepper, that's why.'

'With pepper?'

'Or ground glass and curry powder,' said Wilt. 'Add a soupçon of mustard gas and you'll have the general picture. Or sensation. Something ghastly anyway. And now if you don't mind . . .'

But before he could get to work with the icing syringe again Eva had stopped him. 'There must be an antidote,' she said. 'I'll phone Dr Kores.'

Wilt's eyes bulged in his head. 'You'll do what?' he demanded.

'I said I'll—'

'I heard you,' shouted Wilt. 'You said you'd ring that bloody herbal homothrope Dr Kores and I want to know why.'

Eva looked desperately round the kitchen but there was no comfort now to be found in the Magimix or the le Creuset saucepans hanging by the stove and certainly none in the herb chart on the wall. That beastly woman had poisoned Henry and it was all her own fault for having listened to Mavis. But Wilt was staring at her dangerously and she had to do something immediately. 'I just think you ought to see a doctor,' she said. 'I mean, it could be serious.'

'Could be?' yelled Wilt, now thoroughly alarmed. 'It fucking well is and you still haven't told me—'

'Well, if you must know,' interrupted Eva, fighting back, 'you shouldn't have had so much beer.'

'Beer? My God, you bitch, I knew there was something wrong with the muck,' shouted Wilt and hurled himself at her across the kitchen.

'I only meant—' Eva began, and then dodged round the pine table to avoid the syringe. She was saved by the quads.

'What's Daddy doing with cream all over his genitals?' asked Emmeline. Wilt stopped in his tracks and stared at the four faces in the doorway. As usual, the quads were employing tactics that always nonplussed him. To combine the whimsy of 'Daddy', particularly with the inflection Emmeline gave the word, with the anatomically exact was calculated to disconcert him. And why not ask him instead of referring to him so objectively? For a moment he hesitated and Eva seized her opportunity.

'That's nothing to do with you,' she said and ostentatiously shielded them from the sight. 'It's just that your father isn't very well and—'

'That's right,' shouted Wilt, who could see what was coming, 'slap all the blame on me.'

'I'm not blaming you,' said Eva over her shoulder. 'It's—'

'That you lace my beer with some infernal irritant and bloody well poison me, and then you have the gall to tell them I'm not very well. I'll say I'm not well. I'm—'

A hammering sound from the Gamers' wall diverted his attention. As Wilt hurled the syringe at the Laughing Cavalier his mother-in-law had given them when she'd sold her house and which Eva claimed reminded her of her happy childhood there, Eva hustled the quads upstairs. When she came down again, Wilt had resorted to ice-cubes.

'I do think you ought to see a doctor,' she said.

'I should have seen one before I married you,' said Wilt. 'I suppose you realize I might be dead by now. What the hell did you put in my beer?'

Eva looked miserable. 'I only wanted to help our marriage,' she said, 'and Mavis Mottram said—'

'I'll strangle the bitch!'

'She said Dr Kores had helped Patrick and—'

'Helped Patrick?' said Wilt, momentarily distracted from his ice-packed penis. 'The last time I saw him he looked as if he could do with a bra. Said something about not having to shave so much either.'

'That's what I mean. Dr Kores gave Mavis something to cool his sexual ardour and I thought . . .' She paused. Wilt was looking at her dangerously again.

'Go on, though I'd question the use of "thought".'

'Well, that she might have something that would pep . . .'

'Pep?' said Wilt. 'Why not say ginger and have done with it? And why the hell should I need pepping up anyway? I'm a working man . . . or was, with four damned daughters, not some demented sex pistol of seventeen.'

'I just thought . . . I mean it occurred to me if she could do so much for Patrick . . .' (here Wilt snorted) '. . . she might be able to help us to have a . . . well, a more fulfilling sex life.'

'By poisoning me with Spanish Fly? Some fulfilment that is,' said Wilt. 'Well, let me tell you something now. For your information, I am not some fucking sex processor like that Magimix, and if you want the sort of sex life those idiotic women's magazines you read seem to suggest is your due, like fifteen times a week, you'd better find another husband because I'm buggered if I'm up to it. And the way I feel now, you'll be lucky if I'm ever up to it again.'

'Oh Henry!'

'Sod off,' said Wilt, and hobbled through to the downstairs loo with his mixing bowl of ice cubes. At least they seemed to help and the pain was easing off now.

As the sound of discord inside the house died down, Inspector Hodge and the Sergeant made their way back down Oakhurst Avenue to their car. They hadn't been able to hear what was being said, but the fact that there had been some sort of terrible row had heightened Hodge's opinion that the Wilts were no ordinary criminals. 'The pressure's beginning to tell,' he told Sergeant Runk. 'If we don't find him calling on his friends within a day or two, I'm not the man I think I am.'

'If I don't get some sleep, I won't be either,' said Runk, 'and I'm not surprised that bloke next door wants to sell his house. Must be hell living next to people like that.'

'Won't have to much longer,' said Hodge, but the mention of Mr Gamer had put a new idea in his mind. With a bit of collaboration from the Gamers, he'd be in a

position to hear everything that went on in the Wilts'
house. On the other hand, with their car transformed
into a mobile radio station, he was expecting an early
arrest.

Chapter eleven

All the following day, while Wilt lay in bed with a hot-
water bottle he'd converted into an ice-pack by putting it
into the freezer compartment of the fridge and Inspector
Hodge monitored Eva's movements about Ipford, Flint
followed his own line of investigation. He checked with
Forensic and learnt that the high-grade heroin found in
McCullum's cell corresponded in every way to that discovered in Miss Lynchknowle's flat and almost certainly
came from the same source. He spent an hour with Mrs
Jardin, the prison visitor, wondering at the remarkable
capacity for self-deception that had already allowed her
to put the blame on everyone else for McCullum's death.
Society was to blame for creating the villain, the education authorities for his wholly inadequate schooling, com-
merce and industry for failing to provide him with a
responsible job, the judge for sentencing him . . .
    'He was a victim of circumstances,' said Mrs Jardin.
    'You might say that about everybody,' said Flint,
looking at a corner cupboard containing pieces of silver
that suggested Mrs Jardin's circumstances allowed her
the wherewithal to be the victim of her own senti-
mentality. 'For instance, the three men who threatened to
carve you up with—'
    'Don't,' said Mrs Jardin, shuddering at the memory.
    'Well, they were victims too, weren't they? So's a rabid
dog, but that's no great comfort when you're bitten by
one, and I put drug pushers in that category.' Mrs Jardin

130

had to agree. 'So you wouldn't recognize them again,' asked Flint, 'not if they were wearing stockings over their heads like you said?'

'They were. And gloves.'

'And they took you down the London Road and showed you where the drop was going to be made.'

'Behind the telephone box opposite the turn-off to Brindlay. I was to stop and go into the phone box and pretend to make a call, and then, if no one was about, I had to come out and pick up the package and go straight home. They said they'd be watching me.'

'And I don't suppose it ever occurred to you to go straight to the police and report the matter?' asked Flint.

'Naturally it did. That was my first thought, but they said they had more than one officer on their payroll.'

Flint sighed. It was an old tactic, and for all he knew the sods had been telling the truth. There were bent coppers, a lot more than when he'd joined the force, but then there hadn't been the big gangs and the money to bribe, and if bribery failed, to pay for a contract killing. The good old days when someone was always hanged if a policeman was murdered, even if it was the wrong man. Now, thanks to the do-gooders like Mrs Jardin, and Christie lying in the witness box and getting that mentally subnormal Evans topped for murders Christie himself had committed, the deterrent was no longer there. The world Flint had known had gone by the board, so he couldn't really blame her for giving in to threats. All the same, he was going to remain what he had always been, an honest and hardworking policeman.

'Even so we could have given you protection,' he said, 'and they wouldn't have been bothered with you once you'd stopped visiting McCullum.'

'I know that now,' said Mrs Jardin, 'but at the time I was too frightened to think clearly.'

Or at all, thought Flint, but he didn't say it. Instead, he concentrated on the method of delivery. No one dropped a consignment of heroin behind a telephone kiosk without ensuring it was going to be picked up. Then again, they didn't hang around after the drop. So there had to be some way of communicating. 'What would have happened if you'd been ill?' he asked. 'Just supposing you couldn't have collected the package, what then?'

Mrs Jardin looked at him with a mixture of contempt and bewilderment she evidently felt when faced with someone who concentrated so insistently on practical matters and neglected moral issues. Besides, he was a policeman and ill-educated. Policemen didn't find absolution as victims. 'I don't know,' she said.

But Flint was getting angry. 'Come off the high horse,' he said, 'you can squeal you were forced into being a runner, but we can still charge you with pushing drugs and into a prison at that. Who did you have to phone?'

Mrs Jardin crumbled. 'I don't know his name. I had to call a number and . . .'

'What number?'

'Just a number. I can't—'

'Get it,' said Flint. Mrs Jardin went out of the room and Flint sat looking at the titles in the bookshelves. They meant very little to him and told him only that she'd read or at least bought a great many books on sociology, economics, the Third World and penal reform. It didn't impress Flint. If the woman had really wanted to do something about the conditions of prisoners, she'd have got a job as a wardress and lived on low wages, instead of dabbling in prison visits and talking about the poor calibre of the staff who had to do society's dirty work. Stick up her taxes to build better prisons and she'd soon start squealing. Talk about hypocrisy.

Mrs Jardin came back with a piece of paper.'That's the number,' she said, handing it to him. Flint looked at it. A London phone box.

'When did you have to call?'

'They said between 9.30 and 9.40 at night the day before I had to collect the packet.'

Flint changed direction. 'How many times did you collect?'

'Only three.'

He got to his feet. It was no use. They'd know Mac was dead, even if it hadn't been announced in the papers, so there was no point in supposing they'd make another drop, but at least they were operating out of London. Hodge was on the wrong track. On the other hand, Flint himself couldn't be said to be on the right one. The trail stopped at Mrs Jardin and a public telephone in London. If McCullum had still been alive . . .

Flint left the house and drove over to the prison. 'I'd like to take a look at Mac's list of visitors,' he told Chief Warder Blaggs, and spent half an hour writing names in his notebook, together with addresses.

'Someone in that little lot had to be running messages,' he said when he finished. 'Not that I expect to get anywhere, but it's worth trying.'

Afterwards, back at the Station, he had checked them on the Central Records Computer and cross-referenced for drug dealing, but the one link he was looking for, some petty criminal living in Ipford or nearby, was missing. And he wasn't going to waste his time trying to tackle London. In fact, if he were truthful, he had to admit he was wasting his time even in Ipford except . . . except that something told him he wasn't. It nagged at his mind. Sitting in his office, he followed that instinct. The girl had been seen by her flat-mate down by the marina. Several times. But the marina was just another place like the telephone kiosk on the London Road. It had to be something more definite, something he could check out.

Flint picked up the phone and called the Drug Addiction Study Unit at the Ipford Hospital.

By lunchtime, Wilt was up and about. To be exact, he'd been up and about several times during the morning, in part to get another hot-water bottle from the freezer, but more often in a determined effort not to masturbate himself to death. It was all very well Eva supposing she'd benefit from the effects of whatever diabolical irritant she'd added to his homebrew, but to Wilt's way of thinking, a wife who'd damned near poisoned her husband didn't deserve what few sexual benefits he had to offer. Give her an inkling of satisfaction from this experiment and next time he'd land up in hospital with internal bleeding and a permanent erection. As it was, he had a hard time with his penis.

'I'll freeze the damn thing down,' had been Wilt's first thought and for a while it had worked, though painfully. But after a time he had drifted off to sleep and had woken an hour later with the awful impression that he'd taken it into his head to have an affair with a freshly caught Dover Sole. Wilt hurled himself off the thing and had then taken the bottle downstairs to put it back in the fridge before realizing that this wouldn't be particularly hygienic. He was in the process of washing it when the front doorbell rang. Wilt dropped the bottle on the draining-board, retrieved it from the sink when it slithered off and finally tried wedging it between the upturned teapot and a casserole dish in the drying rack, before going to answer the call.

It was not the postman as he expected, but Mavis Mottram. 'What are you doing at home?' she asked.

Wilt sheltered behind the door and pulled his dressing-gown tightly round him. 'Well, as a matter of fact . . .' he began.

Mavis pushed past him and went through to the kitchen. 'I just came round to see if Eva could organize the food side of things.'

'What things?' asked Wilt, looking at her with loathing. It was thanks to this woman that Eva had consulted Dr Kores. Mavis ignored the question. In her dual rôle as militant feminist and secretary to Mothers Against The Bomb, she evidently considered Wilt to be part of the male sub-species. 'Is she going to be back soon?' she went on.

Wilt smiled unpleasantly and shut the kitchen door behind him. If Mavis Mottram was going to treat him like a moron, he felt inclined to behave like one. 'How do you know she's not here?' he asked, testing the blade of a rather blunt breadknife against his thumb.

'The car's not outside and I thought . . . well, you usually take it . . .' She stopped.

Wilt put the breadknife on the magnetic holder next to the Sabatier ones. It looked out of place. 'Phallic,' he said. 'Interesting.'

'What is?'

'Lawrentian,' said Wilt, and retrieved the icing syringe from a plastic bucket where Eva had been soaking it in Dettol in an attempt to persuade herself she would be able to use the thing again.

'Lawrentian?' said Mavis, beginning to sound genuinely alarmed.

Wilt put the syringe on the counter and wiped his hands. Eva's washing-up gloves caught his eye. 'I agree,' he said and began putting the gloves on.

'What on earth are you talking about?' asked Mavis, suddenly remembering Wilt and the inflated doll. She moved round the kitchen table towards the door and then thought better of it. Wilt in a dressing-gown and no pyjama trousers, and now wearing a pair of rubber gloves and holding a cake-icing syringe, was an extremely disturbing sight. 'Anyway, if you'll ask her to call me, I'll explain about the food side of . . .' Her voice trailed off.

Wilt was smiling again. He was also squirting a yellowish liquid into the air from the syringe. Images of some demented doctor in an early horror movie flickered in her mind. 'You were saying something about her not being here,' said Wilt and stepped back in front of the door. 'Do go on.'

'Go on about what?' said Mavis with a distinct quaver.

'About her not being here. I find your interest curious, don't you?'

'Curious?' mumbled Mavis, desperately trying to find some thread of sanity in his inconsequential remarks. 'What's curious about it? She's obviously out shopping and—'

'Obviously?' asked Wilt, and gazed vacantly past her out of the window and down the garden. 'I wouldn't have said anything was obvious.'

Mavis involuntarily followed his gaze and found the back garden almost as sinister as Wilt with washing-up gloves and that bloody syringe. With a fresh effort, she forced herself to turn back and speak normally. 'I'll be off now,' she said and moved forward.

Wilt's fixed smile crumbled. 'Oh, not so soon,' he said. 'Why not put the kettle on and have some coffee? After all, that's what you'd do if Eva was here. You'd sit down and have a nice talk. And you and Eva had so much in common.'

'Had?' said Mavis and wished to God she'd kept her mouth shut. Wilt's awful smile was back again. 'Well, if you'd like a cup yourself, I suppose I've got time.' She crossed to the electric kettle and took it to the sink. The hot-water bottle was lying on the bottom. Mavis lifted it out and experienced another ghastly frisson. The hot-water bottle wasn't simply not hot, it was icy cold. And behind her Wilt had begun to grunt alarmingly. For a moment Mavis hesitated before swinging round. This time there was no mistaking the threat she was facing. It was staring at her from between the folds of Wilt's dressing-gown. With a squeal, she hurled herself at the back door, dragged it open, shot out and with a clatter of dustbin lids, was through the gate and heading for the car.

Behind her Wilt dropped the syringe back into the bucket and tried to get his hands out of the washing-up gloves by pulling on the fingers. It wasn't the best method and it was some time before he'd rid himself of the wretched things and had grabbed the second bottle from the freezer. 'Bugger the woman,' he muttered as he clutched the bottle to his penis and tried to think of what to do next. If she went to the police . . . No, she wasn't likely to do that but all the same, it would be as well to take precautions. Regardless of hygiene, he flung the bottle from the sink into the freezer and hobbled upstairs. 'At least we've seen the last of Mavis M,' he thought as he got back into bed. That was some consolation for the reputation he was already doubtless acquiring. As usual, he was entirely wrong.

*

Twenty minutes later, Eva, who had been intercepted by Mavis on her way home, drove up to the house.

'Henry,' she shouted as soon as she was inside the front door. 'You come straight down here and explain what you were doing with Mavis.'

'Sod off,' said Wilt.

'What did you say?'

'Nothing. I was just groaning.'

'No, you weren't. I distinctly heard you say something,' said Eva on her way upstairs.

Wilt got out of bed and girded his loins with the water bottle. 'Now you just listen to me,' he said before Eva could get a word in. 'I've had all I can stand from everybody, you, Mavis-moron-Mottram, that poisoner Kores, the quads and the bloody thugs who've been following me. In fact the whole fucking modern world with its emphasis on me being nice and docile and passive and everyone else doing their own thing and to hell with the consequences. (A) I am not a thing, and (B) I'm not going to be done any more. Not by you, or Mavis, or, for that matter, the damned quads. And I don't give a tuppenny stuff what received opinions you suck up like some dehydrated sponge from the hacks who write articles on progressive education and sex for geriatrics and health through fucking hemlock—'

'Hemlock's a poison. No one . . .' Eva began, trying to divert his fury.

'And so's the ideological codswallop you fill your head with,' shouted Wilt. 'Permissive cyanide, page three nudes for the so-called intelligentsia or video nasties for the unemployed, all fucking placebos for them that can't think or feel. And if you don't know what a placebo is, try looking it up in a dictionary.'

He paused for breath and Eva grabbed her opportunity. 'You know very well what I think about video nasties,' she said, 'I wouldn't dream of letting the girls see anything like that.'

'Right,' yelled Wilt, 'so how about letting me and Mr bleeding Gamer off the hook. Has it ever occurred to you that you've got genuine non-video actual nasties, pre-pubescent horrors, in those four daughters? Oh no, not them. They're special, they're unique, they're flipping geniuses. We mustn't do anything to retard their intellectual development, like teaching them some manners or how to behave in a civilized fashion. Oh no, we're your modern model parents holding the ring while those four ignoble little savages turn themselves into computer-addicted technocrats with about as much moral sense as Ilse Koch on a bad day.'

'Who's Ilse Koch?' asked Eva.

'Just a mass murderess in a concentration camp,' said Wilt, 'and don't get the idea I'm on a right-wing, flog 'em and hang 'em reactionary high because I'm not, and those idiots don't think either. I'm just mister stick-in-the-middle who doesn't know which way to jump. But my God I do think! Or try to. Now leave me in peace and discomfort and go and tell your mate Mavis that the next time she doesn't want to see an involuntary erection, not to advise you to go anywhere near Castrator Kores.'

Eva went downstairs feeling strangely invigorated. It was a long time since she'd heard Henry state his feelings so strongly and, while she didn't understand everything he'd said, and she certainly didn't think he'd been fair about the quads, it was somehow reassuring to have him assert his authority in the house. It made her feel better about having been to that awful Dr Kores with all her silly talk about . . . what was it? . . . 'the sexual superiority of the female in the mammalian world'. Eva didn't want to be superior in everything and anyway, she wasn't just a mammal. She was a human being. That wasn't the same thing at all.

Chapter twelve

By the following evening, it would have been difficult to say what Inspector Hodge was. Since Wilt hadn't emerged from the house, the Inspector had spent the best part of two days tracing Eva's progress to and from the school and round Ipford in the bugged Escort.

'It's good practice,' he told Sergeant Runk, as they followed her in a van Hodge had converted to a listening-post.

'For what?' asked the Sergeant, pinning a mark on the town map to indicate that Eva had now parked behind Sainsbury's. She'd already been to Tesco's and Fine Fare. 'So we learn where to get the best discount on washing powder?'

'For when he decides to move.'

'When,' said Runk. 'So far he hasn't been out of the house all day.'

'He's sent her out to check she hasn't got a tail on her,' said Hodge. 'In the meantime, he's lying low.'

'Which you said was just the thing he wasn't doing,' said Runk. 'I said he was and you said . . .'

'I know what I said. But that was when he knew he was being followed. It's different now.'

'I'll say,' said Runk. 'So the sod sends us on a tour of shopping centres and we haven't got a clue what's going on.'

They had that night. Runk, who had insisted on having the afternoon off for some shut-eye if he was to work at night, retrieved the tape from under the seat and replaced it with a new one. It was one o'clock in the morning. Half an hour later, Hodge, whose childhood had been spent in a house where sex was never mentioned, was listening to the quads discussing Wilt's condition with a frankness that appalled him. If anything was needed to convince him that Mr and Mrs Wilt were dyed-in-the-wool criminals, it was Emmeline's repeated demand to know why Daddy had been up in the night putting cake icing on his penis. Eva's explanation didn't help either. 'He wasn't feeling very well, dear. He'd had too much beer and he couldn't sleep, so he went down to the kitchen to see if he could ice cake and . . .'

'I wouldn't like the sort of cake he was icing,' interrupted Samantha. 'And anyway, it was face-cream.'

'I know, dear, but he was practising and he spilt it.'

'Up his cock?' demanded Penelope, which gave Eva the opportunity to tell her never to use that word. 'It's not nice,' she said, 'it's not nice to say things like that and you're not going to tell anyone at school.'

'It wasn't very nice of Daddy to use the icing syringe to pump face-cream up his penis,' said Emmeline.

By the time the discussion was over, and Eva had dropped the quads off at the school, Hodge was ashen. Sergeant Runk wasn't feeling very well either.

'I don't believe it, I don't believe a bloody word of it,' muttered the Inspector.

'I wish to God I didn't,' said Runk. 'I've heard some revolting things in my time but that lot takes the cake.'

'Don't mention that word,' Hodge said. 'I still don't believe it. No man in his right mind would do a thing like that. They're having us on.'

'Oh, I don't know. I knew a bloke once who used to butter his wick with strawberry jam and have his missus—'

'Shut up,' shouted Hodge, 'if there's one thing I can't stand it's filth and I've had my fill of that for one night.'

'So's Wilt, by the sound of it,' said Runk, 'walking about with his prick in a jug of ice cubes like that. Can't have been just face-cream or icing-sugar he had in that syringe.'

'Dear God,' said Hodge. 'You're not suggesting he was fixing himself with a cake-icing syringe, are you? He'd be bloody dead by now, and anyhow the fucking thing would leak.'

'Not if he mixed the junk with cold cream. That'd explain it, wouldn't it?'

'It might do,' Hodge admitted. 'I suppose if people can sniff the filthy muck, there's no knowing what they can do with it. Not that it helps us much what he does.'

'Of course it does,' said the Sergeant, who had suddenly seen a way of ending the tedium of sitting through the night in the van. 'It means he's got the stuff in the house.'

'Or up his pipe,' said Hodge.

'Wherever. Anyway, there's bound to be enough around to haul him in and give him a good going over.'

But the Inspector has his sights set on more ambitious targets. 'A fat lot of good that's going to do us,' he said, 'even if he did crack, and if you'd read what he did to old Flint you'd know better—'

'But this'd be different,' Runk interrupted. 'First off, he'd be cold turkey. Don't have to question him. Leave him in a cell for three days without a fix and he'd be bleating like a fucking baa-lamb.'

'Yes, and I know who for,' said the Inspector. 'His ruddy mouthpiece.'

'Yes, but we'd have his missus too, remember. And anyway this time we'd have hard evidence and it would just be a matter of charging him. He wouldn't get bail on a heroin charge.'

'True,' said Hodge grudgingly, 'if we had hard evidence. "If." '

'Well, there's bound to be with him getting the stuff all over his pyjamas like those kids said. Forensic would have an easy time. Take that cake-icing syringe for a starter. And then there are towels and drying-up cloths. Blimey, the place must be alive with the stuff. Even the fleas on the cat must be addicts the way he's been splashing it round.'

'That's what worries me,' said Hodge. 'Whoever heard of a pusher splashing it round? No way. They're too bloody careful. Especially when the heat's on like it is now. You know what I think?' Sergeant Runk shook his head. In his opinion the Inspector was incapable of thought. 'I think the bastard's trying the old come-on.

Wants us to arrest him. He's trying to trap us into it. That explains the whole thing.'

'Doesn't explain anything to me,' said Runk despairingly.

'Listen,' said Hodge, 'what we've heard on that tape just now is too bizarre to be credible, right? Right. You've never heard of a junkie fixing his cock and I haven't either. But apparently, this Wilt does. Not only that, but he makes a fucking mess, does it in the middle of the night and with a cake-icing syringe and makes sure his kids find him in the kitchen doing it. For why? Because he wants the little bitches to shoot their mouths off about it in public and for us to hear about it. That's why. Well, I'm not falling for it. I'm going to take my time and wait for Mr Clever Wilt to lead me to his source. I'm not interested in single pushers, this time I'm going to pull in the whole ruddy network.'

And having satisfied himself with this interpretation of Wilt's extraordinary behaviour, the Inspector sat on, savouring his eventual triumph. In his mind's eye, he could see Wilt in the dock with a dozen big-time criminals, none of whom the likes of Flint had ever suspected. They'd be moneyed men with large houses who played golf and belonged to the best clubs, and after sentencing him, the Judge would compliment Inspector Hodge on his brilliant handling of the case. No one would ever call him inefficient again. He'd be famous and his photograph would be in all the papers.

Wilt's thoughts followed rather similar lines, though with a different emphasis. The effects of Eva's enthusiasm for aphrodisiacs were still making themselves felt and, more disastrously, had given him what appeared to be a permanent erection. 'Of course I'm confined to the bloody house,' he said when Eva complained that she didn't want him wandering about in his dressing-gown on her weekly coffee morning. 'You don't expect me to go back to the Tech with the thing sticking out like a ramrod.'

'Well, I don't want you making an exhibition of yourself in front of Betty and the others like you did with Mavis.'

'Mavis got what she deserved,' said Wilt. 'I didn't ask the woman into the house, she just marched in, and anyway if she hadn't put you on to poisoner Kores I wouldn't be wandering around with a coat-hanger strapped to my waist, would I?'

'What's the coat-hanger for?'

'To keep the flipping dressing-gown off the inflamed thing,' said Wilt. 'If you knew what it felt like to have stuff like a heavy blanket rubbing against the end of a pressurized and highly sensitive—'

'I don't want to hear,' said Eva.

'And I don't want to feel,' Wilt retorted. 'Hence the coat-hanger. And what's more, you want to try bending your knees and leaning forward at the same time every time you have to pee. It's bloody agony. As it is I've banged my head on the wall twice and I haven't had a crap in two days. I can't even sit down to read. It's either flat on my back in bed with the wastepaper basket for protection or up and about with the coat-hanger. And up and about it is. At this rate, they'll have to build a special coffin with a periscope when I cough it.'

Eva looked at him doubtfully. 'Perhaps you ought to go and see a doctor if it's that serious.'

'How?' snapped Wilt. 'If you think I'm going to walk down the road looking like a pregnant sex-change artist, forget it. I'd be arrested before I was half-way there and the local rag would have a field day. TECH TEACHER ON PERMANENT HIGH. And you'd really love it if I got called Pumpkin Penis Percy. So you have your Tupperware Party and I'll stick around upstairs.'

Wilt went carefully up to the bedroom and took refuge under the wastepaper basket. Presently, he heard voices from below. Eva's Community Care Committee had begun to arrive. Wilt wondered how many of them had already heard Mavis' version of the episode in the kitchen and were secretly delighted that Eva was married to a homicidal flasher. Not that they would ever admit as much. No, it would be 'Did you hear about poor Eva's awful husband?' or 'I can't think how she can bring herself to stay in the same house with that frightful Henry,' but in fact the target for their malice would be Eva herself. Which was just as it should be, considering that she'd doctored his beer with whatever poison Dr Kores had given her. Wilt lay back and wondered about the doctor and presently fell into a daydream in which he sued her for some enormous sum on the grounds of . . . What sort of grounds were there? Invasion of Penisy? Or Deprivation of Scrotal Rights? Or just plain Poisoning. That wouldn't work because Eva had administered the stuff and presumably if you took it in the correct doses it wouldn't have such awful effects. And, of course, the Kores bitch wasn't to know that Eva never did things by halves. In her book, if a little of something was good for you, twice as much was better. Even Charlie, the cat, knew that, and had developed an uncanny knack of disappearing for several days the moment Eva put down a saucer of cream laced with worm powder. But then Charlie was no fool and evidently still remembered the experience of having his innards scoured out by twice the recommended dosage. The poor brute had come limping back into the house after a week in the bushes at the bottom of the garden looking like a tapeworm with fur and had promptly been put on a high-pilchard diet to build him up.

Well, if a cat could learn from experience, there was no excuse for Wilt. On the other hand, Charlie didn't exactly have to live with Eva, but could shove off at the first sign of trouble. 'Lucky blighter,' Wilt muttered and wondered what would happen if he rang up one night and said he wasn't coming home for a week. He could just imagine the explosion on the other end of the line, and if he put the phone down without coming up with a really plausible explanation, he'd never hear the end of it when he did come home. And why? Because the truth was always too insane or incredible. Just about as incredible as the events of the week which had started with that idiot from the Ministry of Education and had gone on through Miss Hare's use of karate in the Ladies' lavatory to McCullum's threats and the men in the car who'd followed him. Add that little lot together with an overdose of Spanish Fly, and you had a truth no one would believe. Anyway, there was no point in lying there speculating about things he couldn't alter.

'Emulate the cat,' said Wilt to himself and went through to the bathroom to check in the mirror how his penis was getting on. It certainly felt better, and when he removed the wastepaper basket, he was delighted to find it had begun to droop. He had a shower and shaved and by the time Eva's little group had broken up, he was able to go downstairs wearing his trousers. 'How did the hen party go?' he asked.

Eva rose to the provocation. 'I see you're back to your normal sexist self. Anyway, it wasn't any sort of party. We're having that next Friday. Here.'

'Here?'

'That's right. It's going to be a fancy-dress party with prizes for the best costume and a raffle to raise money for the Harmony Community Play-Group.'

'Yes, and I'm sending a bill to all the people you're inviting to pay for the insurance in advance. Remember what happened to the Vurkells when Polly Merton sued them for falling downstairs blind drunk.'

'That was quite different,' said Eva. 'It was all Mary's fault for having a loose stair carpet. She never did look after the house properly. It was always a mess.'

'So was Polly Merton when she hit the hall floor. It was a wonder she wasn't killed,' said Wilt. 'Anyway, that's not the point. The Vurkells' house was wrecked and the insurance company wouldn't pay up because he'd been breaking the by-laws by running an illegal casino with that roulette wheel of his.'

'There you are,' said Eva. 'We're not breaking the law by holding a raffle for charity.'

'I'd check it out if I were you, and you can check me out

too,' said Wilt. 'I've had enough trouble with my private parts these last two days without wearing that Francis Drake outfit you rigged me out in last Christmas.'

'You looked very nice in it. Even Mr Persner said you deserved a prize.'

'For wearing your grandmother's camiknickers stuffed with straw, I daresay I did, but I certainly didn't feel nice. In any case, I've got my prisoner to teach that night.'

'You could cancel that for once,' said Eva.

'What, just before the exams? Certainly not,' said Wilt. 'You invite a mob of costumed fools to invade the house for the good of charity without consulting me, you mustn't expect me to stop my charitable work.'

'In that case, you'll be going out tonight then?' said Eva. 'Today's Friday and you've got to keep up the good work, haven't you?'

'Good Lord,' said Wilt, who'd lost track of the days. It *was* Friday and he had forgotten to prepare anything for the lecture to his class at Baconheath. Spurred on by Eva's sarcasm and the knowledge that he'd end up the following Friday in straw-filled camiknickers or even as Puss in Boots in a black leotard which fitted far too tightly, Wilt spent the afternoon working over some old notes on British Culture and Institutions. They were entitled 'The Need For Deference, Paternalism and The Class Structure' and were designed to be provocative.

By six o'clock he had finished his supper, and half an hour later was driving out along the fen roads towards the airbase rather faster than usual. His penis was playing up again and it had only been by strapping it to his lower stomach with a long bandage and a cricket box that he'd been able to make himself comfortable and not provocatively indecent.

Behind him, the two monitoring vans followed his progress and Inspector Hodge was jubilant. 'I knew it. I knew he'd have to move,' he told Sergeant Runk as they listened to the signals coming from the Escort. 'Now we're getting somewhere.'

'If he's as smart as you say he is, it could be up the garden path,' said Runk.

But Hodge was consulting the map. The coast lay ahead. Apart from that, there were only a few villages, the bleak flatness of the fens and . . . 'Any moment he'll switch west,' he predicted. His hopes had turned to certainty. Wilt was heading for the US Airbase at Baconheath and the American connection was complete.

In Ipford prison, Inspector Flint stared into the Bull's face. 'How many years have you still to do?' he asked. 'Twelve?'

'Not with remission,' said the Bull. 'Only eight. I've got good behaviour.'

'Had,' said Flint. 'You lost that when you knocked Mac off.'

'Knocked Mac off? I never did. That's a bloody lie. I never touched him. He—'

'That's not what the Bear says,' interrupted Flint, and opened a file. 'He says you'd been saving up those sleeping pills so you could murder Mac and take over from him. Want to read his statement? It's all down in black and white and nicely signed. Here, take a dekko.'

He pushed the paper across the table but the Bull was on his feet. 'You can't pull that fucking one on me,' he shouted and was promptly pushed back into his chair by the Chief Warder.

'Can,' said Flint, leaning forward and staring into the Bull's frightened eyes. 'You wanted to take over from McCullum, didn't you? Jealous of him, weren't you? Got greedy. Thought you'd grab a nice little operation run from inside and you'd come out in eight years with a pension as long as your arm all safely stashed away by your widow.'

'Widow?' The Bull's face was ashen now. 'What you mean, widow?'

Flint smiled. 'Just as I say. Widow. Because you aren't ever going to get out now. Eight years back to twelve and a life stretch for murdering Mac adds up to twenty-seven by my reckoning, and for all those twenty-seven years, you're going to be doing solitary for your own protection. I can't see you making it, can you?'

The Bull stared at him pathetically. 'You're setting me up.'

'I don't want to hear your defence,' said Flint, and got to his feet. 'Save the blarney for the court. Maybe you'll get some nice judge to believe you. Especially with your record. Oh, and I shouldn't count on the missus to help. She's been shacked up with Joe Slavey for six months, or didn't you know?'

He moved towards the door, but the Bull had broken. 'I didn't do it, I swear to God I didn't, Mr Flint. Mac was like a brother to me. I'd never . . .'

Flint put the boot in again. 'Plead insanity is my advice,' he said. 'You'll be better off in Broadmoor. Buggered if I'd want Brady or the Ripper as a neighbour for the rest of my natural.' For a moment he paused by the door. 'Let me know if he wants to make a statement,' he said to the Chief Warder. 'I mean, I suppose he could help . . .'

There was no need to go on. Even the Bull had got the message. 'What do you want to know?'

It was Flint's turn to think. Take the pressure off too quickly and all he'd get would be garbage. On the other hand, strike while the iron was hot. 'The lot,' he said. 'How the operations work. Who does what. What the links are. You name it, I want it. Every fucking thing!'

The Bull swallowed. 'I don't know everything,' he said, looking unhappily at the Chief Warder.

'Don't mind me,' said Mr Blaggs. 'I'm not here. Just part of the furniture.'

'Start with how Mac got himself junk,' said Flint. It was best to begin with something he already knew. The Bull told him and Flint wrote it all down with a growing sense of satisfaction. He hadn't known about Prison Officer Lane being bent.

'You'll get me slit for this,' said the Bull when he'd finished with Mrs Jardin, the Prison Visitor.

'I don't know why,' said Flint. 'Mr Blaggs here isn't

148

going to say who told him and it doesn't necessarily have to come out at your trial.'

'Christ,' said the Bull. 'You're not still going on with that, are you?'

'You tell me,' said Flint, maintaining the pressure. By the time he left the prison three hours later, Inspector Flint was almost a happy man. True, the Bull hadn't told him everything, but then he hadn't expected him too. In all likelihood, the fool didn't know much more, but he'd given Flint enough names to be going on with. Best of all, he'd grassed too far to back out, even if the threat of a murder charge lost its effect. The Bull would indeed get himself sliced by some other prisoner if the news ever got out. And the Bear was going to be Flint's next target.

'Being a copper's a dirty business sometimes,' he thought as he drove back to the police station. But drugs and violence were dirtier still. Flint went up to his office and began to check out some names.

Ted Lingon's name rang a bell – two bells, when he put his lists together. And Lingon ran a garage. Promising. But who was Annie Mosgrave?

Chapter thirteen

'Who?' said Major Glaushof.

'Some guy who teaches English or something evenings. Name of Wilt,' said the Duty Lieutenant. 'H. Wilt.'

'I'll be right over,' said Glaushof. He put the phone down and went through to his wife.

'Don't wait up, honey,' he said, 'I've got a problem.'

'Me too,' said Mrs Glaushof, and settled back to watch Dallas on BBC. It was kind of reassuring to know Texas was still there and it wasn't damp and raining all the time and goddam cold like Baconheath, and people still thought big and did big things. So she shouldn't have married an Airbase Security Officer with a thing going for German Shepherds. And to think he'd seemed so romantic when she'd met him back from Iran. Some security there. She should have known.

Outside, Glaushof climbed into his jeep with the three dogs and drove off between the houses towards the gates to Civilian Quarters. A group of men were standing well back from Wilt's Escort in the parking lot. Glaushof deliberately skidded the jeep to a stop and got out.

'What is it?' he asked. 'A bomb?'

'Jesus, I don't know,' said the Lieutenant, who was listening to a receiver. 'Could be anything.'

'Like he's left his CB on,' a Corporal explained, 'only there's two of them and they're bleeping.'

'Know any Brit who has two CBs running continuously the same time?' asked the Lieutenant. 'No way, and the frequency's wrong. Way too high.'

'So it could be a bomb,' said Glaushof. 'Why the fuck did you let it in?'

In the darkness and under threat of being blown to bits by whatever diabolical device the car concealed, Glaushof edged away. The little group followed him.

'Guy comes every Friday, gives his lecture, has coffee and goes on home no problem,' said the Lieutenant.

'So you let him drive right through with that lot buzzing and you don't stop him,' said Glaushof. 'We could have a Beirut bomb blast on our hands.'

'We didn't pick up the bleep till later.'

'Too later,' said Glaushof, 'I'm not taking any chances. I want the sand trucks brought up but fast. We're going to seal that car. Move.'

'It ain't no bomb,' said the Corporal, 'not sending like that. With a bomb the signals would be coming in.'

'Whatever,' said Glaushof, 'it's a breach of security and it's going to be sealed.'

'If you say so, Major,' said the Corporal and disappeared across the parking lot. For a moment, Glaushof hesitated and considered what other action he should take. At least he'd acted promptly to protect the base and his own career. As Base Security Officer, he'd always been against these foreign lecturers coming in with their subversive talks. He'd already discovered a geographer who'd sneaked a whole lot of shit about the dangers to bird-life from noise pollution and kerosene into his lectures on the development of the English landscape. Glaushof had had him busted as a member of Greenpeace. A car with radios transmitting continuously suggested something much more serious. And something much more serious could be just what he needed.

Glaushof ran through a mental checklist of enemies of the Free World: terrorists, Russian spies, subversives, women from Greenham Common . . . whatever. It didn't matter. The key thing was that Base Intelligence had fouled things up and it was up to him to rub their faces in the shit. Glaushof smiled to himself at the prospect. If there was one man he detested, it was the Intelligence Officer. Nobody heard of Glaushof, but Colonel Urwin with his line to the Pentagon and his wife in with the Base Commander's so they were invited to play Bridge Saturday nights, oh sure, he was a big noise. And a Yale man. Screw him. Glaushof intended to. 'This guy . . . what did you say his name is?' he asked the Lieutenant.

'Wilt,' said the Lieutenant.

'Where are you holding him?'

'Not holding him anyplace,' said the Lieutenant. 'Called you first thing we picked up the signals.'

'So where is he?'

'I guess he's over lecturing someplace,' said the Lieutenant. 'His details are in the guardhouse. Schedule and all.'

They hurried across the parking lot to the gates to the civilian quarters and Glaushof studied the entry in Wilt's file. It was brief and uninformative. 'Lecture Hall 9,' said the Lieutenant. 'You want me to have him picked up?'

'No,' said Glaushof, 'not yet. Just see no one gets out, is all.'

'No way he can except over the new fence,' said the

Lieutenant, 'and I don't see him getting far. I've switched the current on.'

'Fine,' said Glaushof. 'So he comes out you stop him.'

'Yes, sir,' said the Lieutenant, and went out to check the guards, while Glaushof picked up the phone and called the Security Patrol. 'I want Lecture Hall 9 surrounded,' he said, 'but nobody to move till I come.'

He sat on staring distractedly at the centrepage of *Playgirl* featuring a male nude which had been pinned to the wall. If this bastard Wilt could be persuaded to talk, Glaushof's career would be made. So how to get him in the right frame of mind? First of all, he had to know what was in that car. He was still puzzling over tactics when the Lieutenant coughed discreetly behind him. Glaushof reacted violently. He didn't like the implications of that cough. 'Did you pin this up?' he shouted at the Lieutenant.

'Negative,' said the Lieutenant, who disliked the question almost as much as Glaushof had hated the cough. 'No, sir, I did not. That's Captain Clodiak.'

'That's Captain Clodiak?' said Glaushof, turning back to examine the picture again. 'I knew she . . . he . . . You've got to be kidding, Lieutenant. That's not the Captain Clodiak I know.'

'She put it there, sir. She likes that sort of thing.'

'Yes, well I guess she's a pretty feisty woman,' said Glaushof to avoid the accusation that he was discriminatory. In career prospect terms, it was almost as dangerous as being called a faggot. Not almost; it was worse.

'I happen to be Church of God,' said the Lieutenant, 'and that is irreligious according to my denomination.'

But Glaushof wasn't to be drawn into a discussion. 'Could be,' he said. 'Some other time, huh?' He went out and back to the parking lot where the Corporal, now accompanied by a Major and several men from the Demolition and Excavation section, had surrounded Wilt's car with four gigantic dumpers filled with sand, sweeping aside a dozen other vehicles in the process. As he approached, Glaushof was blinded by two searchlights which had suddenly been switched on. 'Douse those mothers,' he shouted, stumbling about in the glare. 'You want them to know in Moscow what we're doing?' In the darkness that followed this pronouncement, Glaushof banged into the wheelhub of one of the dumptrucks.

'Okay, so I go in without lights,' said the Corporal. 'No problem. You think it's a bomb, I don't. Bombs don't transmit CB.' And before Glaushof could remind him to call him 'Sir' in future, the Corporal had walked across to the car.

'Mr Wilt,' said Mrs Ofrey, 'would you like to elucidate on the question of the rôle of women in British society with particular regard to the part played in professional life by the Right Honorable Prime Minister Mrs Thatcher and . . .'

Wilt stared at her and wondered why Mrs Ofrey always read her questions from a card and why they seldom had anything to do with what he had been talking about. She must spend the rest of the week thinking them up. And the questions always had to do with the Queen and Mrs Thatcher, presumably because Mrs Ofrey had once dined at Woburn Abbey with the Duke and Duchess of Bedford and their hospitality had affected her deeply. But at least this evening he was giving her his undivided attention.

From the moment he'd entered the lecture room, he'd been having problems. The bandage he had wound round his loins had come undone on the drive over, and before he could do anything about it one end had begun to worm its way down his right trouser leg. To make matters worse, Captain Clodiak had come late and had seated herself in front of him with her legs crossed, and had promptly forced Wilt to press himself against the lectern to quell yet another erection or, at least, hide the event from his audience. And by concentrating on Mrs Ofrey, he had so far managed to avoid a second glance at Captain Clodiak.

But there were disadvantages in concentrating so

intently on Mrs Ofrey too. Even though she wore enough curiously patterned knitwear to have subsidized several crofters in Western Scotland, and her few charms were sufficiently muted by wool to make some sort of antidote to the terrifying chic of Captain Clodiak – Wilt had already noted the Captain's blouse and what he took to be a combat skirt in shantung silk – Mrs Ofrey was still a woman. In any case, she evidently liked to be socially exclusive and sat by herself to the left of the rest of the class, and by the time he'd got halfway through his lecture, he'd become positively wry-necked in his regard for her. Wilt had switched his attention to an acned clerk from the PX stores whose other courses were karate and aerobics and whose interest in British Culture was limited to unravelling the mysteries of cricket. That hadn't worked too well either, and after ten minutes of almost constant eye-contact and Wilt's deprecating observations on the effect of women's suffrage on the voting patterns in elections since 1928, the man had begun to shift awkwardly in his chair and Wilt had suddenly realized the fellow thought he was being propositioned. Not wanting to be beaten to pulp by a karate expert, he had tried alternating between Mrs Ofrey and the wall behind the rest of the class, but each time it seemed that Captain Clodiak was smiling more significantly. Wilt had clung to the lectern in the hope that he'd manage to get through the hour without ejaculating into his trousers. He was so worried about this that he hardly noticed that Mrs Ofrey had finished her question. 'Would you say that view was correct?' she said by way of a prompt.

'Well . . . er . . . yes,' said Wilt, who couldn't recall what the question was anyway. Something to do with the Monarchy being a matriarchy. 'Yes, I suppose in a general way I'd go along with you,' he said, wedging himself more firmly against the lectern. 'On the other hand, just because a country has a female ruler, I don't think we can assume it's not male-dominated. After all, we had Queen Boadicea in Pre-Roman Britain and I wouldn't have thought there was an awful lot of Women's Lib about then, would you?'

'I wasn't asking about the feminist movement,' said Mrs Ofrey, with a nasty inflection that suggested she was a pre-Eisenhower American, 'my question was directed to the matriarchal nature of the Monarchy.'

'Quite,' said Wilt, fighting for time. Something desperate seemed to have happened to the cricket box. He'd lost touch with the thing. 'Though just because we've had a number of queens . . . well, I suppose we've had almost as many as we've had kings . . . must have had more, come to think of it? Is that right? I mean, each king had to have a queen . . .'

'Henry VIII had a whole heap of them,' said an astro-navigational expert, whose reading tastes seemed to suggest she would have preferred life in some sort of aircon-ditioned and deodorized Middle Ages. 'He must have been some man.'

'Definitely,' said Wilt, grateful for her intervention. At this rate, the discussion might spread and leave him free to find that damned box again. 'In fact he had five. There was Katherine of . . .'

'Excuse me asking, Mr Wilt,' interrupted an engineer, 'but do old queens count as queens? Like they're widows. Is a king's widow still a queen?'

'She's a queen mother,' said Wilt, who by this time had his hand in his pocket and was searching for the box. 'It's purely titular of course. She—'

'Did you say "titular"?' asked Captain Clodiak, endowing the word with qualities Wilt had never intended and certainly didn't need now. And her voice suited her face. Captain Clodiak came from the South. 'Would you care to amplify what titular means?'

'Amplify?' said Wilt weakly. But before he could answer, the engineer had interrupted again.

'Pardon me breaking in, Mr Wilt,' he said, 'but you've got kind of something hanging out of your leg.'

'I have?' said Wilt, clutching the lectern even more closely. The attention of the entire class was now focused on his right leg. Wilt tried to hide it behind his left.

'And by the look of it I'd say it was something important to you.'

Wilt knew damned well what it was. With a lurch, he let go of the lectern and grabbed his trouser leg in a vain attempt to stop the box but the beastly thing had already evaded him. It hung for a moment almost coyly half out of the trouser cuff and then slid onto his shoe. Wilt's hand shot out and smothered the brute and the next moment he was trying to get it into his pocket. The box didn't budge. Still attached to the bandage by the plaster he had used, it refused to come without the bandage. As Wilt tried to drag it away it became obvious he was in danger of splitting the seam of his trousers. It was also fairly obvious that the other end of the bandage was still round his waist and had no intention of coming off. At this rate, he'd end up half-naked in front of the class and suffering from a strangulated hernia into the bargain. On the other hand, he could hardly stay half-crouching there and any attempt to drag the bloody thing up the inside of his trousers from the top was bound to be misinterpreted. In fact, by the sound of things, his predicament already had been. Even from his peculiar position, Wilt was aware that Captain Clodiak had got to her feet, a bleeper was sounding and the astro-navigator was saying something about codpieces.

Only the engineer was being at all constructive. 'Is that a medical problem you got there?' he asked and missed Wilt's contorted reply that it wasn't. 'I mean, we've got the best facilities for the treatment of infections of the urinogenital tract this side of Frankfurt and I can call up a medic . . .'

Wilt relinquished his hold on the box and stood up. It might be embarrassing to have a cricket box hanging out of his trousers but it was infinitely preferable to being examined in his present state by an airbase doctor. God knows what the man would make of a runaway erection. 'I don't need any doctor,' he squawked. 'It's just . . . well, I was playing cricket before I came here and in a hurry not

156

to be late I forgot . . . Well, I'm sure you understand.'

Mrs Ofrey clearly didn't. With some remark about the niceties of life being wanting, she marched out of the hall in the wake of Captain Clodiak. Before Wilt could say that all he needed was to get to the toilet, the acned clerk had intervened. 'Say, Mr Wilt,' he said, 'I didn't know you were a cricket player. Why, only three weeks ago you were saying you couldn't tell me what you English call a curve ball.'

'Some other time,' said Wilt, 'right now I need to get to . . . er . . . a washroom.'

'You sure you don't want—'

'Definitely,' said Wilt, 'I am perfectly all right. It's just a . . . never mind.'

He hobbled out of the hall and was presently ensconced in a cubicle fighting a battle with the box, the bandage and his trousers. Behind him, the class were discussing this latest manifestation of British Culture with a greater degree of interest than they had shown for Wilt's views on voting patterns. 'I still say he don't know anything about cricket,' said the PX clerk, only to be countered by the navigator and the engineer who were more interested in Wilt's medical condition. 'I had an uncle in Idaho had to wear a support. It's nothing unusual. Fell off a ladder when he was painting the house one spring,' said the engineer. 'Those things can be real serious.'

'I told you, Major,' said the Corporal, 'two radio transmitters, one tape recorder, no bomb.'

'Definitely?' asked Glaushof, trying to keep the disappointment out of his voice.

'Definite,' said the Corporal and was supported in this by the Major from the Demolition and Excavation Section who wanted to know whether he could order his men to move the dumpers back. As they rolled away leaving Wilt's Escort isolated in the middle of the parking lot, Glaushof tried to salvage some opportunity from the situation. After all, Colonel Urwin, the Intelligence

Officer, was away for the weekend and in his absence Glaushof could have done with a crisis.

'He had to come in here with that equipment for some reason,' he said, 'transmitting like that. Any ideas on the matter, Major?'

'Could be it's a dummy run to check if they can bring a bomb in and explode it by remote control,' said the Major, whose expertise tended to make him one-track-minded.

'Except he was transmitting, not receiving,' said the Corporal. 'They'd need signals in, not out, for a bomb. And what's with the recorder?'

'Not my department,' said the Major. 'Explosively, it's clean. I'll go file my report.'

Glaushof took the plunge. 'With me,' he said. 'You file it with me and no one else. We've got to shroud this.'

'We've done that once already with the safety trucks and quite unnecessarily.'

'Sure,' said Glaushof, 'but we still gotta find out what this is all about. I'm in charge of security and I don't like it, some Limey bastard coming in with all this equipment. Either it's a dummy run like you said, or it's something else.'

'It's got to be something else,' said the Corporal, 'obviously. With the equipment he's using, you could tape lice fucking twenty miles away it's that sensitive.'

'So his wife's getting evidence for a divorce,' said the Major.

'Must be goddam desperate for it,' said the Corporal, 'using two transmitters and a recorder. And that stuff's not general issue. I never seen a civilian using homers that sophisticated.'

'Homers?' said Glaushof, who had been preoccupied by the concept of lice fucking. 'How do you mean, homers?'

'Like they're direction indicators. Signals go out and two guys pick it up on their sets and they've got where he is precise.'

'Jesus!' said Glaushof. 'You mean the Russkies could

have sent this guy Wilt in as an agent so they can pin-point right where we are?'

'They're doing that already infra-red by satellite. They don't need some guy coming in waving a radio flag,' said the Corporal. 'Not unless they want to lose him.'

'Lose him? What would they want to do that for?'

'I don't know,' continued the Corporal. 'You're Security, I'm just Technical and why anybody wants to do things isn't my province. All I do know is I wouldn't send any agent of mine any place I didn't want him caught with those signals spelling out he was coming. Like putting a fucking mouse in a room with a cat and it can't stop fucking squeaking.'

But Glaushof was not to be deterred. 'The fact of the matter is this Wilt came in with unauthorized spy equipment and he isn't going out.'

'So they're going to know he's here from those signals,' said the Corporal.

Glaushof glared at him. The man's common sense had become intensely irritating. Here was his opportunity to hit back. 'You don't mean to tell me those radios are still operational?' he shouted.

'Sure,' said the Corporal. 'You tell me and the Major here to check the car for bombs. You didn't say nothing about screwing his transmission equipment. Bombs, you said.'

'Correct,' said the Major. 'That's what you did say. Bombs.'

'I know I said bombs,' yelled Glaushof, 'you think I need telling?' He stopped and turned his attention lividly on the car. If the radios were still working, presumably the enemy already knew they'd been discovered, in which case . . . His mind raced on, following lines which led to catastrophe. He had to make a momentous decision, and now. Glaushof did. 'Right, we're going in,' he said, 'and you're going out.'

Five minutes later, in spite of his protests that he wasn't driving any fucking car thirty miles with fucking spooks following his fucking progress, not unless he had a fucking escort, the Corporal drove out of the base. The tape in the recorder had been removed and replaced with a new one, but in all other respects there was nothing to indicate that the car had been tampered with. Glaushof's instructions had been quite explicit. 'You drive right back and dump it outside his house,' he had told the Corporal. 'You've got the Major here with you to bring you back and if there's any problems, he'll take care of them. Those bastards want to know where their boy is they can start looking at home. They're going to have trouble finding him here.'

'Ain't going to have no trouble finding me,' said the Corporal, who knew never to argue with a senior officer. He should have stuck to dumb insolence.

For a moment, Glaushof watched as the two vehicles disappeared across the bleak night landscape. He had never liked it but now it had taken on an even more sinister aspect. It was across those flatlands that the wind blew from Russia non-stop from the Urals. In Glaushof's mind, it was an infected wind which, having blown around the domes and turrets of the Kremlin, threatened the very future of the world. And now somewhere out there someone was listening. Glaushof turned away. He was going to find out who those sinister listeners were.

Chapter fourteen

'I got the whole place wrapped up, sir, and he's still inside,' said Lieutenant Harah when Glaushof finally reached Lecture Hall 9. Glaushof didn't need telling. He had had enough trouble himself getting through the cordon the Lieutenant had thrown up around the hall and in other circumstances would have expressed himself irritably on the Lieutenant's thoroughness. But the situation was too serious for recrimination, and besides he respected his second-in-command's expertise. As head of the APPS, the Anti Perimeter Penetration Squad, Lieutenant Harah had been through training at Fort Knox, in Panama and had seen action at Greenham Common disguised as a British bobby where he had qualified for a Purple Heart after being bitten in the leg by a mother of four, an experience which had left him with a useful bias against women. Glaushof appreciated his misogyny. At least one man in Baconheath could be relied on not to lay Mona Glaushof and Harah wasn't going to play footsy with any CND women if and when they tried breaking into Baconheath.

On the other hand, he seemed to have gone too far this time. Quite apart from the six hit-squad men in gas masks by the glass fronted door to the lecture hall and a number of others crouching under the windows round the side a small group of women were standing with their heads up against the wall of the next building.

'What are those?' Glaushof asked. He had a nasty suspicion he recognized Mrs Ofrey's Scottish knitwear.

'Suspected women,' said Lieutenant Harah.

'What do you mean "suspected women"?' demanded Glaushof. 'Either they're women or they aren't.'

'They came out dressed as women, sir,' said the Lieutenant, 'doesn't mean to say they are. Could be the terrorist dressed as one. You want me to check them out?'

'No,' said Glaushof, wishing to hell he had given the order to storm the building before he had put in an appearance himself. It wasn't going to look too good spread-eagling the wife of the Chief Administrative Officer against a wall with a gun at her head, and to have her checked out sexually by Lieutenant Harah would really foul things up. On the other hand even Mrs Ofrey could hardly complain about being rescued from a possible hostage situation.

'You sure there's no way he could have got out?'

'Absolute,' said the Lieutenant. 'I got marksmen on the next block in case he makes the roof and the utilities tunnels are sealed. All we got to do is toss a canister of Agent Incapacitating in there and there's going to be no trouble.'

Glaushof glanced nervously at the row of women and doubted it. There was going to be trouble and maybe it would be better if that trouble could be seen to be serious. 'I'll get those women under cover and then you go in,' he said. 'And no shooting unless he fires first. I want this guy taken for interrogation. You got that?'

'Absolute, sir,' said the Lieutenant. 'He gets a whiff of AI he wouldn't find a trigger to pull if he wanted to.'

'Okay. Give me five minutes and then go,' said Glaushof and crossed to Mrs Ofrey.

'If you ladies will just step this way,' he said, and dismissing the men who were holding them hurried the little group round the corner and into the lobby of another lecture hall. Mrs Ofrey was clearly annoyed.

'What do you mean—' she began but Glaushof raised a hand. 'If you'll just let me explain,' he said, 'I realize you have been inconvenienced but we have an infiltration situation on our hands and we couldn't afford the possibility of you being held hostage.' He paused and was glad to see that even Mrs Ofrey had taken the message. 'How absolutely dreadful,' she murmured.

It was Captain Clodiak's reaction that surprised him. 'Infiltration situation? We just had the usual class no problem,' she said, 'I didn't see anybody new. Are you saying there's somebody in there we don't know about?'

Glaushof hesitated. He had hoped to keep the question of Wilt's identity as a secret agent to himself and not have news of it spreading round the base like wildfire. He certainly didn't want it getting out until he had completed his interrogation and had all the information he needed to prove that the Intelligence Section, and in particular that bland bastard Colonel Urwin, hadn't screened a foreign employee properly. That way the Colonel would take a fall and they could hardly avoid promoting Glaushof. Let Intelligence get wind of what was going on and the plan might backfire.

Glaushof fell back on the 'Eyes off' routine.

'I don't think it advisable at this moment in time to elucidate the matter further. This is a top-security matter. Any leak could severely prejudice the defensive capabilities of Strategic Air Command in Europe. I must insist on a total information blackout.'

For a moment the pronouncement had the effect he had wanted. Even Mrs Ofrey looked satisfactorily stunned. Then Captain Clodiak broke the silence. 'I don't get it,' she said. 'There's us and this Wilt guy in there, nobody else. Right?' Glaushof said nothing. 'So you bring up the stormtroopers and have us pinned against the wall as soon as we walk out and now you tell us it's an infiltration situation. I don't believe you, Major, I just don't believe you. The only infiltration I know of is what that bastard sexist lieutenant did up my ass and I intend to formalize a complaint again Lieutenant Harah and you can pull as many phoney agents out of your pinhead imagination as you like, you still aren't going to stop me.'

Glaushof gulped. He could see he'd been right to describe the Captain as a feisty woman and entirely wrong to have allowed Lieutenant Harah to act on his own. He'd also been fairly wrong in his estimation of the Lieutenant's antipathy for women though even Glaushof had to admit that Captain Clodiak was a remarkably attractive woman. In an attempt to save the situation he tried a sympathetic smile. It came out lopsided. 'I'm sure Lieutenant Harah had no intention of—' he began.

'So what's with the hand?' snapped the Captain. 'You think I don't know intentions when I feel them? Is that what you think?'

'Perhaps he was doing a weapon check,' said Glaushof, who knew now he would have to do something really astonishing to regain control of the situation. He was saved by the sound of breaking glass. Lieutenant Harah had waited exactly five minutes before taking action.

It had taken Wilt rather more than five minutes to unravel the bandage and slide it down his trouser leg and reassemble the box in a position where it would afford him some measure of protection from the spasmodic antics of his penis. In the end he had succeeded and had just tied the entire contraption together rather uncomfortably when there was a knock on the door.

'You okay, Mr Wilt?' asked the engineer.

'Yes, thank you,' said Wilt as politely as his irritation allowed. It was always the same with nice idiots. The sods offered to help in precisely the wrong way. All Wilt wanted now was to get the hell out of the base without any further embarrassment. But the engineer didn't understand the situation. 'I was just telling Pete how I had an uncle in Idaho had the same support problem,' said the engineer through the door.

'Really?' said Wilt, feigning interest while actually struggling to pull his zip up. A thread of bandage had evidently got caught in the thing. Wilt tried pulling it down.

'Yea. He went around for years with this bulky thing on until my Auntie Annie heard of this surgeon in Kansas City and she took my Uncle Rolf down there and of course he didn't want to go but he never did regret it. I can give you his name if you like.'

'Fuck,' said Wilt. A stitch on the bottom of his zip sounded as though it had torn.

'Did you say something, Mr Wilt?' asked the engineer.

'No,' said Wilt.

There was a moment's silence while the engineer evidently considered his next move and Wilt tried holding the bottom of the zip to his trousers while wrenching the tag at the same time. 'As I see it, and you've got to understand I'm not a medical man myself I'm an engineer so I know about structural failure, there's muscle deterioration in the lower—'

'Listen,' said Wilt. 'Right now where I've got a structural failure is in the zip on my trousers. Something's got caught in it and it's stuck.'

'Which side?' asked the engineer.

'Which side is what?' demanded Wilt.

'The . . . er . . . thing that's stuck in it?'

Wilt peered down at the zip. In the confines of the toilet it was difficult to see which side anything was. 'How the hell would I know?'

'You pulling it up or down?' continued the engineer.

'Up,' said Wilt.

'Sometimes helps to pull it down first.'

'It's already bloody down,' said Wilt allowing his irritation to get the better of him. 'I wouldn't be trying to pull the fucking thing up if it wasn't down, would I?'

'I guess not,' said the engineer with a degree of bland patience that was even more irritating than his desire to be helpful. 'Just the same if it isn't right down it could be the thing . . .' He paused. 'Mr Wilt, just what is it you've got in the zip?'

Inside the toilet Wilt stared dementedly at a notice which not only instructed him to wash his hands but seemed to suppose he needed telling how to. 'Count to ten,' he muttered to himself and was surprised to find that the zip had freed itself. He'd also been freed from the unwanted helpfulness of the engineer. A crash of breaking glass had evidently disturbed the man's blandness. 'Jesus, what's going on?' he yelled.

It was not a question Wilt could answer. And by the sound of things outside he didn't want to. Somewhere a door burst open and running feet in the corridor were interspersed with muffled orders to freeze. Inside the toilet Wilt froze. Accustomed as he had recently become to the hazards seemingly inherent in going to the lavatory anywhere outside his own house, the experience of being locked in a cubicle with a hit squad of Anti Perimeter Penetration men bursting into the building was new to him.

It was fairly new to the engineer. As the canisters of Agent Incapacitating hit the floor and masked men armed with automatic weapons broke through the door he lost all interest in the problems of Wilt's zip and headed back into the lecture hall only to collide with the navigator and the PX clerk who were dashing the other way. In the confusion that followed Agent Incapacitating lived up to its name. The PX clerk tried to disentangle himself from the engineer who was doing his best to avoid him and the navigator embraced them both under the illusion he was moving in the other direction.

As they fell to the ground Lieutenant Harah loomed over them large and quite extraordinarily sinister in his gas mask.

'Which of you is Wilt?' he yelled. His voice, distorted both by the mask and by the effects of the gas on their nervous systems, reached them slowly. Not even the voluble engineer was able to help him. 'Take them all out,' he ordered and the three men were dragged from the building gurgling sentences that sounded as if a portable recorder with faulty batteries was being played under water.

In his cubicle Wilt listened to the awful noises with growing apprehension. Breaking glass, strangely muffled shouts and the clump of boots had played no part in his previous visits to the airbase and he couldn't for the life of him imagine what they portended. Whatever it was he'd had enough trouble for one evening without wishing to invite any more. It seemed safest to stay where he was and wait until whatever was happening had stopped. Wilt switched off the light and sat down on the seat.

Outside, Lieutenant Harah's men reported thickly that the hall was clear. In spite of the eddies of gas the Lieutenant could see that. Peering through the eyepiece of his gas mask he surveyed the empty seats with a sense of anti-climax. He had rather hoped the infiltrator would put up a show of resistance, and the ease with which the bastard had been taken had disappointed him. On the other hand he could also see that it had been a mistake to bring in the assault dogs without equipping them with gas masks. Agent Incapacitating evidently affected them too. One of them was slithering about the floor snarling in slow motion while another, in an attempt to scratch its right ear, was waving a hindfoot about in a most disturbing manner.

'Okay, that's it,' he said and marched out to question his three prisoners. Like the assault dogs they had been totally incapacitated and he had no idea which was the foreign agent he was supposed to be detaining. They were all dressed in civilian clothes and in no state to say who or what they were. Lieutenant Harah reported to Glaushof. 'I think you better check them out, sir. I don't know which son of a bitch is which.'

'Wilt,' said Glaushof, glaring at the gas mask, 'his name is Wilt. He's a foreign employee. Shouldn't be any difficulty recognizing the bastard.'

'All Limeys look the same to me,' said the Lieutenant, and was promptly rewarded with a chop across his throat and a knee in his groin by Captain Clodiak who had just recognized her sexist assailant through his gas mask. As the Lieutenant doubled up she grabbed his arm and Glaushof was surprised to see how easily his second-in-command was swept off his feet by a woman.

'Remarkable,' he said. 'It's a genuine privilege to witness—'

'Cut the crap,' said Captain Clodiak, dusting her hands and looking as though she would like to demonstrate her expertise in karate on another man. 'That creep said a sexist remark and you said Wilt. Am I right?' Glaushof looked puzzled. He hadn't recognized 'son of a bitch' as being sexist and he didn't want to discuss Wilt in front of the other women. On the other hand he didn't have any idea what Wilt looked like and someone had to identify him. 'Maybe we'd better step outside to discuss this, Captain,' he said and went out the door.

Captain Clodiak followed him warily. 'What do we have to discuss?' she asked.

'Like Wilt,' said Glaushof.

'You're crazy. I heard you just now. Wilt an agent?'

'Incontrovertible,' said Glaushof, pulling brevity.

'How so?' said Clodiak, responding in kind.

'Infiltrated the perimeter with enough radio transmitting equipment hidden in his car to signal our position to Moscow or the moon. I mean it, Captain. What's more it's not civilian equipment you can buy in a store. It's official,' said Glaushof and was relieved to notice the disbelief fade from her face. 'And right now, I'm going to need help identifying him.'

They went round the corner and were confronted by the sight of three men lying face down on the ground in front of Lecture Hall 9 guarded by two incapacitated assault dogs and the APP team.

'Okay, men, the Captain here is going to identify him,' said Glaushof and prodded the PX clerk with his foot. 'Turn over, you.' The clerk tried to turn over but succeeded only in crawling sideways on top of the engineer, who promptly went into convulsions. Glaushof looked at the two contorted figures with disgust before having his attention distracted even more disturbingly by an assault dog that had urinated on his shoe without lifting its leg.

'Get that filthy beast off me,' he shouted and was joined in his protests by the engineer who objected just as strongly though less comprehensibly to the apparent attempts the PX clerk was making to bugger him. By the time the dog had been removed, a process that required the efforts of three men on the end of its chain, and some sort of order was restored on the ground Captain Clodiak's expression had changed again. 'I thought you said you wanted Wilt identified,' she said. 'Well, he's not here.'

'Not here? You mean . . .' Glaushof looked suspiciously at the broken door of the lecture hall.

'They're the men the Lieutenant told us to grab,' said one of the hit-squad. 'There wasn't anyone else in the hall I saw.'

'There's gotta be,' yelled Glaushof. 'Where's Harah?'

'In there where you—'

'I know where he is. Just get him and fast.'

'Yessir,' said the man and disappeared.

'You seem to have got yourself a problem,' said Captain Clodiak.

Glaushof tried to shrug it off. 'He can't have broken through the cordon and even if he has he's going to burn on the fence or get himself arrested at the gate,' he said. 'I'm not worried.'

All the same he found himself glancing round at the familiar dull buildings and the roadways between them with a new sense of suspicion as though somehow they had changed character and had become accomplices to the absent Wilt. With an insight that was alarmingly strange to him he realized how much Baconheath meant to him; it was home, his own little fortress in a foreign land with its comfortable jet noises linking him to his own hometown, Eiderburg, Michigan, and the abattoir down the road where the hogs were killed. As a boy he had woken to the sound of their squeals and an F111 screaming for take-off had the same comforting effect on him. But more than anything else Baconheath with its perimeter fence and guarded gates had been America for him, his own country, powerful, independent and freed from danger by his constant vigilance and the sheer enormity of its arsenal. Squatting there behind the wire and isolated by the flat reaches of the Fens from the old crumbling villages and market towns with their idle, inefficient shopkeepers and their dirty pubs where strange people drank warm, unhygienic beer, Baconheath had been an oasis of brisk efficiency and modernity, and proof that the great US of A was still the New World and would remain so.

But now Glaushof's vision had shifted and for a moment he felt somehow disassociated from the place. These buildings were hiding this Wilt from him and until he found the bastard Baconheath would be infected. Glaushof forced himself out of this nightmare and was confronted by another. Lieutenant Harah came round the corner. He was clearly still paying for his sexist attitude to Captain Clodiak and had to be supported by two APPS men. Glaushof had almost been prepared for that. The garbled noises the Lieutenant was making were something else again and could hardly be explained by a kick in the groin.

'It's the AI, sir,' one of the men explained, 'I guess he must have loosed off a canister in the lobby.'

'Loosed off a canister? In the lobby?' Glaushof squawked, appalled at the terrible consequences to his career such a lunatic action seemed certain to provoke. 'Not with those women—'

'Affirmative,' ejaculated Lieutenant Harah without warning. Glaushof turned on him.

'What do you mean, affirmative?'

'Absolute,' Harah's voice hit a new high. And stuck there. 'Absolute absolute absolute absolute . . .'

'Gag that bastard,' shouted Glaushof and shot round the corner of the building to see what he could do to rescue the situation. It was beyond hope. For whatever insane reason Lieutenant Harah, perhaps in an attempt to defend himself against a second strike from Captain Clodiak, had wrenched the pin from a gas grenade before realizing that his gas mask had come off in his fall. Gazing through the glass doors at the bizarre scenes in the lobby, Glaushof was no longer worried about Mrs Ofrey's interference. Draped over the back of a chair with her hair touching the floor and happily obscuring her face, the wife of the Chief Administrative Executive resembled nothing so much as a large and incontinent highland ewe which had been put rather prematurely through a Fair Isle knitting machine. The rest of the class were in no better shape. The astro-navigation officer lay on her back, evidently re-enacting a peculiarly passive sexual experience, while several other students of British Culture and Institutions looked as though they were extras in some film depicting the end of the world. Once again Glaushof experienced the ghastly sensation of being at odds with his environment and it was only by calling up reserves of approximate sanity that he took control of himself.

'Get them out of there,' he shouted, 'and call the medics. We got a maniac on the loose.'

'Got something,' said Captain Clodiak. 'That Lieutenant Harah's going to have a lot to answer for. I can't see General Ofrey being too pleased with a dead wife. He'll just have to play three-handed bridge with the Commander.'

But Glaushof had had enough of the Captain's objective standpoint. 'You're responsible for this,' he said with a new menace in his voice. 'You talk about questions you're going to have to answer some yourself. Like you deliberately assaulted Lieutenant Harah in the execution of his duty and—'

'Like the execution of his duty includes getting his hand up my . . .' interrupted the Captain furiously and then stopped and stared. 'Oh my God,' she said and Glaushof, who had been preparing for another demonstration of karate, followed her gaze.

In the broken doorway of Lecture Hall 9 a hapless figure was trying to stand up. As they watched, it failed.

Chapter fifteen

Fifteen miles away Wilt's Escort beeped its erratic way towards Ipford. Since no one had thought to provide the Corporal with adequate directions and he had distrusted Glaushof's assurances that he would be well protected by the Major and the men in the truck behind him, he had taken his own precautions before and after leaving the base. He had provided himself with a heavy automatic and had computed a route which would cause maximum confusion to anyone trying to cross-reference his position on their receivers.

He had achieved his object. In short, he had travelled twenty quite extraordinarily complicated miles in no time at all. Half an hour after leaving Baconheath he was still only five miles from the base. After that he had shot off towards Ipford and had spent twenty minutes pretending to change a tyre in a tunnel under the motorway before emerging on a minor road which ran for several miles very conveniently next to a line of high-tension electricity pylons. Two more tunnels and fifteen miles on a road that wound along below the bank of a dyked river, and Inspector Hodge and the men in the other listening van were desperately transmitting messages to one another in an attempt to make out where the hell he had got to. More awkwardly still, they couldn't be entirely sure where they were either.

The Major shared their dilemma. He hadn't expected the Corporal to take evasive action or to drive – when he wasn't lurking in tunnels – at excessive speed along winding roads that had presumably been designed for single-file horse traffic and had been dangerous even then. But the Major didn't care. If the Corporal wanted to take off like a scalded cat that was his problem. 'He wants an armed escort he better stay with us,' he told his driver as they skidded round a muddy ninety-degree bend and nearly landed in a deep water-filled drain. 'I'm not ending my life in a ditch so slow down for Chrissake.'

'So how do we keep up with him?' asked the driver, who had been thoroughly enjoying himself.

'We don't. If he's going any place outside hell its Ipford. I've got the address here. Take the motorway first chance you get and we'll wait for him where he's supposed to be going.'

'Yes sir,' said the driver reluctantly and switched back to the main road at the next turn-off.

Sergeant Runk would have done the same had he been given the chance but the Corporal's tactics had confirmed all Inspector Hodge's wildest dreams. 'He's trying to lose us,' he shouted shortly after the Corporal left the airbase

172

and began to dice with death. 'That must mean he's carrying dope.'

'That or he's practising for the Monte Carlo Rally,' said Runk.

Hodge wasn't amused. 'Rubbish. The little bastard goes into Baconheath, spends an hour and a half and comes out doing eighty along mud roads no one in their right minds would do forty on in daylight and backtrack five times the way he's done – he must have something he values in that car.'

'Can't be his life, and that's for certain,' said Runk who was struggling to keep his seat. 'Why don't we just call up a patrol car and pull him for speeding? That way we can have him searched for whatever he's carrying.'

'Good idea,' said Hodge and had been about to send out instructions when the Corporal had taken radio refuge in the motorway tunnel and they'd lost him for twenty minutes. Hodge had spent the time blaming Runk for failing to have an accurate fix on his last position and calling for help from the second van. The Corporal's subsequent route near the power lines and below the river bank had made matters still more awkward. By then the Inspector had no idea what to do, but his conviction that he was dealing with a master-criminal had been confirmed beyond doubt.

'He's obviously passed the stuff on to a third party and if we go for a search he'll plead innocence,' he muttered.

Even Runk had to agree that all the evidence pointed that way. 'He also happens to know his car's been wired for sound,' he said. 'The route he's following he's got to know. So where do we go from here?'

Hodge hesitated. For a moment he considered applying for a warrant and conducting so thorough a search of the Wilts' house that even the minutest trace of heroin or Embalming Fluid would come to light. But if it didn't . . . 'There's always the tape recorder,' he said finally. 'He may have missed that in which case we'll get the conversations he had with the pick-up artist.'

Sergeant Runk doubted it. 'If you ask me,' he said, 'the

only way you're going to get solid evidence on this bugger is by sending Forensic in to do a search with vacuum-cleaners that'd suck an elephant through a drain pipe. He may be as canny as they come but those lab blokes know their onions. I reckon that's the sane way of going about it.'

But Hodge wasn't to be persuaded. He had no intention of handing the case over to someone else when it was patently obvious he was on the right track. 'We'll see what's on that tape first,' he said as they headed back towards Ipford. 'We'll give him an hour to get to sleep and then you can move in and get it.'

'And have the rest of the bloody day off,' said Runk. 'You may be one of Nature's insomniacs but if I don't get my eight hours I won't be fit for—'

'I am not an insomniac,' snapped the Inspector. They drove on in silence broken only by the bleeps coming from Wilt's car. They were louder now. Ten minutes later the van was parked at the bottom of Perry Road and Wilt's car was announcing its presence from Oakhurst Avenue.

'You've got to hand it to the little sod,' said Hodge. 'I mean you'd never dream to look at him he could drive like that. Just shows you can never tell.'

An hour later Sergeant Runk stumbled out of his van and walked up Perry Road. 'It's not there,' he said when he got back.

'Not there? It's bloody well got to be,' said the Inspector; 'it's still coming over loud and clear.'

'That's as may be,' said Runk. 'For all I care the little shit's tucked up in bed with the fucking transmitters but what I do know is that it's not outside his house.'

'What about the garage?' Runk snorted.

'The garage? Have you ever had a dekko in that garage? It's a ruddy furniture depository, that garage is. Stuffed to the roof with junk when I saw it and if you're telling me he's spent the last two days shifting it all out into the back garden so as he could get his car in there . . .'

'We'll soon see about that,' said Hodge and presently the van was driving slowly past 45 Oakhurst Avenue and the Sergeant had been proved right.

'What did I tell you?' he said. 'I said he hadn't put it in the garage.'

'What you didn't say was he'd parked the thing there,' said Hodge, pointing through the windscreen at the mud-stained Escort which the Corporal, who hadn't been prepared to waste time checking house numbers in the middle of the night, had left outside Number 65.

'Well I'm buggered,' said Runk. 'Why'd he want to do a thing like that?'

'We'll see if that tape has anything to tell us,' said the Inspector. 'You hop out here and we'll go on round the corner.'

But for once Sergeant Runk wasn't to be budged. 'If you want that bloody tape you go and get it,' he said. 'A bloke like this Wilt doesn't leave his car down the road without a good reason and I'm not learning too bleeding late what that reason is, and that's final.'

In the end it was Hodge who approached the car warily and had just started to grope under the front seat when Mrs Willoughby's Great Dane gave tongue inside the house.

'What did I tell you?' said Runk as the Inspector clambered in beside him puffing frantically. 'I knew there was a trap there somewhere but you wouldn't listen.'

Inspector Hodge was too preoccupied to listen to him even now. In his mind's ear he could still hear the baying of that dreadful dog and the sound of its terrible paws on the front door of the Willoughby's house.

He was still shaken by the experience when they arrived back at the station. 'I'll get him, I'll get him,' he muttered as he made his way wearily up the steps. But the threat lacked substance. He had been outwitted yet again and for the first time he appreciated Sergeant

Runk's need for sleep. Perhaps after a few hours his mind would come up with a new plan.

In Wilt's case the need for sleep was paramount too. The effects of Agent Incapacitating on a body already weakened by the administration of Dr Kores' sexual cordial had reduced him to a state in which he hardly knew who he was and was quite incapable of answering questions. He vaguely remembered escaping from a cubicle, or rather of being locked in one, but for the rest his mind was a jumble of images, the sum total of which made no sense at all. Men with masks, guns, being dragged, thrown into a jeep, driven, more dragging, lights in a bare room and a man shouting dementedly at him, all formed kaleidoscopic patterns which constantly rearranged themselves in his mind and made no sense at all. They just happened or were happening or even, because the man shouting at him still seemed somehow remote, had happened to him in some previous existence and one he would prefer not to relive. And even when Wilt tried to explain that things, whatever they were, were not what they seemed, the shouting man wasn't prepared to listen.

It was hardly surprising. The strange noises Wilt was in fact making hardly came into the category of utterances and certainly weren't explanations.

'Scrambled,' said the doctor Glaushof had summoned to try and inject some sense into Wilt's communications system. 'That's what you get with AI Two. You'll be lucky if he ever talks sense again.'

'AI Two? We used standard issue Agent Incapacitating,' said Glaushof. 'Nobody's been throwing AI Two around. That's reserved for Soviet suicide squads.'

'Sure,' said the doctor, 'I'm just telling you what I diagnose. You'd better check the canisters out.'

'I'll check that lunatic Harah out too,' said Glaushof and hurried from the room. When he returned Wilt had assumed a foetal position and was fast asleep.

'AI Two,' Glaushof admitted lugubriously. 'What do we do now?'

'I've done what I can,' said the doctor, dispensing with two hypodermics. 'Loaded him with enough Antidote AI to keep him out of the official brain-death category . . .'

'Brain-death category? But I've got to interrogate the bastard. I can't have him cabbaging on me. He's some sort of infiltrating fucking agent and I got to find out where he's from.'

'Major Glaushof,' said the doctor wearily, 'it is now like zero three hundred hours and there's eight women, three men, one lieutenant and this . . .' he pointed at Wilt, 'and all of them suffering from nerve-gas toxicity and you think I can save any of them from chemically induced psychosis I'll do it but I'm not putting a suspected terrorist wearing a scrotal guard at the head of my list of priorities. If you want to interrogate him you'll have to wait. And pray. Oh yes, and if he doesn't come out of coma in eight hours let me know, maybe we can use him for spare-part surgery.'

'Hold it there, doctor,' he said. 'One word out of any of these people about there being—'

'Gassed?' said the doctor incredulously. 'I don't think you realize what you've done, Major. They're not going to remember a thing.'

'There being an agent here,' shouted Glaushof. 'Of course they've been gassed. Lieutenant Harah did that.'

'If you say so,' said the doctor. 'My business is physical welfare not base security and I guess you'll be able to explain Mrs Ofrey's condition to the General. Just don't call on me to say she and seven other women are naturally psychotic.'

Glaushof considered the implications of this request and found them decidedly awkward. On the other hand there was always Lieutenant Harah . . . 'Tell me, doc,' he said, 'just how sick is Harah?'

'About as sick as a man who's been kicked in the groin and inhaled AI Two can be,' said the doctor. 'And that's not taking his mental condition beforehand into account either. He should have been wearing one of these.' He held up the box.

Glaushof looked at it speculatively and then glanced at Wilt. 'What would a terrorist want with one of those things?' he asked.

'Could be he expected what Lieutenant Harah got,' said the doctor, and left the room.

Glaushof followed him into the next office and sent for Captain Clodiak. 'Take a seat, Captain,' he said. 'Now I want a breakdown of exactly what happened in there tonight.'

'What happened in there? You think I know? There's this maniac Harah . . .'

Glaushof held up a hand. 'I think you should know that Lieutenant Harah is an extremely sick man right now.'

'What's with the now?' said Clodiak. 'He always was. Sick in the head.'

'It's not his head I'm thinking about.'

Captain Clodiak chewed gum. 'So he's got balls where his brain should be. Do I care?'

'I'd advise you to,' said Glaushof. 'Assaulting a junior officer carries a very heavy penalty.'

'Yeah, well the same goes for sexually assaulting a senior one.'

'Could be,' said Glaushof, 'but I think you're going to have a hard time proving it.'

'Are you telling me I'm a liar?' demanded the Captain.

'No. Definitely not. I believe you but what I'm asking is, will anyone else?'

'I've got witnesses.'

'Had,' said Glaushof. 'From what the doctors tell me they're not going to be very reliable. In fact I'd go so far as to say they don't even come into the category of witnesses any longer. Agent Incapacitating does things to the memory. I think you ought to know that. And Lieutenant Harah's injuries have been medically documented. I don't think you're going to be in a position to dispute them. Doesn't mean you have to, but I'd advise you to co-operate with this department.'

Captain Clodiak studied his face. It wasn't a pleasant face but there was no disputing the fact that her situation wasn't one which allowed her too many options. 'What do you want me to do?' she asked.

'I want to hear what this Wilt said and all. In his lectures. Did he give any indications he was a communist?'

'Not that I knew,' said the Captain. 'I'd have reported it if he had.'

'So what did he say?'

'Mostly talked about things like parliament and voting patterns and how people in England see things.'

'See things?' said Glaushof, trying to think why an attractive woman like Ms Clodiak would want to go to lectures he'd have paid money to avoid. 'What sort of things?'

'Religion and marriage and . . . just things.'

At the end of an hour, Glaushof had learnt nothing.

Chapter sixteen

Eva sat in the kitchen and looked at the clock again. It was five o'clock in the morning and she had been up since two indulging herself in the luxury of a great many emotions. Her first reaction when going to bed had been one of annoyance. 'He's been to the pub again and got drunk,' she had thought. 'Well, he won't get any sympathy from me if he has a hangover.' Then she had lain awake getting angrier by the minute until one o'clock when worry had taken over. It wasn't like Henry to stay out that late. Perhaps something had happened to him. She went over various possibilities, ranging from car crashes to his getting arrested for being drunk and disorderly, and finally worked herself up to the point where she knew that something terrible had been done to him at the prison. After all he was teaching that dreadful murderer

McCullum and when he'd come home on Monday night he'd been looking very peculiar. Of course he'd been drinking but all the same she remembered saying . . . No, that hadn't been Monday night because she'd been asleep when he got back. It must have been Tuesday morning. Yes, that was it. She'd said he looked peculiar and come to think of it what she really thought was that he had looked scared. And he'd said he'd left the car in a car park and when he'd come home in the evening he'd kept looking out the front window in the strangest way. He'd had an accident with the car too and while at the time she had just put that down to his usual absent-mindedness now that she came to think about it . . . At that point Eva had turned the light on and got out of bed. Something terrible had been going on and she hadn't even known it.

Which brought her round to anger again. Henry should have told her but he never did tell her really important things. He thought she was too stupid and perhaps she wasn't very clever when it came to arguing about books and saying the right things at parties but at least she was practical and nobody could say that the quads weren't getting a good education.

So the night passed. Eva sat in the kitchen and made cups of tea and worried and was angry and then blamed herself and wondered who to telephone and then decided it was best not to call anyone because they'd only be cross at being woken in the middle of the night and anyway there might be a perfectly natural explanation like the car had broken down or he'd gone to the Braintrees for a drink and had had to stay there because of the police and the breathalyser which would have been the sensible thing to do and so perhaps she ought to go back to bed and get some sleep . . . And always beside this bustle of conflicting thoughts and feelings there was the sense of guilt and the knowledge that she had been stupid to have listened to Mavis or to have gone anywhere near Dr Kores. Anyway, what did Mavis know about sex? She'd never really said what went on between her and Patrick in bed – it wasn't one of those things Eva would have dreamt of asking and even if she had Mavis wouldn't have told her – and all she'd ever heard was that Patrick was having affairs with other women. There might be good reasons for that too. Perhaps Mavis was frigid or wanted to be too dominant or masculine or wasn't very clean or something. Whatever the reason it was quite wrong of her to give Patrick those horrid steroid things or hormones and turn him into a sleepy fat person – well, you could hardly call him a man any longer could you? – who sat in front of the telly every night and couldn't get on with his work properly. Besides, Henry wasn't a bad husband. It was just that he was absent-minded and was always thinking about something or other that had no connection at all with what he was supposed to be doing. Like the time he'd been peeling the potatoes for Sunday lunch and he'd suddenly said the Vicar made Polonius sound like a bloody genius and there's no reason to say that because they hadn't been to church for two Sundays running and she'd wanted to know who Polonius was and he wasn't anyone at all, just some character in a play.

No, you couldn't expect Henry to be practical and she didn't. And of course they'd had their tiffs and disagreements, particularly about the quads. Why couldn't he see they were special? Well, he did, but not in the right way, and calling them 'clones' wasn't helpful. Eva could think of other things he'd said that weren't nice either. And then there was that dreadful business the other night with the cake icer. Goodness only knew what effect that had had on the girls' ideas about men. And that really was the trouble with Henry, he didn't know what romantic meant. Eva got up from the kitchen table and was presently calming her nerves by cleaning out the pantry. She was interrupted at six-thirty by Emmeline in her pyjamas.

'What are you doing?' she asked so unnecessarily that Eva rose to the bait.

'It's perfectly obvious,' she snapped. 'There's no need to ask stupid questions.'

'It wasn't obvious to Einstein,' said Emmeline, using the

well-tried technique of luring Eva into a topic about which she knew nothing but which she had to approve.

'What wasn't?'

'That the shortest distance between two points is a straight line.'

'Well it is, isn't it?' said Eva, moving a tin of Epicure marmalade from the shelf with pilchards and tuna fish on it to the jam section where it looked out of place.

'Of course it isn't. Everyone knows that. It's a curve. Where's Daddy?'

'I don't see how ... What do you mean "Where's Daddy?" ' said Eva, completely thrown by this leap from the inconceivable to the immediate.

'I was asking where he is,' said Emmeline. 'He's not in, is he?'

'No, he isn't,' said Eva, torn now between an inclination to give vent to her irritation and the need to keep calm. 'He's out.'

'Where's he gone?' asked Emmeline.

'He hasn't gone anywhere,' said Eva and moved the marmalade back to the pilchard shelf. Tins didn't look right among the jam-jars. 'He spent the night at the Braintrees.'

'I suppose he got drunk again,' said Emmeline. 'Do you think he's an alcoholic?'

Eva clutched a coffee jar dangerously. 'Don't you dare talk about your father like that!' she snapped. 'Of course he has a drink when he comes home at night. Nearly everyone does. It's quite normal and I won't have you saying things about your father.'

'You say things about him,' said Emmeline, 'I heard you call him—'

'Never mind what I say,' said Eva. 'That's quite different.'

'It isn't different,' Emmeline persisted, 'not when you say he's an alcoholic and anyway I was only asking a question and you're always telling us to—'

'Go up to your room at once,' said Eva. 'You're not speaking to me in that fashion. I won't have it.'

Emmeline retreated and Eva slumped down at the kitchen table again. It was really too trying of Henry not to have instilled some sense of respect in the quads. It was always left to her to be the disciplinarian. He should have more authority. She went back into the larder and saw to it that the packets and jars and tins did exactly what she wanted. By the time she had finished she felt a little better. Finally she chased the quads into dressing quickly.

'We'll have to catch the bus this morning,' she announced when they came in to breakfast. 'Daddy has the car and—'

'He hasn't,' said Penelope, 'Mrs Willoughby has.'

Eva, who had been pouring tea, spilt it. 'What did you say?'

Penelope looked smug. 'Mrs Willoughby has the car.'

'Mrs Willoughby? Yes, I know I've spilt some tea, Samantha. What do you mean, Penny? She can't have.'

'She has,' said Penelope looking smugger still. 'The milkman told me.'

'The milkman? He must have been mistaken,' said Eva.

'He isn't. He's scared stiff of the Hound of Oakhurst Avenue and he only delivers at the gate and that's where our car is. I went and saw it.'

'And was your father there?'

'No, it was empty.'

Eva put the teapot down unsteadily and tried to think what this meant. If Henry wasn't in the car . . .

'Perhaps Daddy's been eaten by the Hound,' suggested Josephine.

'The Hound doesn't eat people. It just tears their throats out and leaves their bodies on the waste ground at the bottom of the garden,' said Emmeline.

'It doesn't. It only barks. It's quite nice if you give it lamb chops and things,' said Samantha, unintentionally dragging Eva's attention away from the frightful possibility that Henry might in his drunken state have mistaken the house and ended up mauled to death by a Great Dane. And then again with Dr Kores' potion still coursing through his veins . . .

Penelope put the idea into words. 'He's more likely to have been eaten by Mrs Willoughby,' she said. 'Mr Gamer says she's sex-mad. I heard him tell Mrs Gamer that when she said she wanted it.'

'Wanted what?' demanded Eva, too stunned by this latest revelation to be concerned about the chops missing from the deep-freeze. She could deal with that matter later.

'The usual thing,' said Penelope with a look of distaste. 'She's always going on about it and Mr Gamer said she was getting just like Mrs Willoughby after Mr Willoughby died on the job and he wasn't going the same way.'

'That's not true,' said Eva in spite of herself.

'It is too,' said Penelope. 'Sammy heard him, didn't you?'

Samantha nodded.

'He was in the garage playing with himself like Paul in 3B does and we could hear ever so easily,' she said. 'And he's got lots of *Playboys* in there and books and she came in and said . . .'

'I don't want to hear,' said Eva, finally dragging her attention away from this fascinating topic. 'It's time to get your things on. I'll go and fetch the car . . .' She stopped. It was clearly one thing to say she was going to fetch the car from a neighbour's front garden, but just as clearly there were snags. If Henry was in Mrs Willoughby's house she'd never be able to live the scandal down. All the same something had to be done and it was a scandal enough already for the neighbours to see the Escort there. With the same determination with which Eva always dealt with embarrassing situations she put on her coat and marched out of the front door. Presently she was sitting in the Escort trying to start it. As usual when she was in a hurry the starter motor churned over and nothing happened. To be exact, something did but not what she had hoped. The front door opened and the Great Dane loped out followed by Mrs Willoughby in a dressing-gown. It was, in Eva's opinion, just the sort of dressing-gown a sex-mad widow would wear. Eva wound down the window to explain that she was just collecting the car and promptly wound it up again. Whatever Samantha's finer feelings might persuade her about the dog, Eva mistrusted it.

'I'm just going to take the girls to school,' she said by way of rather inadequate explanation.

Outside the Great Dane barked and Mrs Willoughby mouthed something that Eva couldn't hear. She wound the window down two inches. 'I said I'm just going to . . .' she began.

Ten minutes later, after an exceedingly acrimonious exchange in which Mrs Willoughby had challenged Eva's right to park in other people's drives and Eva had only been prevented by the presence of the Hound from demanding the right to search the house for her Henry and had been forced to confine herself to a moral critique of the dressing-gown, she drove the quads furiously to school. Only when they had left was Eva thrown back on her own worries. If Henry hadn't left the car at that awful woman's – and she really couldn't see him braving the Great Dane unless he'd been blind drunk and then he wouldn't have held much interest for Mrs Willoughby – someone else must have. Eva drove to the Braintrees and came away even more worried. Betty was sure Peter had said he hadn't seen Henry nearly all week. It was the same at the Tech. Wilt's office was empty and Mrs Bristol was adamant that he hadn't been in since Wednesday. Which left only the prison.

With a terrible sense of foreboding Eva used the phone in Wilt's office. By the time she put it down again panic had set in. Henry not at the prison since Monday? But he taught that murderer every Friday . . . He didn't. He never had. And he wasn't going to teach him on Mondays either now because Mac wasn't a burden on the state, as you might say. But he had given McCullum lessons on Friday. Oh no, he hadn't. Prisoners in that category couldn't have cosy little chats every night of the week, now could they? Yes, he was quite sure. Mr Wilt never came to the prison on Fridays.

Sitting alone in the office, Eva's reactions swung from panic to anger and back again. Henry had been deceiving her. He'd lied. Mavis was right, he had had another woman all the time. But he couldn't have. She'd have known. He couldn't keep a thing like that to himself. He wasn't practical or cunning enough. There'd have been something to tell her like hairs on his coat or lipstick or powder or something. And why? But before she could consider that question Mrs Bristol had poked her head round the door to ask if she'd like a cup of coffee. Eva braced herself to face reality. No one was going to have the satisfaction of seeing her break down.

'No thank you,' she said, 'it's very kind of you but I must be off.' And without allowing Mrs Bristol the opportunity to ask anything more Eva marched out and walked down the stairs with an air of deliberate fortitude. It had almost cracked by the time she had reached the car but she hung on until she had driven back to Oakhurst Avenue. Even then, with all the evidence of treachery around her in the shape of Henry's raincoat and the shoes he'd put out to polish and hadn't and his briefcase in the hall, she refused to give way to self-pity. Something was wrong. Something that proved Henry hadn't walked out on her. If only she could think.

It had something to do with the car. Henry would never have left it in Mrs Willoughby's drive. No, that wasn't it. It was . . . She dropped the car keys on the kitchen table and recognized their importance. They'd been in the car when she'd gone to fetch it and among them on the ring was the key to 45 Oakhurst Avenue. Henry had left her without any warning and without leaving a message but he had left the key to the house? Eva didn't believe it. Not for one moment. In that case her instinct had been right and something dreadful had happened to him. Eva put the kettle on and tried to think what to do.

'Listen, Ted,' said Flint. 'You play it the way you want. If you scratch my back I'll scratch yours. No problems. All I'm saying is—'

'If I scratch your back,' said Lingon, 'I won't have a fucking back to be scratched. Not one you'd want to scratch anyway, even if you could find it under some bloody motorway. Now would you mind just getting out of here?'

Inspector Flint settled himself in a chair and looked round the tiny office in the corner of the scruffy garage. Apart from a filing cabinet, the usual nudey calendar, a telephone and the desk, the only thing it contained of any interest to him was Mr Lingon. And in Flint's view Mr Lingon was a thing, a rather nasty thing, a squat, seedy and corrupt thing. 'Business good?' he asked with as little interest as possible. Outside the glass cubicle a mechanic was hosing down a Lingon Coach which claimed to be de luxe.

Mr Lingon grunted and lit a cigarette from the stub of his last one. 'It was till you turned up,' he said. 'Now do me a favour and leave me alone. I don't know what you're on about.'

'Smack,' said Flint.

'Smack? What's that supposed to mean?'

Flint ignored the question. 'How many years did you do last time?' he enquired.

'Oh Jesus,' said Lingon. 'I've been inside. Years ago. But you sods never let up, do you? Not you. A little bit of breaking and entering, someone gets done over two miles away. You name it, who do you come and see? Who's on record? Ted Lingon. Go and put the pressure on him. That's all you buggers can ever think of. No imagination.'

Flint shifted his attention from the mechanic and looked at Mr Lingon. 'Who needs imagination?' he said. 'A nice signed statement, witnessed and everything clean and above-board and no trade. Much better than imagination. Stands up in court.'

'Statement? What statement?' Mr Lingon was looking uneasy now.

'Don't you want to know who from first?'

'All right. Who?'

'Clive Swannell.'

'That old poove? You've got to be joking. He wouldn't—' He stopped suddenly. 'You're trying it on.'

Flint smiled confidently. 'How about the Rocker then?'

Lingon stubbed his cigarette out and said nothing.

'I've got it down in black and white. From the Rocker too. Adds up, doesn't it? Want me to go on?'

'I don't know what you're talking about, Inspector,' said Lingon. 'And now if you don't mind . . .'

'Next on the list,' said Flint, savouring the pressure, 'there's a nice little piece down Chingford called Annie Mosgrave. Fond of Pakis, she is. And Chinese threesomes. Sort of cosmopolitan, isn't she? But she writes a nice clean hand and she doesn't want some bloke with a meat cleaver coming round one night.'

'You're fucking lying. That's what you're doing,' said Lingon, shifting in his seat and fumbling with the cigarette packet.

Flint shrugged. 'Of course I am. I mean I would be. Stupid old copper like me's bound to lie. Specially when he's got signed statements locked away. And don't think I'm going to do you the favour of locking you away too, Teddie boy. No, I don't like drug buggers. Not one little bit.' He leant forward and smiled. 'No, I'm just going to attend the inquest. Your inquest, Teddie dear. I might even try to identify you. Difficult of course. It will be, won't it? No feet, no hands, teeth all wrenched out . . . that is if there is a head and they haven't burnt it after they've done the rest of what was you over. And they do take their time over it. Nasty really. Remember Chris down in Thurrock. Must have been a terrible way to die, bleeding like that. Tore his—'

'Shut up,' shouted Lingon, now ashen and shaking.

Flint got up. 'For now,' he said. 'But only for now. You don't want to do business: that's fine with me. I'll walk out of here and you won't be seeing me again. No, it'll be some bloke you don't even know comes in. Wants to hire a coach to take a party to Buxton. Money on the table, no hassle and the next fucking thing you know is you'll be wishing it had been me instead of one of Mac's mates with a pair of secateurs.'

'Mac's dead,' said Lingon almost in a whisper.

'So they tell me,' said Flint. 'But Roddie Eaton's still out and about and running things. Funny bloke, Roddie. Likes hurting people, according to my sources, specially when they've got enough knowledge to put him away for life and he can't be certain they won't talk.'

'That's not me,' said Lingon. 'I'm no squealer.'

'Want to bet on it? You'll be screaming your rotten little heart out before they've even begun,' said Flint and opened the door.

But Lingon signalled him back. 'I need guarantees,' he said. 'I got to have them.'

Flint shook his head.. 'I told you. I'm a stupid old copper. I'm not selling the Queen's pardon. If you want to come and see me and tell me all about it, I'll be there. Till one o'clock.' He looked at his watch. 'You've got exactly one hour twelve minutes. After that you'd better shut up shop and buy yourself a shotgun. And it won't do you any good picking up that phone because I'll know. And the same if you leave here to use a call-box. And by five past one Roddie will know too.'

Flint walked out past the coach. The rotten little bastard would come. He was sure of that and everything was fitting nicely, or nastily, into place. And Hodge was screwed too. It was all very satisfactory and only went to prove what he had always said, that there was nothing like years of experience. It helped to have a son in prison for drug smuggling too, but Inspector Flint had no intention of mentioning his sources of information to the Superintendent when he made his report.

Chapter seventeen

'An infiltrating agent?' boomed the Airforce General commanding Baconheath. 'Why wasn't I informed immediately?'

'Yes sir, that's a good question, sir,' said Glaushof.

'It is not, Major, it's a lousy question. It isn't even a question I should have to ask. I shouldn't have to ask any questions. In fact I'm not here to ask questions. I run a tight ship and I expect my men to answer their own questions.'

'And that's the way I took it, sir,' said Glaushof.

'Took what?'

'Took the situation, sir, faced with an infiltrating agent. I said to myself—'

'I am not interested in what you said to yourself, Major. I am only interested in results,' shouted the General. 'And I want to know what results you've achieved. By my count the results you've achieved amount to the gassing of ten Airforce personnel or their dependants.'

'Eleven, sir,' said Glaushof.

'Eleven? That's even worse.'   •

'Twelve with the agent Wilt, sir.'

'Then how come you just told me eleven?' demanded the General, toying with the model of a B52.

'Lieutenant Harah, sir, was gassed in the course of the action, sir, and I am proud to report that without his courage in the face of determined resistance by the enemy we could have encountered heavy casualties and possibly a hostage situation. Sir.'

General Belmonte put the B52 down and reached for a bottle of Scotch before remembering he was supposed to be in command of the situation. 'Nobody told me about a resistance situation,' he said rather more amicably.

'No, sir. It didn't seem advisable to issue a press release in the light of current opinion, sir,' said Glaushof. Having managed to avoid the General's questions he was prepared to apply more direct pressure. If there was one thing the Commander hated it was any mention of publicity. Glaushof mentioned it. 'As I see it, sir, the publicity—'

'Jesus, Glaushof,' shouted the General, 'how many times have I got to remind you there is to be no publicity? That is Directive Number One and comes from the highest authority. No publicity, dammit. You think we can defend the Free World against the enemy if we have publicity? I want that clearly understood. No publicity for Chrissake.'

'Understood, General,' said Glaushof. 'Which is why I've ordered a security blackout, a total no-traffic command to all information services. I mean if it got out we'd had an infiltration problem . . .'

He paused to allow the General to get his strength back for a further assault on publicity. It came in waves. When the bombardment had finished Glaushof produced his real target. 'If you'll permit me to say so, sir, I think we're going to be faced with an informational problem on the Intelligence side.'

'You do, do you? Well, let me tell you something, Major, and this is an order, a top priority directive order, that there is to a security blackout, a total no-traffic command to all information services. That is my order, you understand.'

'Yes, sir,' said Glaushof, 'I'll institute it immediately to the Intelligence Command. I mean if we had a leak to the press there . . .'

'Major Glaushof, that is an order I have given you. I want it instituted pre-immediate to all services.'

'Including Intelligence, sir?'

'Of course including Intelligence,' bawled the General. 'Our Intelligence services are the best in the world and I'm not jeopardizing standards of excellence by exposing them to media harassment. Is that clear?'

'Yessir,' said Glaushof and promptly left the office to order an armed guard to be placed on Intelligence HQ and to instruct all personnel to initiate a total no-traffic command. Since no one knew at all precisely what a no-traffic command was the various interpretations put on it ranged from a ban on all vehicles entering or leaving civilian quarters to a full alert on the airfield, the latter having been intermittently in force throughout the night thanks to wafts of Agent Incapacitating Two sounding off the toxic-weapon-detection sensors. By mid-morning the diverse rumours circulating were so manifestly at odds with one another that Glaushof felt safe enough to bawl his wife out over Lieutenant Harah's sexual insubordination before catching up on his sleep. He wanted to be in good shape to interrogate Wilt.

But when, two hours later, he arrived at the guarded room in the hospital Wilt was evidently in no mood to answer questions. 'Why don't you just go away and let me get some sleep?' he said blearily and turned on his side.

Glaushof glared at his back.

'Give him another shot,' he told the doctor.

'Give him another shot of what?'

'Whatever you gave him last night.'

'I wasn't on duty last night,' said the doctor. 'And anyhow who are you to tell me what to give him?'

Glaushof turned his attention away from Wilt's back and glared instead at the doctor. 'I'm Glaushof. Major Glaushof, doctor, just in case you haven't heard of me. And I'm ordering you to give this commie bastard something that'll jerk him out of that bed so I can question him.'

The doctor shrugged. 'If you say so, Major,' he said and studied Wilt's chart. 'What would you recommend?'

'Me?' said Glaushof. 'How the hell would I know? I'm not a goddam doctor.'

'So happens I am,' said the doctor, 'and I'm telling you I am not administering any further medication to this patient right now. The guy's been exposed to a toxic agent—'

He got no further. With a nasty grunt Glaushof shoved him through the doorway into the corridor. 'Now you just listen to me,' he snarled, 'I don't want to hear no crap about medical ethics. What we've got in there is a dangerous enemy agent and he doesn't even come into the category of a patient. Do you read me?'

'Sure,' said the doctor nervously. 'Sure, I read you. Loud and clear. So now will you take your hands off me?'

Glaushof let go of his coat. 'You just get something'll make the bastard talk and fast,' he said. 'We've got a security problem on our hands.'

'I'll say we have,' said the doctor and hurried away from it. Twenty minutes later a thoroughly confused Wilt was bundled out of the hospital building under a blanket and driven at high speed to Glaushof's office where he was placed on a chair. Glaushof had switched on the tape recorder. 'Okay, now you're going to tell us,' he said.

'Tell you what?' asked Wilt.

'Who sent you?' said Glaushof.

Wilt considered the question. As far as he could tell it didn't have much bearing on what was happening to him except that it had nothing whatsoever to do with reality. 'Sent me?' he said. 'Is what you said?'

'That's what I said.'

'I thought it was,' said Wilt and relapsed into a meditative silence.

'So?' said Glaushof.

'So what?' asked Wilt, in an attempt to restore his morale slightly by combining insult with enquiry.

'So who sent you?'

Wilt sought inspiration in a portrait of President Eisenhower behind Glaushof's head and found a void. 'Sent me?' he said, and regretted it. Glaushof's expression contrasted unpleasantly with that of the late President. 'Nobody sent me.'

'Listen,' said Glaushof, 'this far you've had it easy. Doesn't mean it's going to stay that way. It could get very nasty. Now, are you going to talk or not?'

'I'm perfectly prepared to talk,' said Wilt, 'though I must say your definition of easy isn't mine. I mean being gassed and—'

'You want to hear my definition of nasty?' asked Glaushof.

'No,' said Wilt hastily, 'certainly not.'

'So talk.'

Wilt swallowed. 'Any particular subject you're interested in?' he enquired.

'Like who your contacts are,' said Glaushof.

'Contacts?' said Wilt.

'Who you're working for. And I don't want to hear any crap about teaching at the Fenland College Of Arts and Technology. I want to know who set this operation up.'

'Yes,' said Wilt, once more entering a mental maze and losing himself. 'Now when you say "this operation" I wonder if you'd mind . . .' He stopped. Glaushof was staring at him even more awfully than before. 'I mean I don't know what you're talking about.'

'You don't, huh?'

'I'm afraid not. I mean if I did—'

Glaushof shook a finger under Wilt's nose. 'A guy could die in here and nobody would know,' he said. 'If you want to go that way you've only to say so.'

'I don't,' said Wilt, trying to focus on the finger as a means of avoiding the prospect of his going any way. 'If you'd just ask me some questions I could answer . . .'

Glaushof backed off. 'Let's start with where you got the transmitters,' he said.

'Transmitters?' said Wilt. 'Did you say transmitters? What transmitters?'

'The ones in your car.'

'The ones in my car?' said Wilt. 'Are you sure?'

Glaushof gripped the edge of the desk behind him and thought wistfully about killing people. 'You think you can come in here, into United States territory and—'

'England,' said Wilt stolidly. 'To be precise the United Kingdom of England, Scotland—'

'Jesus,' said Glaushof, 'You little commie bastard, you have the nerve to talk about the Royal Family . . .'

'My own country,' said Wilt, finding strength in the assuredness that he was British. It was something he had never really thought much about before. 'And for your information, I am not a communist. Possibly a bastard, though I like to think otherwise. You have to ask my mother about that and she's been dead ten years. But definitely not a communist.'

'So what's with the radio transmitters in your car?'

'You said that before and I've no idea what you're talking about. Are you sure you're not mistaking me for someone else.'

'You're named Wilt, aren't you?' shouted Glaushof.

'Yes.'

'And you drive a beat-up Ford, registration plates HPR 791N, right?'

Wilt nodded. 'I suppose you could put it like that,' he said. 'Though frankly my wife—'

'You saying your wife put those transmitters in your car?'

'Good Lord no. She hasn't a clue about things like that. Anyway, what on earth would she want to do that for?'

'That's what you're here to tell me, boy,' said Glaushof. 'You ain't leaving till you do, you better believe it.'

Wilt looked at him and shook his head. 'I must say I find that difficult,' he muttered. 'I come here to give a lecture on British Culture, such as it is, and the next thing I know I'm in the middle of some sort of raid and there's gas all over the place and I wake up in a bed with doctors sticking needles into me and . . .'

He stopped. Glaushof had taken a revolver out of the desk drawer and was loading it. Wilt watched him apprehensively. 'Excuse me,' he said, 'but I'd be grateful if you'd put that . . . er . . . thing away. I don't know what you've got in mind but I can assure you I am not the person you should be talking to.'

'No? So who should that be, your controller?'

'Controller?' said Wilt.

'Controller,' said Glaushof.

'That's what I thought you said, though to be perfectly honest I still don't see that it helps very much. I don't even know what a controller is.'

'Then you better start inventing one. Like the guy in Moscow who tells you what to do.'

'Look,' said Wilt, desperately trying to get back to some sort of reality which didn't include controllers in Moscow who told him what to do, 'there's obviously been some terrible mistake.'

'Yeah, and you made it coming in here with that equipment. I'm going to give you one last chance,' said Glaushof, looking along the barrel of the gun with a significance Wilt found deeply alarming. 'Either you spell it out like it is or . . .'

'Quite,' said Wilt. 'Point taken, to use a ghastly expression. What do you want me to tell you?'

'The whole deal. How you were recruited, who you contact and where, what information you've given . . .'

Wilt stared miserably out the window as the list rolled on. He had never supposed the world to be a particularly sensible place and airbases were particularly nonsensical, but to be taken for a Soviet spy by a lunatic American who played with revolvers was to enter a new realm of insanity. Perhaps that's what had happened. He'd gone clean out of his tiny. No, he hadn't. The gun was proof of some kind of reality, one that was taken for granted by millions of people all over the world but which had somehow never come anywhere near Oakhurst Avenue or the Tech or Ipford. In a sense his own little world with its fundamental beliefs in education and books and, for want of a better word, sensibility, was the unreal one, a dream which no one could ever hope to live in for long. Or at all, if this madman with his cliché talk of guys dying in here and nobody knowing had his way. Wilt turned back and made one last attempt to regain the world he knew.

'All right,' he said, 'if you want the facts I'll give them to you but only with men from MI5 present. As a British subject I demand that right.'

Glaushof snorted. 'Your rights ended the moment you passed that guardhouse,' he said. 'You're telling me what you know. I'm not playing footsy with a lot of suspect faggots from British Intelligence. No way. Now talk.'

'If it's all the same to you I think it would be better written down,' said Wilt, playing for time and trying frantically to think what he could possibly confess. 'I mean, all I need is a pen and some sheets of paper.'

For a moment Glaushof hesitated before deciding that there was something to be said for a confession written out in Wilt's own hand. That way no one could say he'd beaten it out of the little bastard. 'Okay,' he said. 'You can use the table.'

Three hours later Wilt had finished and six pages were covered with his neat and practically illegible hand-writing. Glaushof took them and tried to read. 'What you trying to do? Didn't anybody ever teach you to write properly?'

Wilt shook his head wearily. 'If you can't read, take it to someone who can. I've had it,' he said and put his head on his arms on the table. Glaushof looked at his white face and had to agree. He wasn't feeling too good himself. But at least Colonel Urwin and the idiots in Intelligence were going to feel worse. With a fresh surge of energy he went into the office next door, made photocopies of the pages and was presently marching past the guards outside communications. 'I want transcripts made of these,' he told the head of the typists' pool. 'And absolute security.' Then he sat down and waited.

Chapter eighteen

'A warrant? A search warrant for 45 Oakhurst Avenue? You want to apply for a search warrant?' said the Super-intendent.

'Yes, sir,' said Inspector Hodge, wondering why it was that what seemed like a perfectly reasonable request to him should need querying quite so repetitively. 'All the evidence indicates the Wilts to be carriers.'

'I'm not sure the magistrate is going to agree,' said the Superintendent. 'Circumstantial evidence is all it amounts to.'

'Nothing circumstantial about Wilt going out to that airbase and giving us the run-around, and I wouldn't say her going to that herb farm was circumstantial either. It's all there in my report.'

'Yes,' said the Superintendent, managing to imbue the word with doubt. 'What's not there is one shred of hard evidence.'

'That's why we need the search, sir,' said Hodge. 'There've got to be traces of the stuff in the house. Stands to reason.'

'If he's what you say he is,' said the Superintendent.

'Look,' said Hodge, 'he knew he was being tailed when he went out to Baconheath. He had to know. Drives around in circles for half an hour when he comes out and gives us the slip—'

'And that's another thing,' interrupted the Superintendent, 'your bugging the blighter's car without authorization. I consider that highly reprehensible. I want that understood clearly right now. Anyway, he may have been drunk.'

'Drunk?' said Hodge, finding it difficult to make the transition between unauthorized bugging being reprehensible, which in his opinion it wasn't, and Wilt being drunk.

'When he came out of Baconheath. Didn't know whether he was coming or going and went round in circles. Those Yanks drink rye. Sickly muck but it goes down so easily you don't notice.'

Inspector Hodge considered the suggestion and rejected it. 'I don't see how a drunk could drive that fast, not on those roads without killing himself. And choosing a route that'd take him out of radio contact.'

The Superintendent studied the report again. It didn't make comfortable reading. On the other hand there was

198

something in what Hodge had said. 'If he wasn't pissed why leave the car outside someone else's house?' he asked but Hodge had already concocted an answer to that one.

'Shows how clever the little bastard is,' he said. 'Not giving anything away, that bloke. He knows we're onto him and he needs an explanation for all that run-around he's given us so he plays pissed.'

'If he's that bloody clever you're not going to find anything in his house and that's for sure,' said the Superintendent and shook his head. 'No, he'd never have the stuff on his own doorstep. He'd have it stored somewhere miles away.'

'He's still got to move it,' said Hodge, 'and that means the car. Look, sir, Wilt's the one who goes to the airbase, he collects the stuff there and on the way home he hands it over to a third party who distributes it. That explains why he took such pains to lose us. There was a whole twenty minutes when we weren't picking up any signals. That could have been when he was offloading.'

'Could have been,' said the Superintendent, impressed in spite of himself. 'Still, that only goes to prove my point. You go for a search warrant for his house you're going to end up with egg all over your face. More important, so am I. So that's out. You'll have to think of some other way.'

Hodge returned to his office and took it out on Sergeant Runk. 'The way they carry on it's a bloody wonder we ever nick any bugger. And you had to go and sign for those fucking transmitters . . .'

'You don't think they give them out without being signed for,' said Runk.

'You didn't have to land me in the shit by putting "Authorized by Superintendent Wilkinson for covert surveillance." He loved that.'

'Well, wasn't it? I mean I thought you'd got permission . . .'

'Oh no, you didn't. We pulled that stroke in the middle of the night and he'd been home since five. And now we've got to retrieve the bloody things. That's something you can do tonight.'

And having, as he hoped, ensured that the Sergeant would spend the day regretting his indiscretion, the Inspector got up and stared out of the window for inspiration. If he couldn't get a search warrant . . . He was still pondering the question when his attention was distracted by a car parked down below. It looked hideously familiar.

The Wilts' Escort. What the hell was it doing outside the police station?

Eva sat in Flint's office and held back the tears. 'I didn't know who else to come to,' she said. 'I've been to the Tech and phoned the prison and Mrs Braintree hasn't seen him and he usually goes there if he's . . . well, if he wants a change. But he hasn't been there or the hospital or anywhere else I can think of and I know you don't like him or anything but you are a policeman and you have been . . . helpful in the past. And you do know Henry.' She stopped and looked appealingly at the Inspector.

It wasn't a look that held much appeal for Flint and he certainly didn't like the notion that he knew Wilt. He'd tried to understand the blighter, but even at his most optimistic he'd never supposed for one moment that he'd got anywhere near fathoming the horrible depths of Wilt's extraordinary character. The sod came into the category of an enigma made all the more impossible to understand by his choice of Eva as a wife. It was a relationship Flint had always preferred not to think about, but here she was sitting foursquare on a chair in his office telling him, evidently without the slightest regard for his feelings, even as though it were some sort of compliment, that he knew her Henry. 'Has he ever gone off like this before?' he asked, with the private thought that in Wilt's shoes he'd have been off like a flash – before the wedding.

'No, never,' said Eva, 'that's what's so worrying. I

know you think he's . . . peculiar, but he's really been a good husband.'

'I'm sure he has,' said Flint for want of anything more reassuring to say. 'You don't think he's suffering from amnesia.'

'Amnesia?'

'Loss of memory,' said Flint. 'It hits people who've been under strain. Has anything been happening lately that might have caused him to flip . . . to have a nervous breakdown?'

'I can't think of anything in particular,' said Eva, determined to keep any mention of Dr Kores and that dreadful tonic out of the conversation. 'Of course the children get on his nerves sometimes and there was that horrible business at the Tech the other day with that girl dying. Henry was ever so upset. And he's been teaching at the prison . . .' She stopped again as she remembered what had been really worrying her. 'He's been teaching a dreadful man called McCullum on Monday evenings and Fridays. That's what he told me anyway, only when I phoned the prison they said he never had.'

'Had what?' asked Flint.

'Never been there on Fridays,' said Eva, tears welling up in her eyes at this proof that Henry, her Henry, had lied to her.

'But he went out every Friday and that's where he told you he was going?'

Eva nodded dumbly and for a moment Flint almost felt sorry for her. A fat middle-aged woman with four bloody tear-away kids who turned the house into a blooming bearpit and she hadn't known what Wilt was up to? Talk about being as thick as two short planks. Well, it was about time she learnt. 'Look, Mrs Wilt, I know this isn't easy to . . .' he began but to his amazement Eva was there before him.

'I know what you're going to say,' she interrupted, 'but it isn't true. If it had been another woman why did he leave the car in Mrs Willoughby's?'

'Leave the car in Mrs Willoughby's? Who's Mrs Willoughby?'

'She lives at Number 65, and that's where the car was this morning. I had to go and get it. Why would he want to do that?'

It was on the tip of Flint's tongue to say that's what he'd have done in Wilt's place, dump the car down the road and run like hell, when something else occurred to him.

'You wait here,' he said and left the room. In the corridor he hesitated for a moment and tried to think who to ask. He certainly wasn't approaching Hodge but there was always Sergeant Runk. And Yates could find out for him. He turned into the open-plan office where the Sergeant was sitting at a typewriter.

'Got an enquiry for you, Yates,' he said. 'Have a word with your mate Runk and find out where they tailed Wilt last night. I've got his missus in my office. And don't let him know I'm interested, understand? Just a casual enquiry on your part.' He sat on the edge of the desk while Yates was gone five minutes.

'Right balls-up,' said the Sergeant when he returned. 'They followed the little bugger out to Baconheath airbase with a radio tail. He's in there an hour and a half and comes out driving like a maniac. Runkie reckons Wilt knew they were on to him, the way he drove. Anyway they lost him, and when they did find the car it was outside some house down the road from the Wilts' with a fucking big dog trying to tear the front door down to get at Hodge. That's about the strength of it.'

Flint nodded, and kept his excitement to himself. He'd already done enough to make Hodge look the fucking idiot he was; he'd broken the Bull and Clive Swannell and that little shit Lingon, signed statements and all; and all the time Hodge had been harrying Wilt. So why drop him in it any further?

Why not? The deeper the bugger sank the less he'd be likely to surface. And not only Hodge but Wilt too. The bastard had been the original cause of all Flint's misfortunes and to be able to drag him through the mire together with Hodge was justice at its most perfect. Besides, Flint still had to make the catch with Lingon, so a diversion was just what he needed. And if ever there was a diversion ready to hand it was sitting in his office in the shape of Mrs Eva Wilt. The only problem was how to point her in Hodge's direction without anyone learning what he had done. It was a risk he had to take. He'd better check first, though. Flint went to a phone and looked up the Baconheath number.

'Inspector Hodge speaking,' he said, slurring the name so that it might well have been Squash or Hedge, 'I'm calling from Ipford Police Station in connection with a Mr Wilt . . . A Mr Henry Wilt of 45 Oakhurst Avenue, Ipford. I understand he visited you last night.' He waited while someone said he'd check.

It took a long time and another American came on the line. 'You enquiring about someone called Wilt?' he asked.

'That's correct,' said Flint.

'And you say you're police?'

'Yes,' said Flint, noting the hesitancy in the questioner with intense interest.

'If you'll give me your name and the number to call I'll get back to you,' said the American. Flint put the phone down quietly. He'd learnt what he needed and he wasn't having any Yank check his credentials.

He went back to his office and sat down with a calculated sigh. 'I'm afraid you're not going to like what I'm going to tell you, Mrs Wilt,' he said.

Eva didn't. She left the police station white-faced with fury. Not only had Henry lied to her but he'd been cheating her for months and she hadn't had an inkling.

Behind her Flint sat on in his office staring almost ecstatically at a wall-map of Ipford. Henry Wilt, Henry Bloody Wilt, was going to get his comeuppance this time. And he was out there somewhere, somewhere in one of those little streets, holed up with a dolly bird who must have money or he would be back at his job at the Tech.

No, he wouldn't. Not with Eva in pursuit. No wonder

the bugger had left the car down the road. If he'd any sense he'd have left town by now. The bloody woman would murder him. Flint smiled at the thought. Now that *would* be poetic justice, no mistake.

'It's more than my life's worth. I mean I'd do it, I'd happily do it but what if it gets out?' said Mr Gamer.

'It won't,' said Hodge, 'I can give you a solemn assurance on that. You won't even know they're there.'

Mr Gamer looked mournfully round the restaurant. He usually had sandwiches and a cup of coffee for lunch and he wasn't sure how well Boneless Chicken Curry washed down with a bottle of Blue Nun was going to agree with him. Still, the Inspector was paying and he could always get some Solvol on the way back to the shop. 'It's not just me either, it's the wife. If you knew what that woman has been through these last twelve months you wouldn't believe me. You really wouldn't.'

'I would,' said Hodge. If it was anything like what he'd been through in the last four days, Mrs Gamer must be a woman with an iron constitution.

'It's even worse in the school holidays,' Mr Gamer continued. 'Those fucking girls . . . I don't usually swear but there's a point where you've got to . . . I mean you can't begin to know how awful they are.' He stopped and looked closely into Hodge's face. 'One of these days they're going to kill someone,' he whispered. 'They bloody near did for me on Tuesday. I'd have been as dead as a dodo if I hadn't been wearing rubber-soled shoes. Stole my statue from the garden and when I went round to get it . . .'

Hodge listened sympathetically. 'Criminal,' he said. 'You should have reported it to us straight away. Even now if you made a formal complaint . . .'

'You think I'd dare? Never. If it meant having them all carted off to prison straightaway I might but it doesn't work like that. They'd come home from court and . . . it doesn't bear thinking about. Take that poor sod down the road, Councillor Birkenshaw. He had his name up in lights on a french letter with a foreskin on it. Floated right down the street it did and than they went and accused him of showing his privates to them. He had a horrible time trying to prove he hadn't. And look where he is. In hospital. No, it's not worth the risk.'

'I can see what you mean,' said Hodge. 'But this way they wouldn't ever find out. All we need is your permission to—'

'I blame the bloody mother,' Mr Gamer went on, encouraged by the Blue Nun and the Inspector's apparent sympathy. 'If she didn't encourage the little bitches to be like boys and take an interest in mechanical things it'd help. But no, they've got to be inventors and geniuses. Mind you, it takes some sort of genius to do what they did to Dickens' lawnmower. Brand new, it was, and God knows what exactly they did to it. Supercharged it with a camping-gas cylinder and altered the gear ratio too so it went like the clappers. And it's not as though he's a well man. Anyway, he started the bloody thing up and before he could stop it was off down the lawn at about eighty and mowing their new carpet in the lounge. Smashed the piano too, come to think of it. They had to call the fire brigade to put it out.'

'Why didn't he sue the parents?' asked Hodge, fascinated in spite of himself.

Mr Gamer sighed. 'You don't understand,' he said. 'You have to live through it to understand. You don't think they admit what they've done? Of course they don't. And who's going to believe old Dickens when he says four ruddy girls that age could change the sprocket on the driveshaft and superglue the clutch? No one. Mind if I help myself.'

Hodge poured another glass. Clearly Mr Gamer was a broken man. 'All right,' he said. 'Now supposing you know nothing about it. Just suppose a man from the Gas Board comes to check the meter—'

'And that's another thing,' said Mr Gamer almost dementedly, 'gas. The bill! Four hundred and fifty fucking pounds for a summer quarter! You don't believe me, do you? I didn't believe it either. Had that meter changed and checked and it still came to the same. I still don't know how they did it. Must have been while we were on holiday. If only I could find out!'

'Look,' said Hodge, 'you let my man install the equipment and you've a very good chance of getting rid of the Wilts for ever. And I mean that. For ever.'

Mr Gamer gazed into his glass and considered this glorious prospect. 'For ever?'

'For ever.'

'Done,' said Mr Gamer.

Later that afternoon Sergeant Runk, feeling distinctly uncomfortable in a Gas Board uniform, and with Mrs Gamer asking pitifully what could possibly be wrong with the chimney because they'd had it lined when the central heating was put in, was up in the roof space. By the time he left he had managed to feed microphones through a gap in the bricks so that they lay hidden among the insulating chips above the Wilts' bedrooms. 45 Oakhurst Avenue had been wired for sound.

Chapter nineteen

'I think we've got one hell of a problem, sir,' said the Corporal. 'Major Glaushof ordered me to ditch the car back at the Wilt guy's house and I did. All I can say is those transmitters weren't civilian. I had a good look at them and they were hi-tech British.'

Colonel Urwin, Senior Intelligence Officer USAF Baconheath, pondered the problem by looking coolly at a sporting print on the wall. It wasn't a very good one but its depiction of a fox in the far distance, being chased by a motley crowd of thin, fat, pale, or red-faced Englishmen on horseback, always served to remind him that it was as well not to underestimate the British. Better still, it paid to seem to be one of them. To that end he played golf with an ancient set of clubs and spent his idler moments tracing his family tree in the archives of various universities and the graveyards of Lincolnshire churches. In short, he kept an almost subterranean profile and was proud of the fact that he had on several occasions been taken for a master from one of the better public schools. It was a rôle that suited him exactly and fitted in with his professional creed that discretion was the better part of valour.

'British?' he said thoughtfully. 'That could mean anything or nothing. And you say Major Glaushof has put down a security clamp?'

'General Belmonte's orders, sir.'

The Colonel said nothing. In his opinion the Base Commander's IQ was only slightly higher than that of the egregious Glaushof. Anyone who could call four no trumps without a diamond in his hand had to be a cretin. 'So the situation is that Glaushof has this man Wilt in custody and is presumably torturing him and no one is supposed to know he's here. The operative word being "supposed". Obviously whoever sent him knows he never returned to Ipford.'

'Yes, sir,' said the Corporal. 'And the Major's been trying to get a message on line to Washington.'

'See it's coded garbage,' said the Colonel, 'and get a copy to me.'

'Yes, sir,' said the Corporal and disappeared.

Colonel Urwin looked across at his deputy. 'Seems we could have a hornet's nest,' he said. 'What do you make of it?'

Captain Fortune shrugged. 'Could be any number of options,' he said. 'I don't like the sound of that hardware.'

'Kamikaze,' said the Colonel. 'No one would come in transmitting.'

'Libyans or Khomeini might.'

Colonel Urwin shook his head. 'No way. When they hit they don't signal their punches. They'd come in loaded with explosives first time. So who's scoring?'

'The Brits?'

'That's my line of thinking,' said the Colonel, and wandered across to take a closer look at the sporting print. 'The only question is who are they hunting, Mr Henry Wilt or us?'

'I've checked our records and there's nothing on Wilt. CND in the sixties, otherwise non-political.'

'University?'

'Yes,' said the Captain.

'Which one?'

The Captain consulted the computer file. 'Cambridge. Majored in English.'

'Otherwise, nothing?'

'Nothing we know of. British Intelligence would know.'

'And we're not asking,' said the Colonel, coming to a decision. 'If Glaushof wants to play Lone Ranger with the General's consent he's welcome to the fan-shit. We stay clear and come up with the real answer when it's needed.'

'I still don't like that hardware in the car,' said the Captain.

'And I don't like Glaushof,' said the Colonel. 'I have an idea the Ofreys don't either. Let him dig his own grave.' He paused. 'Is there anyone with any intelligence who knows what really happened, apart from that Corporal?'

'Captain Clodiak filed a complaint against Harah for sexual harassment. And she's on the list of students attending Wilt's lectures.'

'Right, we'll start digging back into this fiasco there,' said the Colonel.

'Let's get back to this Radek,' said Glaushof, 'I want to know who he is.'

'I've told you, a Czech writer and he's been dead since God knows when so there is no way I could have met him,' said Wilt.

'If you're lying you will. Shortly,' said Glaushof. Having read the transcripts of Wilt's confession that he had been recruited by a KGB agent called Yuri Orlov and had a contact man called Karl Radek, Glaushof was now determined to find out exactly what information Wilt had passed to the Russians. Understandably it was proving decidedly harder than getting Wilt to admit he was an agent. Twice Glaushof had used the threat of instant death, but without any useful result. Wilt had asked for time to think and had then come up with H-bombs.

'H-bombs? You've been telling this bastard Radek we've got H-bombs stashed here?'

'Yes,' said Wilt.

'They know that already.'

'That's what Radek said. He said they wanted more than that.'

'So what did you give him, the BBs?'

'BBs?' said Wilt. 'You mean airguns?'

'Binary bombs.'

'Never heard of them.'

'Safest nerve-gas bombs in the world,' said Glaushof proudly. 'We could kill every living fucking thing from Moscow to Peking with BBs and they wouldn't even know a thing.'

'Really?' said Wilt. 'I must say I find your definition of safe peculiar. What are the dangerous ones capable of?'

'Shit,' said Glaushof, wishing he was somewhere under-developed like El Salvador and could use more forceful methods. 'You don't talk you're going to regret you ever met me.'

Wilt studied the Major critically. With each unfulfilled threat he was gaining more confidence but it still seemed inadvisable to point out that he already regretted meeting the bloody man. Best to keep things cool. 'I'm only telling you what you want to know,' he said.

'And you didn't give them any other information?'

'I don't know any. Ask the students in my class. They'll tell you I wouldn't know a bomb from a banana.'

'So you say,' muttered Glaushof. He'd already questioned the students and, in the case of Mrs Ofrey, had learnt more about her opinion of him than about Wilt. And Captain Clodiak hadn't been helpful either. The only evidence she'd been able to produce that Wilt was a communist had been his insistence that the National Health Service was a good thing. And so by degrees of inconsequentiality they had come full circle back to this KGB man Radek whom Wilt had claimed was his contact and now said was a Czech writer and dead at that. And with each hour Glaushof's chances of promoting himself were slipping away. There had to be some way of getting the information he needed. He was just wondering if there wasn't some truth drug he could use when he caught sight of the scrotal guard on his desk. 'How come you were wearing this?' he asked.

Wilt looked at the cricket box bitterly. The events of the previous evening seemed strangely distant in these new and more frightening circumstances but there had been a moment when he had supposed the box to be in some way responsible for his predicament. If it hadn't come undone, he wouldn't have been in the loo and . . .

'I was having trouble with a hernia,' he said. It seemed a safe explanation.

It wasn't. Glaushof's mind had turned grossly to sex.

Eva's was already there. Ever since she had left Flint she had been obsessed with it. Henry, her Henry, had left her for another woman and an American airbase slut at that. And there could be no doubt about it. Inspector Flint hadn't told her in any nasty way. He'd simply said that Henry had been out to Baconheath. He didn't have to say any more. Henry had been going out every Friday night telling her he was going to the prison and all the time . . . No, she wasn't going to give way. With a sense of terrible purpose Eva drove to Canton Street. Mavis had been right after all and Mavis had known how to deal with Patrick's infidelities. Best of all, as secretary of Mothers Against The Bomb she hated the Americans at Baconheath. Mavis would know what to do.

Mavis did. But first she had to have her gloat. 'You wouldn't listen to me, Eva,' she said. 'I've always said there was something seedy and deceitful about Henry but you would have it that he was a good, faithful husband. Though after what he tried to do to me the other morning I don't see how . . .'

'I'm sorry,' said Eva, 'but I thought that was my fault for going to Dr Kores and giving him that . . . Oh dear, you don't think that's what's made him do this?'

'No, I don't,' said Mavis, 'not for one moment. If he's been deceiving you for six months with this woman, Dr Kores' herbal mixture had nothing to do with it. Of course he'll try to use that as an excuse when it comes to the divorce.'

'But I don't want a divorce,' said Eva, 'I just want to lay my hands on that woman.'

'In that case, if you're going to be a sexual helot—'

'A what?' said Eva, appalled at the word.

'Slave, dear,' said Mavis, recognizing her mistake, 'a serf, a skivvy who's just there to do the cooking and cleaning.'

Eva subsided. All she wanted to be was a good wife and mother and bring the girls up to take their rightful place in the technological world. At the top. 'But I don't even know the beastly woman's name,' she said, getting back to practicalities.

Mavis applied her mind to the problem. 'Bill Paisley might know,' she said finally. 'He's been teaching out there and he's at the Open University with Patrick. I'll give him a ring.'

Eva sat on in the kitchen, sunk in apparent lethargy. But underneath she was tensing herself for the confrontation. No matter what Mavis said no one was going to take Henry away from her. The quads were going to have a father and a proper home and the best education Wilt's salary could provide, never mind what people said or how much her own pride was hurt. Pride was a sin and anyway Henry would pay for it.

She was going over in her mind what she would say to him when Mavis returned triumphantly. 'Bill Paisley knows all about it,' she said. 'Apparently Henry has been teaching a class of women British Culture and it doesn't take much imagination to see what's happened.' She looked at a scrap of paper. 'The Development of British Culture and Institutions, Lecture Hall 9. And the person to contact is the Education Officer. He's given me the number to call. If you want me to, I'll do it for you.'

Eva nodded gratefully. 'I'd only lose my temper and get agitated,' she said, 'and you're so good at organizing things.'

Mavis went back to the hall. For the next ten minutes Eva could hear her talking with increasing vehemence. Then the phone was slammed down.

'The nerve of the man,' Mavis said, storming back into the kitchen pale-faced with anger. 'First they wouldn't put me through to him and it was only when I said I was from the Library Service and wanted to speak to the Education Officer about the free supply of books that I got to him. And then it was "No comment, ma'am. I'm sorry but no comment." '

'But you did ask about Henry?' said Eva who couldn't see what the Library Service or the free supply of books could possibly have to do with her problem.

'Of course I did,' snapped Mavis. 'I said Mr Wilt had suggested I contact him about the Library Service supplying books on English Culture and that's when he clammed up.' She paused thoughtfully. 'You know I could almost swear he sounded scared.'

'Scared? Why should he be scared?'

'I don't know. It was when I mentioned the name "Wilt",' said Mavis. 'But we're going to drive out there now and find out.'

Captain Clodiak sat in Colonel Urwin's office. Unlike the other buildings at Baconheath which had been inherited from the RAF or which resembled prefabricated and sub-economic housing estates, Intelligence Headquarters was strangely at odds with the military nature of the base. It was in fact a large red-brick mansion built at the turn of the century by a retired mining engineer with a taste for theatrical Tudor, and eye to the value of black fen soil and a dislike for the icy winds that blew from Siberia. As a consequence the house had a mock baronial hall, oak-panelled walls and a highly efficient central-heating system and accorded perfectly with Colonel Urwin's sense of irony. It also set him apart from the rest of the base and lent weight to his conviction that military men were dangerous idiots and incapable of speaking E. B. White's English. What was needed was intelligence, brains as well as brawn. Captain Clodiak seemed endowed with both. Colonel Urwin listened to her account of Wilt's capture with very close interest. It was forcing him to reassess the situation. 'So you're saying that he definitely seemed uneasy right through the lecture?' he said.

'No question,' said Clodiak. 'He kept squirming behind the lectern like he was in pain. And his lecture was all over the place. Incoherent. Usually he takes off on tangents but he comes back to the main theme. This time he rambled and then this bandage came down his leg and he went to pieces.'

The Colonel looked across at Captain Fortune. 'Do we know anything about the need for bandages?'

'I've checked with the medics and they don't know. The guy came in gassed and no other sign of injuries.'

'Let's go back from there to previous behaviour. Anything unusual?' Captain Clodiak shook her head.

'Nothing I noticed. He's hetero, got nice manners, doesn't make passes, he's probably got some hang-ups, like he's a depressive. Nothing I'd class as unusual in an Englishman.'

'And yet he was definitely uneasy? And there's no question about the bandage?'

'None,' said Clodiak.

'Thank you for your help,' said the Colonel. 'If anything else comes to mind come back to us.' And having seen her out into the passage he turned to look at the sporting print for inspiration. 'It begins to sound as though someone's been leaning on him,' he said finally.

'You can bet your life Glaushof has,' said Fortune. 'A guy who confesses that easy has to have had some treatment.'

'What's he confessed to? Nothing. Absolute zero.'

'He's admitted being recruited by this Orlov and having a contact man in a Karl Radek. I wouldn't say that was nothing.'

'The one being a dissident who's doing time in Siberia,' said Urwin, 'and Karl Radek was a Czech writer who died in a Gulag in 1940. Not the easiest man to contact.'

'They could be cover names.'

'Could be. Just. I'd choose something less obviously phoney myself. And why Russians? If they're from the Embassy . . . yes, I suppose so. Except that he met quote Orlov unquote in the bus station in Ipford which is outside Soviet embassy staff permitted radius. And where does he meet friend Radek? Every Wednesday afternoon by the bowling green on Midway Park. Every Wednesday same place same time? Out of the question. Our friends from the KGB may play dumb occasionally but not that dumb. Glaushof's been dealt the hand he asked for and that doesn't happen by accident.'

'Leaves Glaushof up shit creek,' said Fortune.

But Colonel Urwin wasn't satisfied. 'Leaves us all there if we don't take care,' he said. 'Let's go through the options again. Wilt's a genuine Russian probe? Out for the reasons given. Someone running a check on our security? Could be some goon in Washington came up with the idea. They've got Shi'ite suicide squads on the brain. Why use an Englishman? They don't tell him his car's being used to make the test more effective. If so why's he panicking during the lecture? That's what I get back to, his behaviour in that lecture hall. That's where I really begin to pick up the scent. Go from there to this "confession" which only an illiterate like Glaushof would believe and the state of Denmark really is beginning to stink to high heaven. And Glaushof's handling it? Not any more Ed. I'm pulling rank.'

'How? He's got a security blanket from the General.'

'That's where I'm pulling rank,' said the Colonel. 'Old B52 may think he commands this base but I'm going to have to disillusion the old warrior. About a great many things.' He pressed a button on the phone. 'Get me Central Intelligence,' he said.

Chapter twenty

'Orders are no one in,' said the guard on the gate, 'I'm sorry but that's how it is.'

'Look,' said Mavis, 'all we've come to do is speak to the officer in charge of Education. His name is Bluejohn and—'

'Still applies, no one in.'

Mavis took a deep breath and tried to keep calm. 'In that case I'd like to speak to him here,' she said. 'If we can't come in, perhaps he'd be good enough to come out.'

'I can check,' said the guard and went into the gatehouse.

'It's no use,' said Eva, looking at the barrier and the high barbed-wire fence. Behind the barrier a series of drums filled with concrete had been laid out on the roadway to form a zigzag through which vehicles could only wind their way very slowly. 'They're not going to tell us anything.'

'And I want to know why,' said Mavis.

'It might help if you weren't wearing that Mothers Against The Bomb badge,' said Eva.

Mavis took it off reluctantly. 'It's utterly disgusting,' she said. 'This is supposed to be a free country and—'

She was interrupted by the appearance of a lieutenant. He stood in the doorway of the gatehouse and looked at them for a moment before walking over. 'I'm sorry ladies,' he said, 'but we're running a security exercise. It's only temporary so if you come back tomorrow maybe . . .'

'Tomorrow is no good,' said Mavis. 'We want to see Mr Bluejohn today. Now if you'll be good enough to telephone him or give him a message, we'd be most obliged.'

'Sure, I can do that,' said the Lieutenant. 'What do you want me to say?'

'Just that Mrs Wilt is here and would like to make some enquiries about her husband, Mr Henry Wilt. He's been teaching a class here on British Culture.'

'Oh him, Mr Wilt? I've heard of him from Captain Clodiak,' said the Lieutenant, expansively. 'She's been attending his course and she says he's real good. No problem, I'll check with the EO.'

'What did I tell you?' said Mavis as he went back into the guardhouse. '*She* says he's real good. I wonder what your Henry's being so good at now.'

Eva hardly heard. Any lingering doubt that Henry had been deceiving her had gone and she was staring through the wire at the drab houses and prefabricated buildings with the feeling that she was looking ahead into the drabness and barren years of her future life. Henry had run off with some woman, perhaps this same Captain Clodiak, and she was going to be left to bring up the quads on her own and be poor and known as a . . . a one-parent family? But there was no family without a father and where was she going to get the money to keep the girls at school? She'd have to go on Social Security and queue up with all those other women . . . She wouldn't. She'd go out to work. She'd do anything to make up for . . . The images in her mind, images of emptiness and of her own fortitude, were interrupted by the return of the Lieutenant.

His manner had changed. 'I'm sorry,' he said abruptly, 'there's been a mistake. I've got to tell you that. Now if you'll move off. We've got this security exercise on.'

'Mistake? What mistake?' said Mavis, reacting to his brusqueness with all her own pent-up hatred. 'You said Mrs Wilt's husband . . .'

'I didn't say anything,' said the Lieutenant and, turning on his heel, ordered the barrier to be lifted to allow a truck to come through.

'Well!' said Mavis furiously. 'Of all the nerve! I've never heard such a bare-faced lie in my life. You heard what he said just a moment ago and now—'

But Eva was moving forward with a new determination. Henry was in the camp. She knew that now. She'd seen the look on the Lieutenant's face, the changed look, the blankness that had been in such contrast to his previous manner, and she'd known. Without thinking she moved into the drabness of life without Henry, into the desert beyond the barrier. She was going to find him and have it out with him. A figure got in her way and tried to stop her. There was a flurry of arms and he fell. Three more men, only figures in her mind, and she was being held and dragged back. Fron somewhere seemingly distant she heard Mavis shout, 'Go limp. Go limp.' Eva went limp and the next moment she was lying on the ground with two men beside her and a third dragging on an arm.

Three minutes later, covered with dust and with the heels of her shoes scuffed and her tights torn, she was dragged beneath the barrier and dumped on the road. And during that time she had uttered no sound other than to pant with exertion. She sat there for a moment and then got to her knees and looked back into the camp with an intensity that was more dangerous in its implications than her brief battle with the guards.

'Lady, you got no right to come in here. You're just asking for trouble,' said the Lieutenant. Eva said nothing. She helped herself up from the kneeling position and walked back to the car.

'Eva dear, are you all right?' asked Mavis.

Eva nodded. 'Just take me home,' she said. For once Mavis had nothing to say. Eva's strength of purpose needed no words.

Wilt's did. With time running out on him, Glaushof had resorted to a new form of interrogation. Unable to use more forceful methods he had decided on what he considered to be the subtle approach. Since it involved the collaboration of Mrs Glaushof clad in garments

Glaushof and possibly even Lieutenant Harah had found so alluring — jackboots, suspender belts and teatless bras figured high in Glaushof's compendium of erotica — Wilt, who had been hustled yet again into a car and driven to the Glaushof's house, found himself suddenly lying on a heart-shaped bed clad in the hospital gown and confronted by an apparition in black, red and several shades of pink. The boots were black, the suspender belt and panties were red and the bra was black fringed with pink. The rest of Mrs Glaushof was, thanks to her frequent use of a sun lamp, mostly brown and definitely drunk. Ever since Glausie, as she had once called him, had bawled her out for sharing her mixed charms with those of Lieutenant Harah she had been hitting the Scotch. She had also hit a bottle of Chanel No 5 or had lathered herself with the stuff. Wilt couldn't decide which. And didn't want to. It was enough to be cloistered (the word seemed singularly inappropriate in the circumstances) in a room with an alcoholic prostitute who told him to call her Mona.

'What?' said Wilt.

'Mona, baby,' said Mrs Glaushof, breathing whisky into his face and fondling his cheek.

'I am not your baby,' said Wilt.

'Oh, but you are, honey. You're just what momma needed.'

'And you're not my mother,' said Wilt, wishing the hell the woman was. She'd have been dead ten years. Mrs Glaushof's hand strayed down his body. 'Shit,' said Wilt. That damned poison was beginning to work again.

'That's better, baby,' Mrs Glaushof whispered as Wilt stiffened. 'You and me's going to have the best of times.'

'You and I,' said Wilt, frantically trying to find some relief in correct syntax, 'and you may consider — ouch!'

'Is baby going to be good to momma now?' asked Mrs Glaushof, sliding her tongue between his lips. Wilt tried to focus on her eyes and found it impossible. He also found it impossible to reply without unclenching his teeth and Mrs Glaushof's reptilian tongue, tasting as it did of alcohol and tobacco, was so busily exploring his gums that any move that might allow it to go any further seemed inadvisable. For one insane moment it crossed his mind to bite the filthy thing but considering what she had in her hand the consequences didn't bear thinking about. Instead he tried to concentrate on less tangible things. What the hell was he doing lying on a quilted bed with a sex-mad woman clutching his balls when only half an hour ago a homicidal maniac had been threatening to plaster his brains on the ceiling with a .38 unless he talked about binary bombs? It didn't make even the vaguest sense but before he could arrive at any sane conclusion Mrs Glaushof had relinquished her probe.

'Baby's steaming me up,' she moaned and promptly bit his neck.

'That's as maybe,' said Wilt, making a mental note to brush his teeth as soon as possible. 'The fact of the matter is that I . . .'

Mrs Glaushof pinched his cheeks. 'Rosebud,' she whimpered.

'Wosebud?' said Wilt with difficulty.

'Your mouth's like a wosebud,' said Mrs Glaushof, digging her nails still further into his cheeks, 'a lovely wosebud.'

'It doethn't tathte like one,' said Wilt and instantly regretted it. Mrs Glaushof had hoisted herself up him and he was facing a nipple fringed with pink lace.

'Suck momma,' said Mrs Glaushof.

'Thod off,' said Wilt. Further comment was stifled by the nipple and Mrs Glaushof's breast which was worming around on his face. As Mrs Glaushof pressed down on him Wilt fought for breath.

In the bathroom next door Glaushof was having the same problem. Staring through the two-way mirror he'd installed to watch Mrs Glaushof putting on the regalia of his fantasies while he bathed, he had begun to regret his new tactics. Subtle they weren't. The bloody woman had clearly gone clean over the top. Glaushof's own patriotism had led him to suppose that his wife would do her duty by cosying up to a Russian spy, but he hadn't expected her to screw the bastard. What was even worse was that she was so obviously enjoying the process.

Glaushof wasn't. Gritting his teeth he stared lividly through the mirror and tried not to think about Lieutenant Harah. It didn't help. In the end, driven by the thought that the Lieutenant had lain on that same bed while Mona gave him the works he was now witnessing, Glaushof charged out of the bathroom. 'For Chrissake,' he yelled from the landing, 'I told you to soften the son of a bitch up, not turn him on.'

'So what's wrong?' said Mrs Glaushof, in the process of changing nipples. 'You think I don't know what I'm doing?'

'I'm buggered if I do,' squawked Wilt, taking the opportunity to get some air. Mrs Glaushof scrambled off him and headed for the door.

'No, I don't,' said Glaushof, 'I think you're—'

'Screw off,' screamed Mrs Glaushof. 'This guy's got a hard-on for me.'

'I can see that,' said Glaushof morosely, 'and if you think that's softening him up you're fucking crazy.'

Mrs Glaushof divested herself of a boot. 'Crazy, am I?' she bawled and hurled the boot at his head with surprising accuracy. 'So what's an old man like you know about crazy? You couldn't get it up if I didn't wear fucking Nazi jackboots.' The second boot hurtled through the door. 'I got to dress up like I'm fucking Hitler in drag before you're anywhere near a man and that ain't saying much. Like this guy's got a prick like the Washington Monument compared to yours.'

'Listen,' shouted Glaushof, 'lay off my prick. That's a commie agent you got in there. He's dangerous!'

'I'll say,' said Mrs Glaushof now liberating herself from the bra. 'Is he ever.'

'No, I'm not,' said Wilt, lurching away from the bed. Mrs Glaushof staggered out of the suspender belt.

'I'm telling you you could get yourself deep in trouble,' Glaushof called. He'd taken refuge from any further missiles round the corner.

'Deep in it is,' Mrs Glaushof shouted back and slammed the door and locked it. Before Wilt could move she had tossed the key out of the window and was heading for him. 'Red Square here I come.'

'I'm not Red Square. I don't know why everyone keeps thinking—' Wilt began, but Mrs Glaushof wasn't into thought. With an agility that took him by complete surprise she threw him back on to the bed and knelt over him.

'Choo choo, baby,' she moaned and this time there was no mistaking her meaning. Faced with this horrible prospect Wilt lived up to Glaushof's warning that he was a dangerous man and sank his teeth into her thigh. In the bathroom Glaushof almost cheered.

'Countermand my orders? Countermand my orders? You're telling me to countermand my orders?' said General Belmonte dropping several decibels in his disbelief. 'We have an enemy agent infiltration situation with possible bombing implications and you're telling me to countermand my orders?'

'Asking, General,' said the Colonel gently. 'I am simply saying that the political consequences could be disastrous.'

'Having my base blown apart by a fucking fanatic is disastrous too and I'm not standing for it,' said the General. 'No, sir, I am not having a body count of thousands of innocent American service personnel and their dependants on my conscience. Major Glaushof's handling of the situation has been absolutely correct. No one knows we've got this bastard and he can beat the shit out of him for all I care. I am not—'

'Correction, sir,' interrupted the Colonel, 'a number of people know we're holding this man. The British police called in enquiring about him. And a woman claiming to be his wife has already had to be ejected at the main gate. Now if you want the media to get hold—'

'The media?' bellowed the General. 'Don't mention that fucking word in my presence. I have given Glaushof a Directive Number One, Toppest Priority, there's to be no media intervention and I am not countermanding that order.'

'I am not suggesting you do. What I am saying is that the way Glaushof is handling the situation we could find ourselves in the middle of a media onslaught that would get world coverage.'

'Shit,' said the General, cringing at the prospect. In his mind's eye he could already see the television cameras mounted on trucks outside the base. There might even be women. He pulled his mind back from this vision of hell. 'What's wrong with the way Glaushof's handling it?'

'Too heavy,' said the Colonel. 'The security clamp-down's drawing attention to the fact that we do have a problem. That's one. We should cool it all off by acting normal. Two is we are presently holding a British subject and if you've given the Major permission to beat the shit out of him I imagine that's just what—'

'I didn't give him permission to do anything like that, I gave him . . . well, I guess I said he could interrogate him and . . .' He paused and tried the comradely approach. 'Hell, Joe, Glaushof may be a shitass but he has got him to confess he's a commie agent. You've got to hand it to him.'

'That confession's a dummy. I've checked it out and had negative affirmation,' said the Colonel, lapsing into the General's jargon to soften the blow.

'Negative affirmation,' said the General, evidently impressed. 'That's serious. I had no idea.'

'Exactly, sir. That's why I'm asking for an immediate de-escalation of the security directive intelligencewise. I also want this man Wilt handed over to my authority for proper questioning.'

General Belmonte considered the request almost rationally. 'If he isn't Moscow-based, what is he?'

'That's what Central Intelligence intend to find out,' said the Colonel.

Ten minutes later Colonel Urwin left the Airbase Control Centre well satisfied. The General had ordered a security stand-down and Glaushof had been relieved of his custody right to the prisoner.

Theoretically.

In practice getting Wilt out of the Glaushof's house proved rather more awkward. Having visited the Security building and learnt that Wilt had been taken off, still apparently unharmed, to be interrogated at Glaushof's house, the Colonel had driven there with two Sergeants only to realize that 'unharmed' no longer applied. Ghastly noises were emanating from upstairs.

'Sounds like someone's having themselves a whole heap of fun,' said one of the Sergeants as Mrs Glaushof threatened to castrate some horny bastard just as soon as she stopped bleeding to death and why didn't some other cocksucker open the fucking door so she could get out. In the background Glaushof could be heard telling her plaintively to keep her cool, he'd get the door undone, she didn't have to shoot the lock off and would she stop loading that fucking revolver.

Mrs Glaushof replied she didn't intend shooting the fucking lock off, she had other fucking objects in fucking mind, like him and that fucking commie agent who'd bit her and they weren't going to live to tell the tale, not once she'd got that magazine fucking loaded and why didn't shells go in the way they were fucking supposed to? For an instant Wilt's face appeared at the window, only to vanish as a bedside lamp complete with a huge lampshade smashed through the glass and hung upside-down from its cord.

Colonel Urwin studied the thing with horror. Mrs Glaushof's language was foul enough but the shade, covered with a collage of sado-masochistic images cut from magazines, pictures of kittens in baskets and puppy dogs, not to mention several crimson hearts and flowers, was aesthetically so disgusting that it almost unnerved him.

The action had the opposite effect on Glaushof. Less concerned about the likelihood of his drunken wife murdering a Russian spy with a .38 she had been trying to load with what he hoped was 9 mm. ammunition than with the prospect of having his entire house torn apart and its peculiar contents revealed to the neighbours he left the comparative safety of the bathroom and charged the bedroom door. His timing was bad. Having foiled any hope Wilt might have held of escaping by the window Mrs Glaushof had finally loaded the revolver and pulled the trigger. The shot passed through the door, Glaushof's shoulder, and one of the tubes in the hamster's complicated plastic burrow on the staircase wall before embedding in the tufted carpet.

'Jesus Christ,' screamed Glaushof, 'you meant it! You really meant it.'

'What's that?' said Mrs Glaushof, almost as surprised by the consequences of simply pulling the trigger, though definitely less concerned. 'What you say?'

'Oh God,' moaned Glaushof, now slumped to the floor.

'You think I can't shoot the fucking lock off?' Mrs Glaushof enquired. 'You think that? You think I can't?'

'No,' yelled Glaushof. 'No, I don't think that. Jesus, I'm dying.'

'Hypochondriac,' Mrs Glaushof shouted back, evidently paying off an old domestic score. 'Stand back, I'm coming out.'

'For fuck's sake,' squealed Glaushof, eyeing the hole she'd already made in the door near one of the hinges, 'don't aim at the lock.'

'Why not?' Mrs Glaushof demanded.

It wasn't a question Glaushof was prepared to answer. In one final attempt to escape the consequences of her next fusillade he rolled sideways and hit the stairs. By the time he'd crashed to the bottom even Mrs Glaushof was concerned.

'Are you OK, Glausie?' she asked and simultaneously pulled the trigger. As the second shot punched a hole in a Liberace-style bean bag, Wilt acted. In the knowledge that her next shot might possibly do to him what it had already done to Glaushof and the bag, he picked up a pink furbelowed stool and slammed it down on her head.

'Macho man,' grunted Mrs Glaushof, inappropriate to the end, and slid to the floor. For a moment Wilt hesitated. If Glaushof were still alive, and by the sound of breaking glass downstairs it seemed as though he was, there was no point in trying to break the door down. Wilt crossed to the window.

'Freeze!' shouted a man down below. Wilt froze. He was staring down at five uniformed men crouched behind handguns. And this time there was no question what they were aiming at.

Chapter twenty-one

'Logic dictates,' said Mr Gosdyke, 'that we should look at this problem rationally. Now I know that's difficult but until we have definite proof that your husband is being held at Baconheath against his will there really isn't any legal action we can take. You do see that?'

Eva gazed into the solicitor's face and saw only that she was wasting time. It had been Mavis' idea that she should consult Mr Gosdyke before she did anything hasty. Eva knew what 'hasty' meant. It meant being afraid of taking real risks and doing something effective.

'After all,' Mavis had said, as they drove back, 'you may be able to apply for a court order or habeas corpus or something. It's best to find out.'

But she didn't need to find out. She'd known all along that Mr Gosdyke wouldn't believe her and would talk about proof and logic. As if life was logical. Eva didn't even know what the word meant, except that it always produced in her mind the image of a railway line with a train running along it with no way of getting off it and going across fields and open countryside like a horse. And anyway when you did reach a station you still had to walk to wherever you really wanted to go. That wasn't the way life worked or people behaved when things were really desperate. It wasn't even the way the Law worked with people being sent to prison when they were old and absent-minded like Mrs Reeman who had walked out of the supermarket without paying for a jar of pickled onions and she never ate pickles. Eva knew that because she'd helped with Meals on Wheels and the old lady had said she never touched vinegar. No, the real reason had been that she'd had a pekinese called Pickles and he'd died a month before. But the Law hadn't seen that, any more than Mr Gosdyke could understand that she already had the proof that Henry was in the airbase because he hadn't been there when the officer's manner had changed so suddenly.

'So there's nothing you can do?' she said and got up.

'Not unless we can obtain proof that your husband really is being held against . . .' But Eva was already through the door and had cut out the sounds of those ineffectual words. She went down the stairs and out into the street and found Mavis waiting for her in the Mombasa Coffee House.

'Well, did he have any advice?' asked Mavis.

'No,' said Eva, 'he just said there was nothing he could do without proof.'

'Perhaps Henry'll telephone you tonight. Now that he knows you've been out there and they must have told him . . .'

Eva shook her head. 'Why should they have told him?'

'Look, Eva, I've been thinking,' said Mavis, 'Henry's been deceiving you for six months. Now I know what you're going to say but you can't get away from it.'

'He hasn't been deceiving me the way you mean,' said Eva. 'I know that.'

Mavis sighed. It was so difficult to make Eva understand that men were all the same, even a sexually subnormal one

226

like Wilt. 'He's been going out to Baconheath every Friday evening and all that time he's been telling you he's got this prison job. You've got to admit that, haven't you?'

'I suppose so,' said Eva, and ordered tea. She wasn't in the mood for anything foreign like coffee. Americans drank coffee.

'The question you have to ask yourself is why didn't he tell you where he was going?'

'Because he didn't want me to know,' said Eva.

'And why didn't he want you to know?'

Eva said nothing.

'Because he was doing something you wouldn't like. And we all know what men don't think their wives would like to know, don't we?'

'I know Henry,' said Eva.

'Of course you do but we none of us know what even those closest to us are really like.'

'You knew all about Patrick's chasing other women,' said Eva, fighting back. 'You were always going on about his being unfaithful. That's why you got those steroid pills from that beastly Dr Kores and now all he does is sit in front of the telly.'

'Yes,' said Mavis, cursing herself for ever mentioning the fact. 'All right, but you said Henry was undersexed. Anyway that only goes to prove my point. I don't know what Dr Kores put in the mixture she gave you . . .'

'Flies,' said Eva.

'Flies?'

'Spanish flies. That's what Henry called them. He said they could have killed him.'

'But they didn't,' said Mavis. 'What I'm trying to get across is that the reason he wasn't performing adequately may have been—'

'He's not a dog, you know,' said Eva.

'What's that got to do with it?'

'Performing. You talk as though he were something in a circus.'

'You know perfectly well what I meant.'

227

They were interrupted by the arrival of the tea. 'All I'm saying,' Mavis continued when the waitress had left, 'is that what you took for Henry's being undersexed—'

'I said he wasn't very active. That's what I said,' said Eva.

Mavis stirred her coffee and tried to keep calm. 'He may not have wanted you, dear,' she said finally, 'because for the last six months he has been spending every Friday night in bed with some American servicewoman at that airbase. That's what I've been trying to tell you.'

'If that had been the case,' said Eva, bridling, 'I don't see how he could have come home at ten thirty, not if he was teaching as well. He never left the house until nearly seven and it takes at least three-quarters of an hour to drive out there. Two three-quarters make . . .'

'One and a half hours,' snapped Mavis. 'That doesn't prove anything. He could have had a class of one.'

'Of one?'

'One person, Eva dear.'

'They're not allowed to have only one person in a class,' said Eva. 'Not at the Tech. If they don't have ten . . .'

'Well, Baconheath may be different,' said Mavis, 'and anyway they fiddle these things. My bet is that Henry's teaching consisted of taking off his clothes and—'

'Which just shows how much you know about him,' interrupted Eva. 'Henry taking his clothes off in front of another woman! That'll be the day. He's too shy.'

'Shy?' said Mavis, and was about to say that he hadn't been so shy with her the other morning. But the dangerous look had come back on to Eva's face and she thought better of it. It was still there ten minutes later when they went out to car park to fetch the quads from school.

'Okay, let's take it from there,' said Colonel Urwin. 'You say you didn't shoot Major Glaushof.'

'Of course I didn't,' said Wilt. 'What would I do a thing like that for? She was trying to blow the lock off the door.'

'That's not the version I've got here,' said the Colonel,

referring to a file on the desk in front of him, 'according to which you attempted to rape Mrs Glaushof orally and when she refused to co-operate you bit her leg. Major Glaushof tried to intervene by breaking the door down and you shot him through it.'

'Rape her orally?' said Wilt, 'What the hell does that mean?'

'I prefer not to think,' said the Colonel with a shudder.

'Listen,' said Wilt, 'if anyone was being raped orally I was. I don't know if you've ever been in close proximity to that woman's muff but I have and I can tell you the only way out was to bite the bitch.'

Colonel Urwin tried to erase this awful image. His security classification rated him 'highly heterosexual' but there were limits and Mrs Glaushof's muff was unquestionably off them. 'That doesn't exactly gel with your statement that she was attempting to escape from the room by blowing the lock off with a .38, does it? Would you mind explaining what she was doing that for?'

'I told you she was trying . . . well, I've told you what she was trying to do and as a way out I bit her. That's when she got mad and went for the gun.'

'It still doesn't explain why the door was locked and she had to blow the lock. Are you saying Major Glaushof had locked you in?'

'She'd thrown the fucking key out of the window,' said Wilt wearily, 'and if you don't believe me go and look for the thing outside.'

'Because she found you so sexually desirable she wanted to rape you . . . orally?' said the Colonel.

'Because she was drunk.'

Colonel Urwin got up and consulted the sporting print for inspiration. It wasn't easy to find. About the only thing that rang true was that Glaushof's ghastly wife had been drunk. 'What I still don't understand is why you were there in the first place.'

'You think I do?' said Wilt. 'I came out here on Friday night to give a lecture and the next thing I know I've been gassed, injected, dressed up like something that's going to be operated on, driven all over the place with a fucking blanket over my head and asked insane questions about radio transformers in my car—'

'Transmitters,' said the Colonel.

'Whatever,' said Wilt. 'And told if I don't confess to being a Russian spy or a fanatical raving Shi'ite Muslim I'm going to have my brains plaster all over the ceiling. And that's just for starters. After that I'm in a horrible bedroom with a woman dressed up like a prostitute who hurls keys out of the window and shoves her dugs in my mouth and then threatens to suffocate me with her cunt. And you're asking me for an explanation?' He sank back in his chair and sighed hopelessly.

'That still doesn't—'

'Oh, for God's sake,' said Wilt. 'If you want insanity explained go and ask that homicidal maniac Major. I've had a bellyful.'

The Colonel got up and went out the door. 'What do you make of him?' he asked Captain Fortune who had been sitting with a technician recording the interview.

'I've got to say he convinces me,' said Fortune. 'That Mona Glaushof would screw a fucking skunk if there weren't nothing better to hand.'

'I'll say,' said the technician. 'She's been humping Lieutenant Harah like he's a human vibrator. The guy's been taking mega-vitamins to keep up.'

'Dear God,' said the Colonel, 'and Glaushof's in charge of security. What's he doing letting Mona Messalina loose on this one for?'

'Got a two-way mirror in the bathroom,' said the Captain. 'Could be he gets his thrills through it.'

'A two-way mirror in the bathroom? The bastard's got to be sick watching his wife screwing a guy he thinks is a Russian agent.'

'Maybe he thought the Russkies have got a different technique. Something he could learn,' said the technician.

'I want a check run on that key outside the house,' said the Colonel and went out into the passage.

'Well?' he asked.

'Nothing fits,' said the Captain. 'That Corporal in Electronics is no fool. He's certain the equipment he saw in the car was British classified. Definitely non-Russian. No record of it ever being used by anyone else.'

'Are you suggesting he was under surveillance by British Security?'

'It's a possibility.'

'It would be if he hadn't demanded MI5 attendance the moment Glaushof started putting the heat on,' said Urwin. 'Have you ever heard of a Moscow agent calling for British Intelligence when he's been blown? I haven't.'

'So we go back to your theory that the Brits were running an exercise on base security systems. About the only thing that adds up.'

'Nothing adds up for me. If it had been a routine check they'd have come to his rescue by now. And why has he clammed? No point in sweating it out. Against that we've got those transmitters and the fact that Clodiak says he was nervous and agitated all through the lecture. That indicates he's no expert and I don't believe he ever knew his car was tagged. Where's the sense?'

'You want me to question him?' asked the Captain.

'No, I'll go on. Just keep the tape running. We're going to need some help in this.'

He went back into his office and found Wilt lying on the couch fast asleep. 'Just a few more questions, Mr Wilt,' he said. Wilt stared blearily up at him and sat up.

'What questions?'

The Colonel took a bottle from a cupboard. 'Care for a Scotch?'

'I'd care to go home,' said Wilt.

Chapter twenty-two

In Ipford Police Station Inspector Flint was savouring his triumph. 'It's all there, sir,' he told the Superintendent, indicating a pile of folders on the desk. 'And it's local. Swannell made the contact on a skiing trip to Switzerland. Nice clean place, Switzerland, and of course he says he was the one who was approached by this Italian. Threatened him, he says, and of course our Clive's a nervous bloke as you know.'

'Could have fooled me,' said the Superintendent. 'We nearly did the bugger for attempted murder three years ago. Got away because the bloke he scarred wouldn't press charges.'

'I was being ironical, sir,' said Flint. 'Just saying his story for him.'

'Go on. How did it work?'

'Simple really,' continued Flint, 'nothing too complicated. First they had to have a courier who didn't know what he was doing. So they put the frighteners on Ted Lingon. Threaten him with a nitric acid facial if he doesn't co-operate with his coach tours to the continent. Or so he claims. Anyway he's got a regular run to the Black Forest with overnight stops. The stuff's loaded aboard at Heidelberg without the driver knowing, comes through to Ostend and the night ferry to Dover and halfway across one of the crew dumps the muck over the side. Always on the night run so no one sees. Picked up by a friend of Annie Mosgrave's who happens to be in his floating gin palace nearby and . . .'

'Hang on a minute,' said the Superintendent. 'How the hell would anyone find a package of heroin in mid-Channel at night?'

'The same way Hodge has been keeping tabs on Wilt. The muck's in a bloody great suitcase with buoyancy and a radio signal that comes on the moment it hits the water.

Bloke beams in on it, hauls it aboard and brings it round to a marker buoy in the Estuary and leaves it there for a frogman to pick up when the gin palace is back in the marina.'

'Seems a risky way of going about things,' said the Superintendent, 'I wouldn't trust tides and currents with that amount of money involved.'

'Oh, they did enough practice runs to feel safe and tying it to the chain of the marker buoy made that part easy,' said Flint. 'And after that it was split three ways with the Hong Kong Charlies handling the London end and Roddie Eaton fixing this area and Edinburgh.'

The Superintendent studied his fingernails and considered the implications of Flint's discoveries. On the whole they seemed entirely satisfactory, but he had a nasty feeling that the Inspector's methods might not look too good in court. In fact it was best not to dwell on them. Defending counsel could be relied on to spell them out in detail to the jury. Threats to prisoners in gaol, murder charges that were never brought . . . On the other hand if Flint had succeeded, that idiot Hodge would be scuppered. That was worth a great many risks.

'Are you quite certain Swannell and the rest haven't been spinning you a yarn?' he asked. 'I mean I'm not doubting you or anything but if we go ahead now and they retract those statements in court, which they will do—'

'I'm not relying on their statements,' said Flint. 'There's hard evidence. I think when the search warrants are issued we'll find enough heroin and Embalming Fluid on their premises and clothing to satisfy Forensic. They've got to have spilt some when they were splitting the packages, haven't they?'

The Superintendent didn't answer. There were some things he preferred not to know and Flint's actions were too dubious for comfort. Still if the Inspector had broken a drug ring the Chief Constable and the Home Secretary would be well satisfied, and with crime organized the way it was nowadays there was no point in being too scrupulous. 'All right,' he said finally. 'I'll apply for the warrants.'

'Thank you, sir,' said Flint and turned to go. But the Superintendent stopped him.

'About Inspector Hodge,' he said. 'I take it he's been following a different line of investigation.'

'American airbases,' said Flint. 'He's got it into his head that's where the stuff's been coming in.'

'In that case we'd better call him off.'

But Flint had other plans in mind. 'If I might make a suggestion, sir,' he said, 'the fact that the Drug Squad is pointing in the wrong direction has its advantages. I mean Hodge has drawn attention away from our investigations and it would be a pity to put up a warning signal until we've made our arrests. In fact it might help to encourage him a bit.'

The Superintendent looked at him doubtfully. The last thing the head of the Drug Squad needed was encouraging. He was demented enough already. On the other hand . . .

'And how exactly is he to be encouraged?' he asked.

'I suppose you could say the Chief Constable was looking for an early arrest,' said Flint. 'It's the truth after all.'

'I suppose there's that to it,' said the Superintendent wearily. 'All right, but you'd better be right with your own cases.'

'I will be, sir,' said Flint and left the room. He went down to the car pool where Sergeant Yates was waiting.

'The warrants are all settled,' he said. 'Have you got the stuff?'

Sergeant Yates nodded and indicated a plastic packet on the back seat. 'Couldn't get a lot,' he said, 'Runkie reckoned we'd no right to it. I had to tell him it was needed for a lab check.'

'Which it will be,' said Flint. 'And it's all the same batch?'

'It's that all right.'

234

'No problem then,' said Flint as they drove out, 'we'll look at Lingon's coach first and then Swannell's boat and the back garden and leave enough for Forensic to pick up.'

'What about Roddie Eaton?'

Flint took a pair of cotton gloves from his pocket. 'I thought we'd leave these in his dustbin,' he said. 'We'll used them on the coach first. No need to bother going to Annie's. There will be something there anyway, and besides, the rest of them will try to get lighter sentences by pointing the finger at her. All we need is three of them as guilty as sin and facing twenty years and they'll drop everyone else in the shit with them.'

'Bloody awful way of going about police work,' said Yates after a pause. 'Planting evidence and all.'

'Oh, I don't know,' said Flint. 'We know they're traffickers, they know it, and all we're doing is giving them a bit of their own medicine. Homeopathic, I call it.'

That wasn't the way Inspector Hodge would have described his work. His obsessive interest in the Wilts' extraordinary domestic activities had been alarmingly aggravated by the noises coming from the listening devices installed in the roof space. The quads were to blame. Driven up to their rooms by Eva who wanted them out of the way so that she could think what to do about Henry, they had taken revenge by playing long-playing records of Heavy Metal at one hundred watts per channel. From where Hodge and Runk sat in the van it sounded as though 45 Oakhurst Avenue was being blown apart by an endless series of rythmic explosions.

'What the fuck's wrong with those bugs?' Hodge squealed, dragging the earphones from his head.

'Nothing,' shouted the operator. 'They're highly sensitive . . .'

'So am I,' yelled Hodge, stubbing his little finger into his ear in an attempt to get his hearing back, 'and something's definitely wrong.'

'They're just picking up one hell of a lot of interference. Could be any number of things produce that effect.'

'Like a fifty-megaton rock concert,' said Runk. 'Bloody woman must be stone deaf.'

'Like hell,' said Hodge. 'This is deliberate. They must have scanned the place and spotted they were being bugged. And turn that damned thing off. I can't hear myself think.'

'Never known anyone who could,' said Runk. 'Thinking doesn't make a sound. It's an—'

'Shut up,' yelled Hodge, who didn't need a lecture on the workings of the brain. For the next twenty minutes he sat in comparative silence trying to figure out his next move. At every stage of his campaign he had been out-manoeuvred and all because he hadn't been given the authority and back-up he needed. And now the Superintendent had sent a message demanding an immediate arrest. Hodge had countered with a request for a search warrant and had been answered with a vague remark that the matter would be considered. Which meant, of course, that he'd never get that warrant. He was on the point of returning to the station and demanding the right to raid the house when Sergeant Runk interrupted his train of thought.

'That jam session's stopped,' he said. 'Coming through nice and quiet.'

Hodge grabbed the earphones and listened. Apart from a rattling sound he couldn't identify (but which came in fact from Emmeline's hamster Percival getting some exercise in her wheel) the house in Oakhurst Avenue was silent. Odd. The place hadn't ever been silent before when the Wilts were at home. 'The car still outside?' he asked the technician.

The man turned to the car monitor. 'Nothing coming through,' he muttered and swung the aerial. 'They must have been using that din to dismantle the transmitters.'

Behind him Inspector Hodge verged on apoplexy.

'Jesus, you moron,' he yelled, 'you mean you haven't been checking that fucking car all this time?'

'What do you think I am? A bleeding octopus with ears?' the radio man shouted back. 'First I have to cope with all those stupid bugs you laced the house with and at the same time I've got two direction indicators to listen in to. And what's more I'm not a moron.'

But before Hodge could get into a real fight Sergeant Runk had intervened. 'I'm getting a faint signal from the car,' he said. 'Must be ten miles away.'

'Where?' yelled Hodge.

'East, as before,' said Runk. 'They're heading back to Baconheath.'

'Then get after them,' Hodge shouted, 'this time the shit isn't going to get back home before I've nabbed him. I'll seal that fucking base off if it's the last thing I do.'

Oblivious of the ill-feeling building up behind her Eva drove steadily towards the airbase. She had no conscious plan, only the determination to force the truth, and Wilt, out of somebody even if that meant setting fire to the car or lying naked in the roadway outside the gates. Anything to gain publicity. And for once Mavis had agreed with her and been helpful too. She had organized a group of Mothers Against The Bomb, some of whom were in fact grandmothers, had hired a coach and had telephoned all the London papers and BBC and Fenland Television to ensure maximum coverage for the demonstration.

'It gives us an opportunity to focus the world's attention on the seductive nature of capitalist military-industrial world domination,' she had said, leaving Eva with only the vaguest idea what she meant but with the distinct feeling that Wilt was the 'It' at the beginning of the sentence. Not that Eva cared what anyone said; it was what they did that counted. And Mavis's demonstration would help divert attention away from her own efforts to get into the camp. Or, if she failed to do that, she would see to it that the name Henry Wilt reached the millions of viewers who watched the news that night.

'Now I want you all to behave nicely,' she told the quads as they drove up to the camp gates. 'Just do what Mummy tells you and everything is going to be all right.'

'It isn't going to be all right if Daddy's been staying with an American lady,' said Josephine.

'Fucking,' said Penelope, 'not staying with.'

Eva braked sharply. 'Who said that?' she demanded, turning a livid face on the quads in the back seat.

'Mavis Motty did,' said Penelope. 'She's always going on about fucking.'

Eva took a deep breath. There were times when the quads' language, so carefully nurtured towards mature self-expression at the School for the Mentally Gifted, seemed appallingly inappropriate. And this was one of those times. 'I don't care what Mavis said,' she declared, 'and anyway it isn't like that. Your father has simply been stupid again. We don't know what's happened to him. That's why we've come here. Now you behave yourselves and—'

'If we don't know what's happened to him how do you know he's been stupid?' asked Samantha, who had always been hot on logic.

'Shut up,' said Eva and started the car again.

Behind her the quads silently assumed the guise of four nice little girls. It was misleading. As usual they had prepared themselves for the expedition with alarming ingenuity. Emmeline had armed herself with several hatpins that had once belonged to Grandma Wilt; Penelope had filled two bicycle pumps with ammonia and sealed the ends with chewing-gum; Samantha had broken into all their piggy banks and had then bought every tin of pepper she could from a perplexed green-grocer; while Josephine had taken several of Eva's largest and most pointed Sabatier knives from the magnet board in the kitchen. In short the quads were happily looking forward to disabling as many airbase guards as they could and were only afraid that the affair would pass off peacefully. In the event their fears were almost realized.

As they stopped at the gatehouse and were approached by a sentry there were none of those signs of preparedness that had been so obvious the day before. In an effort to maintain that everything was normal and in a 'No Panic Situation' Colonel Urwin had ordered the removal of the concrete blocks in the roadway and had instilled a fresh sense of politeness in the officer in charge of entry to civilian quarters. A large Englishwoman with permed hair and a carload of small girls didn't seem to pose any threat to USAAF security.

'If you'll just pull over there I'll call up the Education Office for you,' he told Eva who had decided not to mention Captain Clodiak this time. Eva drove past the barrier and parked. This was proving much easier than she had expected. In fact for a moment she doubted her judgement. Perhaps Henry wasn't there after all and she had made some terrible mistake. The notion didn't last long. Once again the Wilts' Escort had signalled its presence and Eva was just telling the quads that everything was going to be all right when the Lieutenant appeared from the guardhouse with two armed sentries. 'Pardon me, ma'am,' he said, 'but I'd be glad if you'd step over to the office.'

'What for?' asked Eva.

'Just a routine matter.'

For a moment Eva gazed blankly up at his face and tried to think. She had steeled herself for a confrontation and words like 'stepping over to the office' and 'a routine matter' were somehow threateningly bland. All the same she opened the door and got out.

'And the children too,' said the Lieutenant. 'Everybody out of there.'

'Don't you touch my daughters,' said Eva, now thoroughly alarmed. It was obvious she had been tricked into the base. But this was the opportunity the quads had been waiting for. As the Lieutenant reached for the door

239

handle Penelope poked the end of the bicycle pump through the window and Josephine pointed a carving knife. It was Eva's action that saved him from the knife. She wrenched at his arm and at the same time the ammonia hit him. As the stuff wafted up from his soaked jacket and the two sentries hurled themselves on Eva, the Lieutenant gasped for air and dashed for the guard-house vaguely aware of the sound of girlish laughter behind him. It sounded demonic to him. Half suffocated he stumbled into the office and pressed the Alert button.

'It rather sounds as if we have another problem,' said Colonel Urwin as sirens wailed over the base.

'Don't include me,' said Wilt. 'I've got problems of my own like trying to explain to my wife what the hell's been happening to me the last God knows how many days.'

But the Colonel was on the phone to the guardhouse. For a moment he listened and then turned to Wilt. 'Your wife a fat woman with four daughters?'

'You could put it like that, I suppose,' said Wilt, 'though frankly I'd leave the "fat" bit out if you meet her. Why?'

'Because that's what just hit the main gate,' said the Colonel and went back to the phone. 'Hold everything . . . What do you mean you can't? She's not . . . Jesus . . . Okay, okay. And cut those fucking sirens.' There was a pause and the Colonel held the phone away from his ear and stared at Wilt. Eva's shouted demands were clearly audible now that the sirens had stopped.

'Give me back my husband,' she yelled, 'and take your filthy paws off me . . . If you go anywhere near those children . . .' The Colonel put the phone down.

'Very determined woman, is Eva,' said Wilt by way of explanation.

'So I've gathered,' said the Colonel, 'and what I want to know is what she's doing here.'

'By the sounds of things, looking for me.'

'Only you told us she didn't know you were here. So how come she's out there fighting mad and . . .' He stopped. Captain Fortune had entered the room.

'I think you ought to know the General's on the line,' he announced. 'Wants to know what's going on.'

'And he thinks *I* know?' said the Colonel.

'Well, someone has to.'

'Like him,' said the Colonel, indicating Wilt, 'and he's not saying.'

'Only because I haven't a clue,' said Wilt with increasing confidence, 'and without wishing to be unnecessarily didactic I'd say no one in the whole wide world knows what the hell's going on anywhere. Half the world's population is starving and the overfed half have a fucking death-wish, and—'

'Oh for Chrissake,' said the Colonel, and came to a sudden decision. 'We're taking this bastard out. Now.'

But Wilt was on his feet. He had watched too many American movies not to have ambivalent feelings about being 'taken out'. 'Oh no you're not,' he said backing up against the wall. 'And you can cut the bastard abuse too. I didn't do anything to start this fucking madhouse and I've got my family to think about.'

Colonel Urwin looked at the sporting print hopelessly. He'd been right to suspect the British of having hidden depths he would never understand. No wonder the French spoke of 'perfidious Albion'. The bastards would always behave in ways one least expected. In the meantime he had to produce some explanation that would satisfy the General. 'Just say we've got a purely domestic problem on our hands,' he told the Captain, 'and rout Glaushof out. Base security is his baby.'

But before the Captain could leave the room Wilt had reacted again. 'You let that maniac anywhere near my kids and someone's going to get hurt,' he shouted, 'I'm not having them gassed like I was.'

'In that case you better exercise some parental control yourself,' said the Colonel grimly, and headed for the door.

Chapter twenty-three

By the time they reached the parking lot by the gates it was clear that the situation had deteriorated. In an entirely unnecessary effort to rescue their mother from the sentries – Eva had already felled one of the men with a knee-jerk to the groin she had learnt at a Rape Resistance Evening Class – the quads had abandoned the Wilts' car and, by dusting the second sentry with pepper, had put him out of action. After that they had occupied the gatehouse itself and were now holding the Lieutenant hostage inside. Since he had torn off his uniform to escape the ammonia fumes and the quads had armed themselves with his revolver and that of the sentry writhing on the ground outside, they had been able to isolate the guardhouse even more effectively by threatening the driver of an oil tanker which had made the mistake of arriving at the barrier and forcing him to offload several hundred gallons of fuel oil on to the roadway before driving tentatively into the base.

Even Eva had been appalled at the result. As the stuff swilled across the tarmac Lieutenant Harah had driven up rather too hurriedly in a jeep and had tried to brake. The jeep was now enmeshed in the perimeter fence and Lieutenant Harah, having crawled from it, was calling for reinforcements. 'We have a real penetration situation here,' he bawled into his walkie-talkie. 'A bunch of leftist terrorists have taken over the guardhouse.'

'They're not terrorists, they're just little girls,' Eva shouted from inside, only to have her words drowned by the Alert siren which Samantha had activated.

Outside in the roadway Mavis Mottram's busload of Mothers Against The Bomb had gathered in a line and had handcuffed themselves together before padlocking the ends of the line to the fence on either side of the gateway and were dancing something approximate to the can-can and chanting 'End the arms race, save the human' in full view of three TV cameras and a dozen photographers. Above their heads an enormous and remarkable balloon, shaped and veined like an erect penis, swung slowly in the breeze exposing the rather confusing messages, 'Wombs Not Tombs' and 'Screw Cruise Not Us' painted on opposite sides. As Wilt and Colonel Urwin watched, the balloon, evidently force-fed by a hydrogen cylinder, shed its few human pretensions in the shape of an enormous plastic foreskin and turned itself into a gigantic rocket.

'This is going to kill old B52,' muttered the Colonel who had until then been enjoying the spectacle of Lieutenant Harah covered in oil and trying to get to his feet. 'And I can't see the President liking it too much either. That fucking phallus has got to hit prime time with all those cameras.'

A fire truck shot round the corner past them and in a jeep behind it came Major Glaushof, his right arm in a sling and his face the colour of putty.

'Jesus,' said Captain Fortune, 'if that fire truck hits the oil we're going to have a body count of thirty of the Mothers.'

But the truck had stopped and men were deploying hoses. Behind them and the human chain Inspector Hodge and Sergeant Runk had driven up and were staring wildly about them. In front the women still kicked up their legs and chanted, the firemen had begun to spray foam on to the oil and Lieutenant Harah, and Glaushof was gesticulating with one hand to a troop of Anti Perimeter Penetration Squad men who had formed up as near the Mothers Against The Bomb as they could get and were preparing to discharge canisters of Agent Incapacitating at them.

'For fuck's sake hold it,' yelled Glaushof but his words were drowned out by the Alert Siren. As the canisters dropped into the roadway at the feet of the human chain Colonel Urwin shut his eyes. He knew now that Glaushof was a doomed man, but his own career was in jeopardy. 'We've got to get those fucking kids out of there before the cameras start playing on them,' he bawled at Captain Fortune. 'Go in and get them.'

The Captain looked at the foam, the oil and the drifting gas. Already a number of MABs had dropped to the ground and Samantha had added to the hazards of approaching the guardhouse by accidentally-on-purpose firing a revolver through one of the windows, an action which had drawn answering fire from Glaushof's APP Squad.

'You think I'm risking my life . . .' the Captain began but it was Wilt who took the initiative. Wading through the oil and foam he made it to the guardhouse and presently four small girls and a large woman came out with him. Hodge didn't see them. Like the cameramen his attention was elsewhere, but unlike them he was no longer interested in the disaster taking place at the gates. A canister of AI had persuaded him to leave the scene as quickly as possible. It had also made it difficult to drive. As the police van backed into the bus and then shot forward and ricocheted off a cameraman's car before sliding off the road and onto its side, he had a moment of understanding. Inspector Flint hadn't been such an old fool after all. Anyone who tangled with the Wilt family had to come off worst.

Colonel Urwin shared his feelings. 'We're going to get you out of here in a chopper,' he told Wilt as more women slumped across the gateway.

'And what about my car?' said Wilt. 'If you think I'm leaving . . .'

But his protest was shouted down by the quads. And Eva.

'We want to go up in a helicopter,' they squealed in unison.

'Just take me away from all this,' said Eva.

Ten minutes later Wilt looked down from a thousand

feet at the pattern of runways and roads, buildings and bunkers and at the tiny group of women being carried from the gate to waiting ambulances. For the first time he felt some sympathy for Mavis Mottram. For all her faults she had been right to pit herself against the banal enormity of the airbase. The place had all the characteristics of a potential extermination camp. True, nobody was being herded into gas chambers and there was no smoke rising from crematoria. But the blind obedience to orders was there, instilled in Glaushof and even in Colonel Urwin. Everyone in fact, except Mavis Mottram and the human chain of women at the gate. The others would all obey orders if the time came and the real holocaust would begin. And this time there would be no liberators, no successive generations to erect memorials to the dead or learn lessons from past horrors. There would be only silence. The wind and the sea the only voices left. And it was the same in Russia and the occupied countries of Eastern Europe. Worse. There Mavis Mottram was already silenced, confined to a prison or a psychiatric ward because she was idiosyncratically sane. No TV cameras or photographers depicted the new death camps. And twenty million Russians had died to make their country safe from genocide, only to have Stalin's successors too afraid of their own people to allow them to discuss the alternatives to building more machines to wipe life off the face of the earth.

It was all insane, childish and bestial. But above all it was banal. As banal as the Tech and Dr Mayfield's empire-building and the Principal's concern to keep his own job and avoid unfavourable publicity, never mind what the staff thought or the students would have preferred to learn. Which was what he was going back to. In fact nothing had changed. Eva would go on with her wild enthusiasms; the quads might even grow up to be civilized human beings. Wilt rather doubted it. Civilized human beings were a myth, legendary creatures who existed only in writers' imaginations, their foibles and faults expurgated and their occasional self-sacrifices magnified. With the quads that was impossible. The best that could be hoped was that they would remain as independent and uncomfortably non-conforming as they were now. And at least they were enjoying the flight.

Five miles outside the base the helicopter set down beside an empty road.

'You can drop off here,' said the Colonel, 'I'll try and get a car out to you.'

'But we want to go all the way home by helicopter,' shouted Samantha above the roar of the rotors, and was joined by Penelope who insisted she wanted to parachute onto Oakhurst Avenue. It was too much for Eva. Grabbing the quads in turn she bundled them out onto the beaten grass and jumped down beside them. Wilt followed. For a moment the air around him was thick with the downblast and then the helicopter had lifted off and was swinging away. By the time it had disappeared Eva had found her voice.

'Now look what you've been and done,' she said. Wilt stared round at the empty landscape. After the interrogation he had been through he was in no mood for Eva's whingeing.

'Let's start walking,' he said. 'Nobody's coming out to pick us up and we'd better find a bus stop.'

He climbed the bank onto the road and set off along it. In the distance there was a sudden flash and a small ball of flame. Major Glaushof had fired a tracer round into Mavis Mottram's inflated penis. The fireball and the little mushroom cloud of smoke above it would be on the evening TV news in full colour. Perhaps something had been achieved after all.

Chapter twenty-four

It was the end of term at the Tech and the staff were seated in the auditorium, as evidently bored as the students they themselves had previously lectured there. Now it was the Principal's turn. He had spent ten excruciating minutes doing his best to disguise his true feelings for Mr Spirey of the Building Department who was finally retiring, and another twenty trying to explain why financial cuts had ended any hope of rebuilding the engineering block at the very time when the College had been granted the staggering sum of a quarter of a million pounds by an anonymous donor for the purchase of textbooks. In the front row Wilt sat poker-faced among the other Heads of Departments and feigned indifference. Only he and the Principal knew the source of the donation and neither of them could ever tell. The Official Secrets Act had seen to that. The money was the price of Wilt's silence. The deal had been negotiated by two nervous officials from the United States Embassy and in the presence of two rather more menacing individuals ostensibly from the legal division of the Home Office. Not that Wilt had been worried by their attitude. Throughout the discussion he had basked in the sense of his own innocence and even Eva had been overawed and then impressed by the offer of a new car. But Wilt had turned that down. It was enough to know that the Principal, while never understanding why, would always be unhappily aware that the Fenland College of Arts and Technology was once again indebted to a man he would have liked to fire. Now he was lumbered with Wilt until he retired himself.

Only the quads had been difficult to silence. They had enjoyed pumping ammonia over the Lieutenant and disabling sentries with pepper too much not to want to make their exploits known.

'We were only rescuing Daddy from that sexy woman,' said Samantha when Eva rather unwisely asked them to promise never to talk about what had happened.

'And you'll have to rescue your Mother and me from Dartmoor if you don't keep your damned traps shut,' Wilt had snapped. 'And you know what that means.'

'What?' asked Emmeline, who seemed to be looking forward to the prospect of a prison break.

'It means you'll be taken into care by horrible foster parents and not as a bloody group either. You'll be split up and you won't be allowed to visit one another and . . .' Wilt had launched into a positively Dickensian description of foster homes and horrors of child abuse. By the time he'd finished the quads were cowed and Eva had been in tears. Which was the first time that had happened and was another minor triumph. It wouldn't last, of course, but by the time they spilled the beans the immediate dangers would be over and nobody would believe them anyway.

But the argument had aroused Eva's suspicions again. 'I still want to know why you lied to me all those months about teaching at the prison,' she said as they undressed that night.

Wilt had an answer for that one too. 'You heard what those men from MI5 said about the Official Secrets Act.'

'MI5?' said Eva. 'They were from the Home Office. What's MI5 got to do with it?'

'Home Office, my foot, Military Intelligence,' said Wilt. 'And if you choose to send the quads to the most expensive school for pseudo-prodigies and expect us not to starve . . .'

The argument had rumbled on into the night but Eva hadn't needed much convincing. The officials from the Embassy had impressed her too much with their apologies and there had been no talk of women. Besides, she had her Henry home again and it was obviously best to forget that anything had happened at Baconheath.

And so Wilt sat on beside Dr Board with a slight sense of accomplishment. If he was fated to fall foul of other people's stupidity and misunderstanding he had the satisfaction of knowing that he was no one's victim. Or only temporarily. In the end he beat them and circumstances. It was better than being a successful bore like Dr Mayfield – or worse still, a resentful failure.

'Wonders never cease,' said Dr Board when the Principal finally sat down and they began to file out of the auditorium, 'a quarter of a million in actual textbooks? It must be a unique event in British education. Millionaires who give donations usually provide better buildings for worse students. This one seems to be a genius.'

Wilt said nothing. Perhaps having some common sense was a form of genius.

At Ipford Police Station ex-Inspector Hodge, now merely Sergeant Hodge, sat at a computer terminal in Traffic Control and tried to confine his thoughts to problems connected with flow-patterns and off-peak parking systems. It wasn't easy. He still hadn't recovered from the effects of Agent Incapacitating or, worse still, from the enquiry into his actions the Superintendent had started and the Chief Constable had headed.

And Sergeant Runk hadn't been exactly helpful. 'Inspector Hodge gave me to understand the Superintendent had authorized the bugging of Mr Wilt's car,' he said in evidence. 'I was acting on his orders. It was the same with their house.'

'Their house? You mean to say their house was bugged too?'

'Yes, sir. It still is for all I know,' said Runk, 'we had the collaboration of the neighbours, Mr Gamer and his wife.'

'Dear God,' muttered the Chief Constable, 'if this ever gets to the gutter press . . .'

'I don't think it will, sir,' said Runk, 'Mr Gamer has moved out and his missus has put the house up for sale.'

'Then get those bloody devices out of there before someone has the place surveyed,' snarled the Chief Constable before dealing with Hodge. By the time he had finished the Inspector was on the verge of a breakdown himself and had been demoted to Sergeant in the Traffic Section with the threat of being transferred to the police dog training school as a target if he put his foot wrong just once again.

To add insult to injury he had seen Flint promoted to Head of the Drug Squad.

'The chap seems to have a natural talent for that kind of work,' said the Chief Constable. 'He's done a remarkable job.'

The Superintendent had his reservations but he kept them to himself. 'I think it runs in the family,' he said judiciously.

And for a fortnight during the trial Flint's name had appeared almost daily in the *Ipford Chronicle* and even in some of the national dailies. The police canteen too had buzzed with his praises. Flint the Drug Buster. Almost Flint the Terror of the Courtroom. In spite of all the efforts the defence counsel had made, with every justification, to question the legality of his methods, Flint had countered with facts and figures, times, dates, places and with exhibits, all of which were authentic. He had stepped down from the witness box still retaining the image of the old-fashioned copper with his integrity actually enhanced by the innuendoes. It was enough for the public to look from him to the row of sleazy defendants in the dock to see where the interests of justice lay. Certainly the Judge and jury had been convinced. The accused had gone down with sentences that ranged from nine years to twelve and Flint had gone up to Superintendent.

But Flint's achievement led beyond the courtroom to areas where discretion still prevailed.

'She brought the stuff back from her cousins in California?' spluttered Lord Lynchknowle when the Chief Constable visited him. 'I don't believe a word of it. Downright lie.'

'Afraid not, old chap. Absolutely definite. Smuggled the muck back in a bottle of duty-free whisky.'

'Good God. I thought she'd got it at that rotten Tech. Never did agree with her going there. All her mother's fault.' He paused and stared vacuously out across the rolling meadows. 'What did you say the stuff was called?'

'Embalming Fluid,' said the Chief Constable, 'Or Angel Dust. They usually smoke it.'

'Don't see how you can smoke embalming fluid,' said Lord Lynchknowle. 'Mind you, there's no understanding women, is there?'

'None at all,' said the Chief Constable and with the assurance that the coroner's verdict would be one of accidental death he left to deal with other women whose behaviour was beyond his comprehension.

In fact it was at Baconheath that the results of Hodge's obsession with the Wilt family were being felt most keenly. Outside the airbase Mavis Mottram's group of Mothers Against The Bomb had been joined by women from all over the country and had turned into a much bigger demonstration. A camp of makeshift huts and tents was strung out along the perimeter fence, and relations between the Americans and the Fenland Constabulary had not been improved by scenes on TV of middle-aged and largely respectable British women being gassed and dragged in handcuffs to camouflaged ambulances.

To make matters even more awkward Mavis' tactics of blockading the civilian quarters had led to several violent incidents between US women who wanted to escape the boredom of the base to go souvenir-hunting in Ipford and Norwich and MABs who refused to let them out or, more infuriatingly, allowed them to leave only to stop

251

them going back. These fracas were seen on TV with a regularity that had brought the Home Secretary and the Secretary of State for Defence into conflict, each insisting that the other was responsible for maintaining law and order.

Only Patrick Mottram had benefited. In Mavis' absence he had come off Dr Kores' hormones and had resumed his normal habits with Open University students.

Inside the airbase, too, everything had changed. General Belmonte, still suffering from the effect of seeing a giant penis circumcise itself and then turn into a rocket and explode, had been retired to a home for demented veterans in Arizona where he was kept comfortably sedated and could sit in the sun dreaming of happy days when his B52 had blasted the empty jungle in Vietnam. Colonel Urwin had returned to Washington and a cat-run garden in which he grew scented narcissi to perfection and employed his considerable intelligence to the problem of improving Anglo-American relations.

It was Glaushof who had suffered the most. He had been flown to the most isolated and radioactive testing ground in Nevada and consigned to duties in which his own personal security was in constant danger and his sole responsibility. And sole was the word. Mona Glaushof with Lieutenant Harah in tow had hit Reno for a divorce and was living comfortably in Texas on the alimony. It was a change from the dank Fenlands and the sun never ceased to shine.

It shone too on Eva and 45 Oakhurst Avenue as she bustled about the house and wondered what to have for supper. It was nice to have Henry home and somehow more assertive than he had been before. 'Perhaps,' she thought as she Hoovered the stairs, 'we ought to get away by ourselves for a week or two this summer.' And her thoughts turned to the Costa Brava.

*

But it was a problem Wilt had already solved. Sitting in The Pig In A Poke with Peter Braintree he ordered two more pints.

'After all I've been through this term I'm not having my summer made hellish in some foul camp site by the quads,' he said cheerfully. 'I've made other arrangements. There's an adventure school in Wales where they do rock-climbing and pony-trekking. They can work their energy off on that and the instructors. I've rented a cottage in Dorset and I'm going down there to read *Jude The Obscure* again.'

'Seems a bit of a gloomy book to take on holiday,' said Braintree.

'Salutary,' said Wilt, 'a nice reminder that the world's always been a crazy place and that we don't have such a bad time of it teaching at the Tech. Besides, it's an antidote to the notion that intellectual aspirations get you anywhere.'

'Talking about aspirations,' said Braintree, 'what on earth are you going to do with the thirty thousand quid this lunatic philanthropist has allotted your department for textbooks?'

Wilt smiled into his pint of best bitter. 'Lunatic philanthropists' was just about right for the Americans with their airbases and nuclear weapons, and the educated idiots in the State Department who assumed that even the most ineffectual liberal do-gooder must be a homicidal Stalinist and a member of the KGB – and who then shelled out billions of dollars trying to undo the damage they'd done.

'Well, for one thing I'm going to donate two hundred copies of *Lord of the Flies* to Inspector Flint,' he said finally.

'To Flint? Why him of all people? What's he want with the damned things?'

'He's the one who told Eva I was out at . . .' Wilt stopped. There was no point in breaking the Official Secrets Act. 'It's a prize,' he went on, 'for the first copper to arrest the Phantom Flasher. It seems an appropriate title.'

'I daresay it does,' said Braintree. 'Still, two hundred copies is a bit disproportionate. I can't imagine even the most literate policeman wanting to read two hundred copies of the same book.'

'He can always hand them out to the poor sods at the airbase. Must be hell trying to cope with Mavis Mottram. Not that I disagree with her views but the bloody woman is definitely demented.'

'Still leaves you with a hell of a lot of new books to buy,' said Braintree. 'I mean, it's all right for me because the English Department needs books but I shouldn't have thought Communication and—'

'Don't use those words. I'm going back to Liberal Studies and to hell with all that bloody jargon. And if Mayfield and the rest of the social-economic structure merchants don't like it, they can lump it. I'm having it my way from now on.'

'You sound very confident,' said Braintree.

'Yes,' said Wilt with a smile.

And he was.

Tom Sharp
Wilt £1.95

'Henry Wilt works humbly at his Polytechnic dinning Eng. Lit. into the unreceptive skulls of rude mechanicals, but spends his nights in fantasies of murdering his gargantuan, feather-brained wife, half-consummated when he dumps a life-sized inflatable doll in a building site hole, and is grilled by the police, his wife being missing, stranded on a mud bank with a gruesome American dyke' GUARDIAN

'Superb farce' TRIBUNE

'. . . triumphs by a slicing wit' DAILY MIRROR

Blott on the Landscape £1.95

'Skulduggery at stately homes, dirty work at the planning inquiry, and the villains falling satisfactorily up to their ears in the minestrone . . . the heroine breakfasts on broken bottles, wears barbed wire next to her skin and stops at nothing to protect her ancestral seat from a motorway construction' THE TIMES

'Deliciously English comedy' GUARDIAN